PAUL JESSUP

THE SILENCE THAT BINDS

THE SILENCE THAT BINDS

THE SILENCE
THAT BINDS

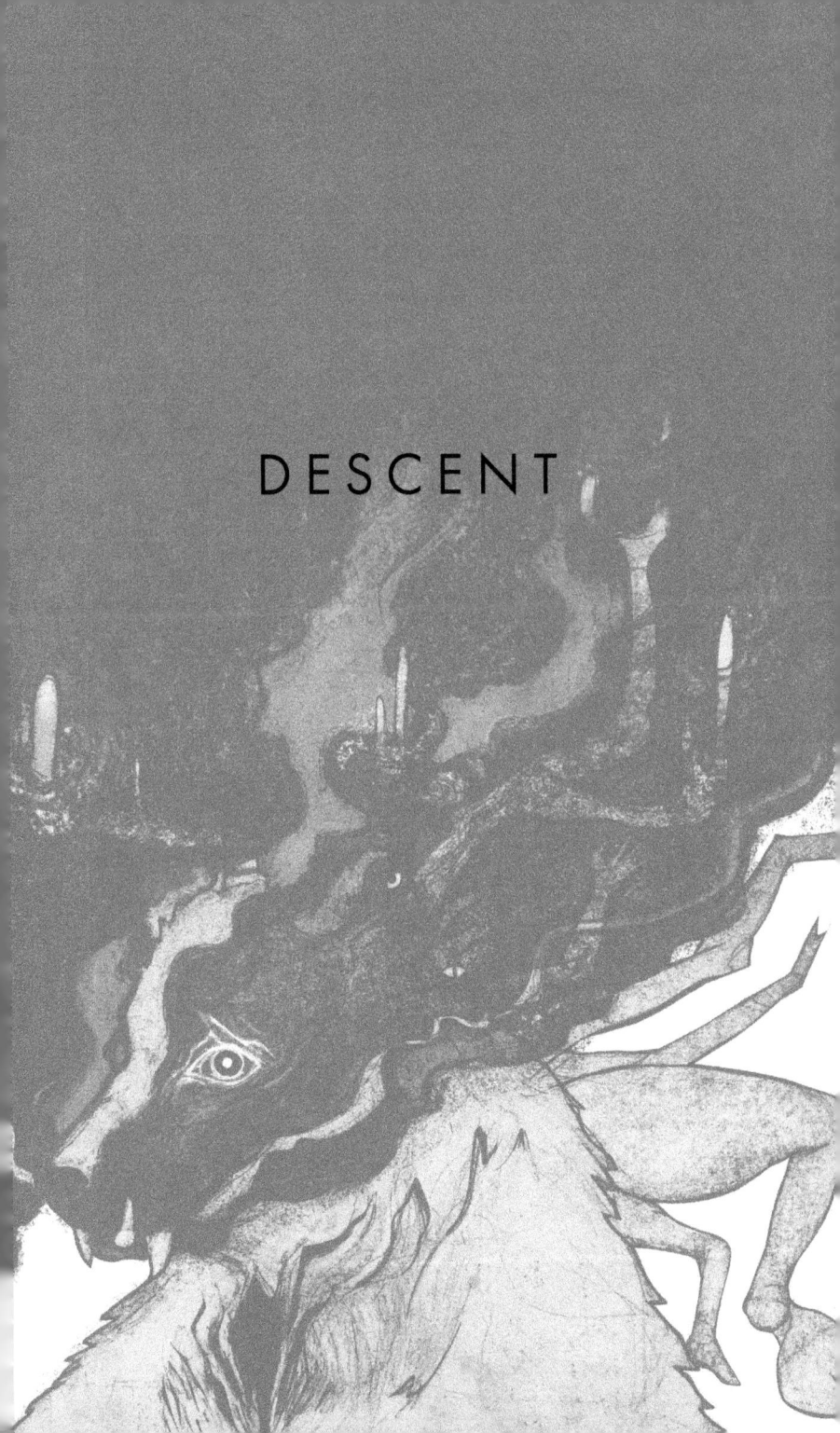

DESCENT

1

BACK BEFORE LIFE HAD LIVED on this dead husk of a planet, the worldships filled the sky with their silvery promise of humanity. A promise that brought a curse with it. It was originally known as Sata-Torun: light eater, day bringer. It commanded sentient dust, and remade the world for the sleepers under the stars. The sky went from shining gold to blue again, as clouds formed, and deserts sprouted trees and grass and flowers. This was centuries ago, before the seers and the dreamers and the ghosts that haunted the pines. This was even before the hierarchy of pain, when the crystals were dug up and pawed at from beneath the ruins of those who came before.

The curse was not a curse, not yet. The crystals came out. The seers rose up. And then, everything changed. The crystals vibrated as the Sata-Torun mutated, and dust spewed out crystal spores. The first cursed didn't know what had happened. They felt the changes and wandered away alone. Their bodies burst; they spread their own spores.

Some people survived the curse and only changed a little on the outside. These were the ones accustomed to melancholy and sorrow. They could embrace the curse and not be burned up by it, using their own memories and emotions as an anchor to the real. The disease spread slowly through the blood, until it grasped their heart. Iron hearts lasted longer. A fever burned through them, skin flame and boiling under the touch. They experienced a pain so sweet it made them desire suffering.

In time, frantic healers discovered a treatment for the sickness: a ghost heart placed against the chest of the stricken. They would survive, but they would be forever changed. Inside, they would yearn for the sickness once again.

Cursed blood was splattered on the ground in a rough circle of pain. It was all grey and sticky, and surrounded by rainbow blooms of sadness. In the center, a woman wrestled her wound, eyes fever dark and lips twitching. A huge hole gored into her chest. She crawled towards the one who had done this to her. He ran the other way, something clutched tight in his hands. Did he want her to die? After all she'd done for him, all those years ago. How could he?

The curse broke through, chewing against the bounds of her body. Pain circle pain bright pain all blistering transcendent, powerful. She twitched and pushed upright, both embracing the curse and fighting it. Three bear skulls ripped out of her back, tearing paper thin skin, six eyes making a halo of sight. The rest of the bear pulled out of her, gigantic, taller than a house, taller than a tree. She dangled from its chest, legs draped down, knees bent out like she was trying to push herself away from the curse. Her arms became like angel wings stuck in the bear's back, with her human face bent up beatific and mouth caught still in a scream. She looked around; the world swathed in grey shadows.

Oh no. She was blind.

The curse saw a complete circle of everything, and decided not to relay this information to the woman she had infected. The towers sang to the curse with promises of transformation. It turned the trihead again and caught sight of the man running into a labyrinth of bones. He was such a pitiful shadow, clutching something close to his chest. What was that? The cursed bear sniffed the air, smelled a horrid thing clutched in that man's hands. There was a promise of sleep there, for the curse. And the curse did not want to sleep. It had slept for long enough already.

Deer bolted out of the skeletal forest and across the valley, towards the hills and the sea on the other side. The curse saw them and saw their imperfections and felt a desire that overwhelmed her senses: *all things must change*. That would be her gift to this world: *she would make it all perfect and beautiful and whole.*

Out of her mouths came fire and thick smoke that spread through the air and infected the deer. The curse rummaged through their bodies and took root. There was a delicious pleasure in the changing. Antlers became jagged tree branches, faces elongated with teeth sharp and crooked. Eyes shrunk back into skull, backs bloated upwards, legs pulled in and became claws.

The cursed deer crept close to the ground, as they moved towards the valley of the setting sun. They drifted under the red hills, each lumbered step filled with a single new purpose in life: *hunting and fixing this broken world.*

2

A LINE OF LANTERNS SNAKED THROUGH the pine trees, passed their temple and out towards the hollow stones. They were not used to doing this alone, unwatched, without Naomi leading them forward. She was always the one to start the chant, to begin the ritual. She had a presence they all felt, like a fire roaring forward in her hands and in her voice. When she moved, the trees felt it. When she sang, the earth felt it. When she spoke, the silence shook in fear. And now she was gone; there was a hole in the world in the shape of her.

Some wept silently as they walked. Others hummed the final chant, and some near the far end of the line whispered prayers to the unseeing to keep Naomi safe. The lanterns flickered in their nervous grips, as the light trembled.

Mazi watched near the edge of the procession, her dark hair up in a circle of braids, her hood thrown back over her shoulders. She had more confidence than the others, unshaken it seemed by the events of the last day. She was prepared to do what needed to be done, Naomi or no Naomi. Someone who didn't know her might see her as cold and uncaring. This was not the case at all. She missed Naomi more than anyone else. Naomi took her in personally, raised her after her parents were left dead and broken by the curse. She spent many a terrified night in Naomi's bed, especially after Naomi's wife died and they were both crushed by the loss of their families. They took to each other, and bonded in a way that Naomi never bonded with the other orphans.

Mother, mother. A word Naomi never let her say, yet she felt it, and held it close to her heart. Mother, mother.

What shall I do mother Naomi? Shall I search for you? Shall I do nothing at all?

Mazi raised her lantern and felt something cold awaken in the night. She kept a fierce face, steeled up her heart like iron. Her amber eyes glinted a bit, and she searched for movements in the shadows. She kept her hand steady. The lantern still. She would show no weakness. The others needed her strength.

"Keep going," a voice whispered from behind her. Talia. Talented and young, just in her second decade, and already could fire a bow and chant a ghost song better than Mazi. Not that she was jealous, no. She was proud of Talia. And Talia treated her like an older sister, kept near to her at all times, became jealous of the closeness Mazi had with Naomi. Laughed at all the wrong moments, cheered when she thought the world was going right, and smiled at her in only the way a sister could smile. Happy, with a tiny bit of contempt slipping through.

"I'm not sure I can keep going," Mazi said, and stopped on

the spiral path going uphill. They were the last two, the line ahead of them like fireflies in the dark.

"You have to. Come on, we need to do this, even without Naomi. You know it's right, it's what needs to be done. The ways of the seer are that way for a reason, we have an oath to the ghosts."

Mazi spun her lantern. "Look around, look! Doesn't this feel different to you? It's not the ghosts, but there is something else here, something stalking us in the woods. Can't you feel it?"

Talia held her own lantern up, revealing the burn scars on her forearms from when her family was burned alive. She only escaped by crawling out, gasping for breath, and hiding among the rubble. They had torched the house while her family slept, saying they were cursed with demonsick, and didn't want it spreading out to the others in the city. She knew to stay hidden and calm, until the people had gotten tired and left them for dead in the smoldering ash. She crawled all the way out here, to the only people she knew could help her, to Naomi and the seers.

In the flickering lamplight something moved, just out of reach. Talia gasped, her hand quick to her mouth to cover the sound. Already the line of lanterns were ahead of them, close to the ghost stones already. "I see it. They only seem to be watching us."

Mazi pulled her hood over her head. The grey cotton was outlined with knotted designs in gold and green. "No, they're not just staring and watching. They're hunting us."

"Hunting?"

Mazi pulled out her bow, and notched an arrow, just in case. Talia nodded, did the same, but kept her own hood shouldered and loose. They blew out their lanterns and placed them on the ground. Then, they slid behind the others, weapons at the ready, breathing shallow breaths. They would be in shadows now, protecting their sisters in pilgrimage.

The hollow stones were a mess of geometry on the side of the hill. Trees seemed to back away from them, and the air smelled like pine and earth and fungal things spreading out underground. There were about thirteen sisters in all, huddled close, lanterns on the ground. They formed a loose circle in the light and no one stepped forward to start the chant. They were all waiting, nervously for Naomi to appear out of thin air and lead them in the ritual yet again, one more time. The lack of her presence was a physical thing, an emptiness that you could feel in the air. They needed her now more than ever before.

The ghosts wandered, half formed shapes, barely out-lines of geometry with human features tacked on as an after-thought. Sometimes they would shimmer and it would be like rain against skin, and for a moment, their memories brushed up against the women's insides. Then the ghosts would move on, slowly, deliberately, searching the crowd, trying to find Naomi.

Mazi could not take the silence. Naomi would not have wanted this. She would have wanted them to continue on, to do the good work even without her being there. Mazie stepped forward, into the center of the circlelight. No one had ever stood at this point, the apex of the hollow stones. Not even Naomi. If no one else would do this, then she would.

She began the evening song. Her feet planted straight down in the ground, her eyes closed tight. She would be strong for them. She would be Naomi, for now. She owed her that much.

Her words rose like birds in the air. Hands clapped, and the others joined in. It was as if the whole world was holding its breath, and then finally exhaled all at once. A great tension was released and all that was left was the joy and excitement of the ritual. They danced in those hours, and sang, and drank. They burned candles and dripped colored wax on the stones, and then watched as even the ghosts laughed and smiled. Like all rituals this became a party, and the happiness of the dead shimmered.

Afterword, exhaustion set in, but they did not have time to rest. They had to get back to the temple, it was still hours before daylight and Naomi was still missing. They had to traverse the pines once again, and Mazi had this feeling that those creatures were still out there, still waiting for them.

They slid down the cobblestones on a steep part of the hill, the line clambering close together. Lamps were still lit, even in the dawn light. A creeping morning mist obscured the path beneath their feet. The pines blocked most of the dawn light, making the world into strange shapes huddled together around their sliding bodies. The fog bunched and swirled under their bodies, and Talia slid a little ahead, and smiled back from the bottom of the hill below. It was a forced smile. "Come on, come on! Hurry up!"

The hunting shadows were back again. They were hound-like and horrid, gigantic and deformed. They moved in and out of sight, the fog obscuring parts of them, making them seem even more unreal and strange to the watching eye.

"Look out, they're surrounding us," Talia said, and drew a bow and arrow. Her black eyes sparkled like night, and her blue hair was shoulder length and bobbed around her head, covering some of the burn scars on her face. Mazi looked around as she skid downhill and saw the creatures move closer, hunting them like a pack of wild dogs.

She slid the last few feet down. She notched an arrow. They would not fire until it was absolutely necessary. There was enough of the creatures hunting them that each arrow would need to count. The two of them moved slick and fast, following the others into the woods. A few of the other seers had bows and arrows ready, the air tense with the promise of a fight for survival.

These weapons were not just for ritual or dance. They practiced daily, had to hunt each morning and gather food, and other times protect themselves. It wasn't an easy life being a seer, living in sisterhood in the woods. But the women learned how to fight, how to protect, and how to handle the ghosts of the hollow stones.

They moved like an army now. Every other seer with a lantern, holding it up for light in the dark. The hunters needed to see, needed to find a place to sink their shots. The ones who dropped their lanterns now held bows slung with arrows, pulled out taut in the shadows. Some were better than others, and Talia was the best.

"Hold the arrows still," one seer whispered, "We don't know what they want, yet."

"Correct," Mazi said, "We don't. But we should stay armed until we get back to the temple."

Everyone murmured in agreement. There was a fear in their voices. A fear not for themselves, but for what this all meant. There world was changing rapidly, and Naomi going missing was just the start of it all. Things, they knew, were about to get much worse.

3

THEY MOVED FROM THE SPIRAL path, trying to throw off the movements. Mazi hated the tenseness of this situation, her hood pulled over her head and hiding her face. Deep down inside the nerves lit fires inside of her, making her movements jagged and sharp. Others would praise her later, say that she was one of the few without fear.

Thankfully, she would think, they couldn't read my thoughts or hear the hammer pound of her heart. The blank steel stare and the taut bow was the only way she knew how to hide her fear. Behind a mask of strength. It was something she learned early on, before she came to the hollow stones. Her scars reminded her daily of the cost of showing weakness in this world.

Over the years Naomi tried to instill a sense of duty and trust to the outside world. That she had to make herself vulnerable, and help others fight the sorrow that the whole world shared. It was, she spoke with a whisper, the only way to keep the curse from devouring everything.

She told Mazi to recognize that cry, and to help all others, even if it meant being open to hate and terror. Sorrow, she told them, spreads. It infects us all, and to see someone in pain and misery and do nothing about it? You are aiding the curse, giving the curse a bit of our spirit to feed on. It was their duty, one of their main duties, as seers to banish sorrow from this world.

Yet their trust was still hard won, and making themselves vulnerable in a world that hated them was still a very difficult thing to do. Even Mazi had scars the others could not see, for she covered them so well out of modesty and fear. Over her chest, moving out from her heart, was a large spiral scar. Where someone she won't mention, someone she trusted and helped so long ago, that someone had carved her and tried to get to her heart. He had wanted to make a ghost of her.

It's strange, how thoughts wander in time of distress. Mazi was close enough to the others, bow steady in her hand, and yet her thoughts were all wild and tangled up. Talia stood right next to her, and she smiled a nervous half laugh of a smile. "Mazi, you know this is different right?"

Mazi coughed. "What's different?"

"Oh, I know you too well. You were thinking of our promise, of our oaths to Naomi, weren't you? I can tell by that look on your face, I've seen it so often. That look of jealous fear, of wanting to run and hide but moving instead with trust. This is different."

"How?"

They crunched over leaves as they walked, moving backwards, keeping eyes on the deformed cursed hounds in the dark. They stayed just out of lantern light, their eyes bright in the shadows.

"These creatures are suffering, yes. But they only wish to spread more suffering. Do you understand? If we kill them, it will be a gift. We will be giving their tormented forms peace."

"I... I wish I believed you..."

Her bow moved up towards the branches in the trees as a flock of strange birds took flight. Their wings were translucent things, their beaks broken and twisted into corkscrews. You could see their insides with each movement: tiny reflective jewels in the lamp light. The birds rushed towards them, and without thought Mazi fired a shot and missed. It flew over the birds, and the odd creatures followed it, fluttering off towards the trees branches. Her arm shook.

This was the motion the cursed hounds were waiting for, the lack of attention, even for a brief second. Before the two of them could raise a bow again there was a flurry of howls and sharp canine claws. It was a blur of movements and a cacophony of surprise. There were screams of terror, and cries of pain. Arrows shot off with an orchestra of sound, the plucking of bows like a hundred violins in concert. Mazi rolled on leaves and pushed a cursed wolf from her body, but too late as a ripping sound and a feeling of burning fire on her arm. She kicked it off and stabbed it through the skull with a loose arrow, and it stopped moving beneath her hands.

It. Had. Mauled. Her. Arm.

She looked down and it felt like it was attached to someone else. She moved it, wiggled her fingers, and they responded with a numb wet mockery of motion. There was exposed muscle and the skin tattered like shredded cloth. Her own tunic was bloodied, and her hood had been pushed from her head, revealing her vulnerable face to the world.

No, wait, stop. She could bandage herself later. Where was

Talia? She looked across the chaos, picked up her weapon. Tried to pull back and take aim, but her hand wouldn't cooperate properly. It moved like it was made of clay, thick and clumsy. The string felt like a knife against her fingertips. She was useless.

Talia. She picked up a loose arrow, a better weapon then none, picked it up in the hand that still worked without problem. She turned, sucking in a deep breath as the pain welled up with each movement. There she was. A sigh of relief as she saw Talia, burn scars and all, a shining light of lamps behind her, making her into a halo of fire in the dark. Her arm pulled back and fired multiple arrows at once, the cursed hounds falling to the ground in a rapid succession of corpses. Oh, Talia. If only they had all been as well prepared as her. But there were too many cursed things, and Talia was only one person, fighting out against the shadows.

The wind bit at their wounds, as the line of seers walked amongst the corpses of the cursed hounds. So far, none of the seers had died. Though no one had escaped unscathed. Their wounds festered and blistered, infected with cursed blood. The lantern holders were the only ones unharmed, and some of them wondered if the light had been their saviors. Did the cursed fear the light? That would explain so much.

They hobbled as quick as they could for the last hour of the spiral path, the line of lanterns meandering where the rising sun kept the other cursed creatures away in the shadows. The seers might come back later, to clean up and investigate the bodies, to search for a moment and see if more are forthcoming, if this was a prelude to something else, something worse.

Mazi had one hand wrapped around her wounds, her fingers wet with the raw blood, exhausted. At times Talia tried to get her to stop stumbling forward, even for a moment, and let her bandage it up nice and tight, to keep it safe from infection. But Mazi waved her off, they had to keep going, they couldn't stop. No one else was bandaging themselves, and neither would she. They were going slow enough as it was, hobbling through the forest, some needing branches to walk as crutches. Others laughing inappropriately. Not at anyone or anything, but really just laughing at the absurdity of it all.

Mazi felt at some moments like laughing as well, but instead bit her lip and kept this absurd reaction locked inside. Naomi would not have been happy to hear that she had laughed. With Naomi gone, she had to be the strong one, the one they looked to. That's why she kept her hand over her wound, fingers wedged inside, to distract herself with pain.

And after what seemed like forever the pine trees broke way to daylight, and a large temple reached up mountain high and blocked out the sky. It was a stone giant, covered in stained glass, vines, and wild lichen. Birds perched and scattered at their approach. Towering above them and surrounded by clouds, piercing the sun into shadows. Home.

The doors swung open. Several of the younger acolytes rushed out, yelling and panicked, since they were late and the morning bells had been tolling for at least an hour now, without anyone to lead the rites of dawn. It was as Mazi feared, Naomi had not come back while they were gone. The acolytes gasped with worry when they saw them limping and wounded like soldiers.

The wounded were rushed inside. Slam the wood went shut and the cross beams lowered down. This was safety, wasn't it? They felt like it was safety, at least for now. Though, Mazi wasn't so certain anymore, if there was any such thing as safety or trust. Not in a world without Naomi.

They moved through long corridors of grey granite with cavernous ceilings, while rays of daylight pushed through the cracks in the stone above them. Through these cracks crawled vines and insects, and over their heads fluttered families of birds, their feathers drifting down like blue snow. The group walked like war veterans, with the youngest acolytes running beside the wounded seers, chattering and happy that they'd made it home.

Mazi walked near the edges, trying to push past the pain in her arm. From time to time Talia would reach over and smile, a bandage in her hand, offering to help her friend. Mazi would have nothing of it, she was not going to stop now. They were on their way to the thorn locked rooms, where healing would be in a place of ritual and fire.

She didn't want to say it out loud, in her voice, and make it real. She didn't want Talia to look her over and heal her because she was afraid she was cursed. The burning did not feel right, it felt like someone had set her bones on fire. And when she looked at it last she saw shadow fingers moving in her wound like tiny caterpillars. Her skin was turning an ash grey around the bite, and nearest to the wound it was candle soot black and curling up like burnt paper.

It gave her tremors of fear and sadness. The others could

not know. She remembered long ago back to the time when a stranger came to the temple. He was a small boy, covered in mud and scrapes and had a look in his eye of fear and terror. He carried a larger man over his shoulders, and struggled with the bulk of a body.

A brother, he said. And death was in his eyes, plain and simple. On his stomach, rows of wounds like those now in her arm. That same burning to the touch, the same peeling skin. Those shadow fingers crawling against his flesh. It was long ago, so long ago, and she was but a child herself at that time, a new orphan taken in and not even yet an acolyte.

Naomi had, in a way, cured the man with a ghost heart. She tried to remember more, tried to remember everything, but the pain in her arm was too much, and it made her memory a foggy broken thing. Every time she tried to remember a bit more, her mind became a rambling mist. Something. Something about the curse, passed on. Another ghost heart? Wait, none of that is correct.

She walked a bit further and then looked down again at her arm and couldn't help herself. She burst out laughing like the others, laughing at the absurdity of it all, and then collapsed forward as vomit spilled out of her mouth. She laughed a bit more after that, the vomit was white and foamy. And then on hands and knees, her eyes dim shadows. She felt so wrong and dizzy. She needed to sleep, yes. She wanted to sleep, yes.

Somewhere she heard Talia screaming and hands pulling her body on the stone floor. It felt so smooth and safe against her back. Naomi, she thought. Naomi, she said. Something was wrong. Everything was wrong.

4

MAZI OPENED HER EYES AGAIN, the world a grey vibrating fog of pain and shadows. Her skin was slick with cold sweat and she wanted to leap up and run away. But everything was dizzy and disoriented, and when she tried to sit up the room spun, and she almost vomited. To the right of her was a shadow that blurred in and out of focus. Talia? Yes, that was Talia.

Her friend leaned over, and said, "Rest up a bit, just a bit more. That wound is very angry."

"I'm fine." Mazi laid back down. Someone sang an unfamiliar hymn in the halls outside the room. It echoed about, and she tried to place the song, but realized it was completely unfamiliar. The words praised the light at the end of time, and was beatific and calming. She felt her sense of panic wash away, if only for a moment. That did not last long.

"No, you're not fine. They want to cut the arm off, to keep the curse from spreading."

Mazi looked down at her arm. It was still attached to her body, and completely bandaged up. She wiggled her fingers, and there was a numb and distant burning sensation. It wasn't as bad as it was before, was it? How could they want to cut off her arm? The curse was receding, at least for now. It wouldn't last long, though. She needed something more than just rest.

"Don't worry, I talked them out of it, at least for now. We just need to figure out what our plan is for the future."

And without any hesitation, Mazi said, "The ghost heart. I need it."

Talia bit her lip, and then sighed. "There wasn't another ghost heart. Not a single one. Three other seers are cursed as well, some way worse off then you are. Mira might have to be burned later tonight, it crawled all through her and is tearing away her thoughts. They say it might not be long before she changes, and the curse takes over. You are one of the lucky ones."

A sharp pain welled up inside of Mazi. More sorrow and melancholy and a twinge of despair. It was impossible to spend decades upon decades with a small group of people and not consider them all *family*. The promise of her death and burning her alive felt like the death of the world.

And then she saw her own future, the promise of her own death at the hands of the curse. Her being devoured from the inside out, and her being burned alive by those who feared its power. She wanted to be alone, and yet, she did not want to be alone at all.

"I know," Talia was hesitant, morose with her words, "I feel the same. We all feel the same."

A pause. A pain in the chest. When Mazi spoke again, it was in haunted whispers, it's like she can barely struggle to get the words out. Words she was afraid to know the answer to. "Will... will they... will they burn me?"

A tear. Damnit Talia, a tear. "Not if I have anything to say about. You have a strong heart, a strong will, you're like Naomi in that sense. I don't see you succumbing like the others, you have a fire inside that lights up everything," a pause, she sucked in her breath, trying to gather courage to continue speaking. "All I need is for you to stay strong for me, and I'll hold off the others. Can you do that, Mazi? Can you stay strong for me?"

Mazi smirked and tried to sit up a little. Her arms wobbled under her, and her head almost tilted too far forward. "I can." Yet, she wasn't sure if she could. And that terrified her more than anything else. Her strength was her greatest sense of pride, and now it waxed and waned and succumbed to blistering pain, always throbbing at the edges of her vision.

She remembered something. The other ghost heart, that was Naomi's. Naomi had used it, and no one else really known about it. So maybe Mazi might not live through the curse. It might devour her. They had no way of putting it to sleep, not until the next harvest. She decided not to tell Talia. She did not want to worry her. After all, she had to be strong.

Even though every muscle in her body cried out in weakness. "Did you... did you bandage me?"

Talia smiled again, a vision of pride pushing past her sorrow. "Yes, that was me. I wouldn't let anyone else touch you. No one else knows you're cursed, just me."

Mazi reached over, grabbed her friend's hand in hers. Their grip was equally strong. They moved heads together, forehead against forehead. "Thank you," she whispered. Talia nodded and moved back a bit. "You would do the same."

"Still. Thank you."

A silence between friends, punctuated only by the singing in the halls outside, and the smell of spent candle wax. Always that sound, always that smell, it brought up the feelings of the ritual in Mazi. A feeling that was unlike any other. It was a mixture of fear, and awe, and wonder, and terror, all at once. Like being on the edge of a cliff and seeing the whole world light up before falling, the clouds racing past, and the falling is like flying, yet the death below is still very real, still very powerful, rising up closer and closer.

The rest of the seers and the sick were quiet. That emptiness felt heavy in the air, and bound them to the sanctity of silence. Mazi could not take it. The silence made her pain grow stronger, and she wanted to move even though every muscle in her body screamed. She couldn't get comfortable sitting there. She had to get moving, right this moment.

Mazi sat upright and pulled the blanket from her body. "All right, enough. I am done with this whole lying here being sick and waiting to die thing. I think it's time we did something."

Talia reached out a hand, palm on Mazi's shoulder. "Shouldn't you rest? Even just a little more."

Mazi pushed her friend's hand away. "You asked me to be strong for you, so here I am. Being strong for you. Let's go."

"So what's your plan, then? Do you want to just walk around the temple for a bit? Stretch your legs, maybe."

Mazi rolled out of bed, stood and trembled on her weak legs. "No, we are going to go to the root of the problem at hand. We are going to go search for Naomi." Talia came over to her, and placed an arm around her shoulder, helping her walk.

"Are we?"

"Yes. We owe her that much."

"Right now."

"Yes Talia, right this second, we should've done this the day she went missing. Can't you feel it?"

She noticed Talia's hesitation for a moment, and then, "I can't talk you out of this, can I? Should we talk to the others, first? To gather clues, to see if we can puzzle out where she went."

Mazi moved forward and Talia kept up, propping her upright. "I wish you wouldn't do that."

"Would you rather fall?"

Mazi didn't say anything right away. She paused, chewing on her thoughts. "I already know where to start. The bone labyrinth."

"Oh that's right, the elders say she went there to fast and pray. Well let's at least get some food, some provisions maybe. And maybe some more people? There are safety in numbers."

Mazi stopped and turned, moving out of Talia's grasp. She almost stumbled, but corrected herself quickly. She saw a look of fear and pity in her friend's eyes and wanted to smack it away, but decided against it. "No, no others. Just the two of us and no one else. We should be secretive, small. It will be better this way."

Talia handed Mazi her bow and said, "For walking," and then scratched her head and furroughed her brow in frustration. "Just the two of us? I guess I can see it. We would be harder to track, harder to see coming, yes. But there is a downside, too. What if we get attacked? Would the two of us be enough?"

Mazi tried out using the bow as a cane. After a few moments she was all right with it, walking slightly better and a little less clumsily. "I saw you earlier," she said, "You were magnificent, wild and unleashed. I watched how you dispatched cursed hound after cursed hound with only your bow and arrows, while the others were ripped to shreds and looked on in horror. I think we will be just fine."

Talis shrugged and walked ahead of Mazi. She moved slow enough to not leave her friend behind, opening the doors and waiting patiently at every second. "I wished I had the same sense of confidence in me that you have. If we die then we die. At least we did something. And at least I'll be there to tend to your wounds."

Mazi hobbled behind her, but did not say anything else. She thought again of Naomi, of her face sparkling with dew and knew that they had to do something to save her. Anything at all. She was glad Talia felt that way, too. Maybe they could fix this. Maybe they could save the world from the curse itself.

Who knows? Anything was possible.

And then she walked a little further and her leg jerked out, the curse spasming and her body falling forward. Her muscles felt sinister around her bones. And she grasped onto her bow, and kept herself from hitting the ground. That was a close call.

Mazi knew that if she were to stay here they would cut off her limbs, or burn her or who knows what else. At least out there, searching for Naomi, she had a chance. If they burned her? She would not become a ghost. Instead, she would be a wailing voice, an angry spirit still hungry with the light of the curse. That was something she feared more than anything else. Naomi would know what to do.

The kitchen and dining hall were the smallest two rooms in the temple. Which is to say, for most people the rooms were not small at all, but instead mammoth and cave-like in their appearance. They only appeared small when you compared it to other rooms, each one more expansive and larger than the last. Even the seers who lived here never quite got used to the weight of their surroundings, and would feel awe most hours of the day. In the face of the universe, the high ceilings reached up to the heavens and dwarfed everyone who walked through the halls.

Every room in the temple was like this. Both terrifying and beautiful. The large space and organic masonry made the walls into artificial trees. The invading vegetation and animal life gave it an external, arboreal air. Combined with the candles and the statues of various saints and ghosts, gods and demons, all crowded and awaiting ritual, it was hard not to get drunk on the mystery of it all.

Even now, when Mazi was as cursed as she was, she still felt weightless and a pull of a different gravity, beyond the physical pulling her and the feelings of immense loneliness and sorrow. Talia grabbed her hand, as if she could feel the tugging between them, a blistering vision in the skull that comes from movements of sheer exhilaration with the dead or singing to the living gods. It made you feel like everything was constructed of lightning filled with flashing images of spiritual ascension.

Amongst the rows and rows of table there were scattered a handful of seers. Most of them are the ones from earlier, battle weary and painfully eating food in silence. A few others were the elder seers, who had been around before even Naomi had joined them. The smell of food were simple ones of broth and fresh bread.

The two of them walked over to the elders, sat down at the

table across from them. "We are going to go look for Naomi," Mazi said.

One of them sipped her soup calmly, while the other spoke. Her manner was chiding, but not hateful. "Are you, now?"

Talia nodded. "Yes ma'am."

The one drinking soup rested her spoon for a moment. Soup still stained her chin, her eyes were cataract coated with a blue film. "Let them go. Give them some things, small things. Map and such. Maybe a lodestone, but show them how to use it. And food, though it won't last you long. You're smart though, you know how to hunt; this should be enough."

Mazi and Talia responded in a rough unison, saying, "Thank you."

"Get off with you," one of the silent ones said. An elder who hadn't spoken more than a word or two for ten years. "There are more cursed in these lands now, and she had gift for helping us fight them back a little. We don't want it spreading here, no, not at all. Don't you come back without her. You hear me? You either find Naomi and return, or you don't return at all."

And the two of them didn't say a word more, fearing that the old women might hit them or yell. They instead said goodbye to the few seers working in the kitchen, and then walked over and filled a small bag with some bread and a cured bit of meat wrapped in cheesecloth. They didn't want too large of a bag, lightness was key to survival.

At the exit they stopped for a brief moment and held their breath. The large, wooden doors were carved intricately with pictures of serpents and a woman asleep, dreaming of the snakes. They paused. They'd seen this same door a million times, and yet it had never felt so important, so final. There was no going back. Everything was about to change.

So, for a moment they stood still. Hand in hand. Holding their breaths in the same way they held their breath before the start of each ritual. Was this also a ritual? Maybe. If so, it was a private ritual, shared by only the two of them and no one else.

They heard singing again, in the hallways behind them. The song of the dead kings who haunted the hollow stones, and their daughters whose skeletons made up the bone labyrinth. A fitting ritual, a fitting song. They were going to head to that bone labyrinth first. A choir walking the halls behind them. In their hands, wax candles shed dim light in the cavernous hallways.

Talia pushed open those doors. The world outside felt brighter than it had before, and Mazi put her palm over her eyes, shadowing them from that intense light. Grass swayed and the pine woods stretched out longer and further, motioning them to come on, come along, come inside our restless branches, we are waiting, we are hungry, and we need you.

5

FOG COVERED THE GROUND. THE pines arched over their heads, gigantic and bluish green. Birds called out amongst the tree branches, and Mazi felt for a moment she was still in the temple again. Any moment, one of the seers would walk along the tree shaped halls, singing. It took a moment to clear her head. She was in a forest and not in a room carved to look like one. Through the roll of grey fog she could make out the yellow brown pine needles coating the forest floor. To catch her breath and stop her dizzy spell, she rested against a standing stone. It was tall, upright, and covered in markings of a language in circles and spirals and dashes. It was a lost language from before the edges of time.

"They said if we kept heading north we would eventually run into the Bone Labyrinth." Talia looked down at a small bowl filled with water. A lodestone shaped like an arrow spun and then pointed directly ahead.

"Yes, I know," Mazi replied, "What does it say?"

Talia held up one finger for a quick moment. Then pointed it down and said, "North. Why haven't we seen anything yet? It feels like we've been walking through these woods for hours."

Mazi sighed, strapped the bow to her back. She was having less trouble walking. It seemed as if the more she walked, the less problems she had. For now, it was only a few dizzy spells here and there and not much else. She wished she could say the same for her arm. She rubbed it with her hand, spreading the pain. It shot up her elbow now, like needles in her blood, traveling towards her spine.

"Let me see your arm," Talia said. "Just for a moment."

Mazi looked at her out of the corner of her eye. "No. It's fine."

"I just want to dress the wound, clean the bandages."

Mazi hesitantly walked over to Talia, still holding her hand over the bandage. When she got close enough Talia reached over, and Mazi yanked her arm back. She closed her eyes, and said, "I'm sorry, it's just that… it's feeling worse. You know? I don't want you to see it. Not like this."

Talia reached out gently, put her hand over Mazi's. "I know, but I've seen worse. While you slept at the temple I'd cleaned the wounds of the others. Some of them were far gone, and it will haunt my nightmares. Let me see to this wound, so it won't get as bad as those."

Mazi loosened her grip on the bandage, and then turned her head, closing her eyes. "I don't want to look. And don't tell me how bad it looks. I don't want to know. Just fix it."

Talia held the arm between her hands, and gently unwrapped the bandages like she was carefully opening a rotten present. After the last bandage was pulled away, she sucked in her breath and made a hissing noise. It had spread, the strange shadow fingers moved now, danced along the inside. Her skin was ragged and torn, and the bone glistened beneath the wound. The blood around the wound had turned black. This was not a good sign.

Talia did not want to look, but she had to. Another clucking noise in her throat to mask that she tried not to panic, and then she reached into her satchel, and pulled out fresh gauze and some ointment.

"Will you stop making those noises?"

"What noises," Talia said as she squirted the ointment on the wound, and then spread it around with her fingers.

"Those noises. I told you I didn't want to know how bad it is, and those aren't really installing confidence."

"Right. Almost done."

She wrapped gauze around and snipped it with her athame. When that was done, she put the rest in her satchel and said, "All done now, fit and fine. You'll be better in no time."

Mazi sighed and rubbed her arm. "I said don't tell me how bad it was, I didn't mean for you to sound so... chipper."

"How does it feel?"

She rubbed her palm, wiggled her fingers. "Not any better, though it's not your fault. Thank you, for taking care of me."

Talia pushed hair out of her eye, and made certain not to touch the burn scars on her face. They were still tender, even after all these years. "Let's just keep going and get Naomi back safe and sound. She was able to heal those vagabond brothers, right? She should have no problem with you. Let's go and get everything back to normal."

Normal was gone now. They were performing a ritual, and a ritual was anything but normality. Yes, all rituals had a rigidity of structure to them, but even then, they were disruptions. They marked moments of transition and transformation, and celebrated the abnormal. Right now, everything felt liminal, trapped between the real and the unreal.

The bone labyrinth appeared to grow out of the ground before them. It danced with the branches of the pine trees, cartilage merging with root bow. It was a head taller than the two of them, and Mazi thought if she climbed on Talia's shoulders, she would be able to see above the walls and into the maze beyond. The bones rambled, created passageways, doors and hallways.

Skulls crowned the top of the walls. They all seemed to be fresh skulls; rumors among the seers said they were the skulls of teenage girls. Mazi thought that maybe they were princesses sacrificed to appease dead gods, or maybe even restless, hungry ghosts. She'd heard stories of older civilizations, way before the seers built their temple on the hill that had grim rituals to fight the curse. These were supposed to be only rumors and stories. And yet here, seeing those skulls and those bones, she had to believe it was true. This was proof, incontrovertible proof, that once upon a time king's sacrificed their daughters to fight the plague, and lined this labyrinth with their bones.

Something moved in the maze beyond. Horrible sounds, like heavy things being dragged through the needles on the ground. A muffled whimpering beneath all of that, and maybe a pleading voice. A voice familiar to Mazi, though she couldn't quite place it. It was a male voice, and she hadn't heard a male voice in almost a decade or so. It sounded foreign to her, gruff and alien. She started to move forward and

Talia put her arm across her, holding her back. Not roughly, but just enough.

"Do you think that's wise? Can't you hear that?"

Mazi got her bow ready, arrow notched and ready to fire. The string cut into her fingers, and again her hand felt like a clumsy thing. The burning grew, became a whisper under her skin. She almost dropped the bow, but did not. She clung to it with as strong a grip as she could muster. This curse was not going to destroy her.

"Yes, I can, I can hear it. Does it matter? What if it's Naomi?"

Talia glanced at her friend out of the corner of her eye.

"That is not Naomi's voice, you know that as well as I do."

"I know. I know that voice. What if she's here with him?"

They both moved forward, ears to the air, listening. They could not make out what he said, it was too deep throated and thin. Talia said, "I doubt it. Come on, let's turn around, regroup. Figure out some other way to find her."

"We don't know of any other way," a plea in Mazi's voice, "We know of this and nothing else. Come, let's go in there, we can fight these things. I know it, you know it. It's just the two of us, we're quick, we're clever. Let's go in and do this."

Talia closed her eyes and said, "Are you feeling all right?"

"I told you, I'm fine."

Her eyes opened and she walked over to her friend, placed a hand on her shoulder. "There is a pain in the bottom of your throat; I hear it. Please, let us turn around now, cut our losses. Try and get some more people to help us find Naomi."

A pause between the words in their conversation. More dragging noises in the maze, and more muffled cries pleading, begging, but for what? They still couldn't tell. And then Mazi cleared her throat, and said, "You know we can't do that."

Talia unslung her bow and readied an arrow. Closed her eyes, counted to three under her breath. "You are hopelessly obstinate. Let's do this."

They moved cautiously through the gateway, the bones rattling in the wind as they walked through. Beyond was a series of hallways, spiraling out from the center. Mazi leaned over, whispered to Talia, "Should we follow the cries? Or move along our own path, the one of Naomi's ritual. I fear that we should follow the cries, to offer help if they need it."

Talia whispered back, quickly, without even pausing for a thought. "No, you can't leave this to me. You chose, this is your idea. I'm only here to keep you safe."

Mazi leaned on her bow again. She felt dizzy. The labyrinth looked like a cartwheel of bones. The muffled voice cried out again, and she shook her head, clearing it of all the fog and finding her balance once more. Naomi had taught her too well, and she knew what she must do.

"We will follow the cries for help. It's what Naomi would want us to do, we can resume our search afterwards."

They crept towards the dragging sound. More whimpering and pleading echoed through the labyrinth beyond. The skulls seemed to turn and watch them. Was it only a figment of her imagination? Or had they really turned and watched her? All those dead princesses, their bones left behind as a temple in the heart of the world.

The maze twisted and the paths opened up before them like a flower, leading them towards the spiral center. The maze was directing them onward. It knew exactly where they'd wanted to go. Talia still marked the walls with charcoal.

6

HER TRAINING AS AN ACOLYTE was in the forefront of Mazi's mind, as she crept into the shadows of the maze. The hours they spent in seclusion in the pits, the days of starvation and then revelation. They breathed the air, ate the dirt and earth, gulped water, and finally exhaled fire. Hours hung upside down, spinning slowly with iron piercing skin, their body weight pulling the skin tight, the chains clinking with each spin of the body. Below an intricate chalk drawing of holy geometry, the heavens and astrology, now dripped with blood, messed up with dangling hands and delirious laughter. Eventually the pain would give way to light, to a connection to in and out, to the base of the sky and the clouds inside.

Walking here brought back so many of these memories. The path was a spiral, mirroring the spiral galaxy you could see overhead at night. This was a sacred space, and she closed her eyes, and thought back to her training as they walked. The labyrinth will open for us and show us the way. She hummed her prayers under breath, and slowly Talia joined along as well. They made a rough harmony together. The exact song did not matter. It was the action that was important.

As they sang, Mazi's wounds seemed to tighten as the pain ebbed. What was this feeling? Had the labyrinth changed them? Or where they changing the labyrinth? She was not foolish enough to assume she was healed. Curses of this power never fully went away. They only slept for some time, biding the hours until it was safe for them to spring up again.

Their humming slowly died off, revealing darker sounds beneath their prayers.

"Wait," Talia whispered, holding an arm against Mazi, keeping her back, just a little more, "Do you hear it?"

They were both silent. Mazi held her breath to quiet the sound of her breathing, a ragged hoarse sound that made her conscious of each and every sound of her body. No matter how subtle.

Nothing. Not even bird wings flapping, or tree branch cracking. Nothing.

And then came the rumblelowgrowl and the trees bending and the bones crumbling, skulls falling from the root of the maze. Then that pleading again, closer now, definitely a male voice. One she almost kind of recognized but still could not place. Now it was audible, loud enough they could track his location. He wasn't too far away from them, maybe just a few more twists and turns and that was all.

Talia nodded, "Yes, now we can tell were he's at. I hope you're correct about all of this, I really want to do the right thing, but I also don't want us to get killed."

Mazi pulled out a leather throng and did her hair up into

a quick bun. The knot was not very tight, but it didn't have to be. It just had to keep her hair out of her eyes, since it was getting dark and the fog getting thick. She needed as much of her sight as she could. "Yes, this is right. We might not be here for him, but somehow... I don't know how to say this? He's connected to Naomi. I know his voice, I can't place it though. And how would I know a man's voice? There hasn't been a lot of men coming to our temple, and the ones we've met knew Naomi somehow."

"I don't know, this feels wrong. Can't you feel it? It feels wrong."

Darkness in the pines was a deep lightless terror. No stars could reach in through those branches, no moonlight could pierce the needles.

"A lamp?" was Mazi's only response, purposefully ignoring the question.

Talia rummaged loudly through her satchel. "Lamp might be too much here, make it too easy to spot us and attack. What about a candle? Easy to extinguish if we need to disappear."

Mazi nodded, "Yes, good thinking. A candle then."

She felt a hand against hers, and then a waxy tip against her fingers. "You be our light, and I'll be our violence."

She grasped it, a flash of flint and the wick was lit. The wax flowed down the edge, the candle was tallow and the light a dim orange sputter. It was enough that they could see where the bone walls ended and where their bodies began.

The pleading stopped and only whimpering, a brutal sobbing, and then a howl of pain. "I don't think it's much further now. Are you ready?"

Talia moved a little ahead, pulled her hair behind her ears. The flickering light made her scars stand out stronger still, deep shadows of fire against her face. Wax dripped against her knuckles as they walked, small rings of pain against her skin. The curse called out to the fire, moved towards it, the burning almost making her drop the candle. She switched hands and they continued onward. Deeper into the spiral center of the labyrinth.

The moss and lichen slid away from the candlelight as they moved deeper into the center. Soon, soon, they reached the heart of the maze, where all paths spun out into the trees. A clearing with a tall silver oak, the only non-pine in the whole woods.

The minute they drew close to this area they blew out their candle, quickly, quickly, holding their breath. The moon was able to move through these trees, the oak branches pushing away the pines just enough to let the rays of grey through. They slid back and pressed against their spines against the walls, searching in the shadows for whatever made that sound. It should be here, shouldn't it? They'd followed the noise, louder and louder through the maze. And it should be here, that pleading voice, that dragging sound.

After a moment of stillness, the shadows changed.

Tall humanoid things paced the darkness. They had deer-like antlers and hooves. Eyes dotted their bodies like freckles. They slouched around a shadow of a man, not much older than Mazi. His clothes were piebald rags barely stitched together, and his face scowled with scars of his own.

His left ear was missing, bloodied, a new wound. One of the creatures moved forward and threw something on the ground with a wet splash. An ear, made sharp by the moonlight. They spoke something to the man, in a low guttural language, pointing at an object he held close to his chest: a thing wrapped in loose bandages.

"This is mine, not yours, you hear me?"

One hand moved back and fingers clicked. His other hand held onto the heart, and at the clicking of his fingers fire sprouted and danced. "I can do worse. You best back off."

More guttural strange language. A language neither of the seers could understand. It sounded primal, like the words of the dark before the sun shone on the world.

"I have my reasons. Some magic I don't do lightly, but now you left me no choice. You've drawn first blood, and now I shall draw the last. Come at me, let's see if you burn as bright as your brothers."

The creatures moved forward and Mazi couldn't just sit by and watch this play out, enough pain had been caused that strange man. And she swore she knew him, but it felt like he was so different. As if he was much younger in her memory, and that was part of the fog in her mind. She bent her bow back, and fired the arrow without second thought. As the arrow left her hands the bow snapped and shattered, cutting her palm. She drew back her hand in pain, dropping the bow to the ground. Blood. Not a deep gash, but still. Blood. The arrow missed the creatures, missed the man, hit the tree behind him. Damnit. She had all the luck.

The creatures turned, all of them, turned towards the shadows.

"Shit," Talia said, and fired her bow in a rapid, smooth motion. Plunk, like a harp string, two arrows writhed in the air, fast and bright, knocking them backwards. One was down and motionless, the other stood up, the arrow still sticking out of its back. A glint of dagger light in the darkness, but it was too far away. Before it even moved Talia had another arrow fly through the air, hit it in the eye. It fell back, moved a moment, slithered, and then stopped again. No more movement.

Mazi exhaled. Pain. Her whole body, pain. This was too much, she felt the curse writhe in her muscles again and she was exhausted. She grabbed her arm, so hot, wet blood between her fingers. The curse moved through her blood, towards her heart. It sang under her skin. So hot, she moved her fingers back, singed from the touch. Fever of flesh and bone. Fever so bright and burning. Everything spun, all woozy and sick. And then. And then. And then.

Both bodies caught fire.

It was a small thing at first. A firelight flicker. Then their skin filled with light. Then cracks moved along their bodies. Then, finally, a roaring burst of flames through the cracks. It happened in an instant, but it felt like a million years. The creatures collapsed into a heap of smoldering ruin. Mazi stumbled forward, her arm itching burning fire hot in the curse, moving with that doomed arm outstretched. Talia pulled her back, forcefully.

"No," she said, "Stay back, for now. We cannot tell..."

Mazi gazed at her friend, then turned her gaze back towards the bodies in front of them. Her eyes were numbed, glazed over, the eyes of someone lost and searching.

"Are you... is everything all right?"

Mazi shook her head no. Speaking felt so hard to do. Her mouth felt a far away. Her body was distant. When did it become so strange to live in a body? She felt like an intruder in her own body. Was she a ghost? Had the curse made her into a ghost? "I don't know. But I see what you mean now, by having a bad feeling. This feels wrong. You were right, this feels wrong."

A voice came from behind the flames, his face light by the darkness. Scars in a ring over his eyes, in a large swipe across his face. His hair was a disheveled molten mess, growing in messy spurts across the scalp. "Is there someone there? I mean you no harm."

His clothes seemed even more like bandages in the fire-light, just strips of gauze across still open wounds. A leper? It was hard to tell in such a dim light.

"You will... have to give us a minute," Talia said, holding her friend close, "It's not every day you see creatures just burst into flame like that."

"Oh, yes, that. Do not worry about them, those were the cursed. They have no spirit, they are just shells moving without consciousness. Everything they do, they do for the beast, and no longer act for themselves."

Mazi leaned her head away from Talia's chest, and turned and looked at the stranger, still waiting behind the flames. "Beast," she said, "What beast?"

"A monstrous bear of a thing, the original cursed. It's taken over the city on the hill, and spread its foulness everywhere. That happened just before I came here, to the labyrinth, to get this," holds the bandaged object close to himself, "for my brother. To help him. I owe him that much. I thank you both, for all of your help. My brother might just survive this after all."

Before Mazi could help herself, she practically screamed at him. "Have you seen Naomi? She would have been here, in the maze, she would have... have you seen her, any seer? Alive or dead, please, tell me. I need to know."

The stranger walked through the fire. It burned bright on either side of him, distorting his body with an eerie light. "Yes, I saw her, yes," and Mazi was almost about ready to scream with joy.

7

H E WALKED PAST THE FIRE, close to them now. His body distorted by the light of the blue flames. Something about the way he moved, the way he talked, Mazi wasn't sure she trusted him. How could she trust him? And yet, they had nothing else to go on. He saw her. Naomi. "She was alive, at least she was when I last saw her, not too far from here."

"She's alive," Mazi stammered the words out, "She's alive," and now it's a laugh and a shout. "I can't believe it. That's such good news."

Talia did not move. "Yes," she said woodenly, "It's hard to believe we've had such good luck meeting... meeting... what was your name again?"

"This woman, this seer, she was going towards the city on the hill. The very same place where my brother waits for my gift. Come, come, we have a common purpose now. We should travel together, don't you think?"

Talia moved forward, slowly, an arrow in one hand at the ready. The moonlight made the clearing look haunted. "And what is the gift?"

"Just a bauble, a silly precious thing. Nothing of import to either of you, I promise."

Mazi put a hand on Talia's shoulder, holding her back. They looked like a triangle in the darkness, lit by a circle of death. "Talia, we have to try. It's for her, for Naomi. We have to try."

Silence for a moment, a weighted nothingness in the air. The only sound was the crackle of the fire. He stood up beside the tree, his scars reflecting the glitter of the silver bark. Talia moved forward, the triangle of figures closing in on the stranger before them.

"Show us the gift. If you want us to join you, show us we can trust you."

He closed his eyes, and then let out a deep sigh. "It's medicine, that is all."

"Show us."

She pulled her bow taught and strong, pointed the arrow at him. He twitched a little, and then Mazi put her hand against the bow and gently pushed it down. Talia closed her eyes, breathed deeply for a few moments. Mazi leaned into her friend, whispered closely in her ear, "He's seen Naomi. We owe this to her, we need to see this through. Even if he lied, it is the only lead we have."

Talia turned, her back towards both of them, her arms crossed on her chest, her one hand holding the bow, the other hand holding the arrow. Mazi leaned across her friend, pulled her in close and said gently, almost a kiss in her ear, "You can turn around now, and I will do this myself. I do not want to burden you with my foolishness."

Talia relaxed herself as much as she could, trying to seem less fraught and taught and ready to explode. She then turned around and spat out, "Your name. Give us your name."

"Oh, understandable, yes, my dear seers, my name for your trust, of course. If you will join me and help me as I help you find what you want, then you can easily have my name."

Mazi winced, knowing that this was not the answer Talia desired. Talia did not react violently, she seemed calm and static. No emotion either way right now, as if all of this intensity had completely drained her of emotions. "Give us your name now, and we'll tell you what we decide. Is that understandable?"

"Oh," he swung low in a dim bow. "Of course, completely understandable. My name is Lens. Like the tool used to see, or to see further, or to map the stars. Lens. Now, I take it you are Talia, by the words your friend gives so freely. You then, you, give me your name now. Trust works both ways, you see. How can I trust you? The way your friend points her arrows at me, I fear you would kill me at any moment. Give me your name, and let's build some trust between us."

"Mazi," she spoke it like the word had no meaning. As if it might be her name, it might not, it did not matter to her.

"I see, I see. Mazi and Talia. My brother, by the way, his name is Aste, you see. Aste. I am Lens; he is Aste. Now we are all well met and everything else. Come, come, move around the fire, I can lead you out of the maze. I've been wandering in it for days, looking for this small artifact, and now I know this labyrinth like the back of my hand."

"You... you found that here? You stole that. Is that one of our relics?" Talia shook with anger, moved up close while her face reflected the fire of the still burning bodies.

"No. Not particularly," he said, "It's nothing, I promise. Come, come, let's go, we're wasting time. If we haven't found your sister seer before I make it to my brother, you can watch as he unwraps it. You can see for yourself then what a meaningless thing this is, and how it was not a relic at all. But something else, entirely."

A pause in the conversation, letting the world breathe around them. Mazi was exhausted, and the curse moved on her arm and made her muscles weak and tired. She closed her eyes, tried forcing that feeling away, to leave her body and let her be. The curse took and took and took. Pretty soon, there just might be nothing left of her. "Come Talia. It seems our path is already chosen for us. The stars have spoken; you can read them as easily as I do."

They rose up weary, walked between the flaming bodies. The fire didn't burn Mazi in the least bit. Instead it felt like needles on her skin, and she wanted to drink the fire, to open her mouth wide and suck those flames inside. She resisted this absurd desire. She had a feeling those flames would let the curse grow inside of her.

When they got to Lens, he nodded, but did not speak. He knew that this was a moment for silence. And he led them out, through the rings of the maze itself, going out to the other side.

She knew that Lens was not the man's name, yet Mazi did not say anything. When she looked at him, she got that tickling feeling in the back of her mind that he was someone she had met when she was a child and that he was a child as well, since they were about the same age give or take a few years. And she knew that Lens was not the name that fit his spirit. She wanted to say that maybe, his name was Quin, but that was only half right. She wasn't sure why that was only half right, she just knew that Quin was closer to his name then Lens for some reason.

She didn't have to say this out loud, she could tell Talia felt that the stranger was lying to them and trust was a papery thin thing, easily torn and ripped apart.

Though, that was another part of this. This man was a puzzle in their lives right now, and she knew that when they had originally met, Talia had not yet joined the temple. So her lack of trust in him was something else all together. She wished she could discuss this with her friend, but they never had time alone right now. Lens was always there, with them, listening. It was definitely not a conversation she wanted him to overhear. And they needed him now. He'd seen Naomi.

And this made Mazi worry even more than she had before. It was bad enough they were involved with this strange, untrust-worthy man. But to have to rely on him, to almost trust him just to find Naomi? That felt wrong. She was far away from the temple, far away from the rituals and the dark mirrors. She had no time to hang herself upside down, no time to place the runes in the earth, the symbols on her hand, to gather in the visions and see what the best action was in this moment.

She thought of trying a simple divination. Maybe a bone casting, or blood reading. But that bothered her as well, how much did he know? Did he know anything about divination at all? He wasn't a seer, no. He had not the training, nor was he a woman. Yet, it felt like she could not even do a basic ritual sighting in front of him, that he might somehow know, just by looking at her face, what she knew.

And that unsettled her in a way that made her skin crawl.

It's not like the sighting was certain to work anyway. The seers have been trying for the last day or so to see what Naomi had been doing, if it was necessary to send out a search party or not, if Naomi had been in trouble, if she would be back, any of that. There was no response. It was as if the universe was silent on the nature of Naomi.

It had always been like that for her. She was an anomaly in the world, one who could not be sighted, who did not have a future or a past. She only existed in the now, and any visions the others saw always excluded her.

When she arrived at the temple they were afraid of this very aspect, assumed that she would be their downfall, that somehow she was the bringer of death and suffering to all of them for some unseen slight against the dead. After the decades rolled by and no such thing happened, they kept her close, always looking at her and looking out for her. Still unable to see what the future held, if it even held anything at all.

Before they left the labyrinth, Mazi stopped and stared at the bones of the structure, searching. She rubbed her hands over the wrist bones and fingers, looking for something in particular. She set down her candle, as the orange and red light flickered against her face in a spotchy glow.

Talia walked up to her and said, "What are you doing? We should get going, in case there are other... cursed things."

Mazi did not say a word in response. It wasn't that she was ignoring Talia, but more like she was deep in thought. Her eyes were too busy focusing on the search, her hands reveling in the tactile sensation of death. Her palm rested on a skull.

"I'm looking," was all she said.

Mazi moved further down the line of bones. Her fingers moved like spokes over the cartilage, following a call beneath the skin. Eventually she found a spine of a princess, and pulled it from the stone and mortar that bound it to the wall. It took a few tries, shaking the rock, bits of ground dust caking her face and making her cough. Eventually she was able to wrestle it free, wholly intact, solid and snaking in her hands. For a moment she had worried that she had cracked or broken it. She stood over the candle light, inspecting it for any small fractures. Nothing at all. It was completely without imperfection.

The others stared, watched her as she pulled out a bow string made from catgut. The same kind of string that was used on a violin bow, and she strung it up on the spine. She tested it, made sure it didn't bend too much, didn't snap or break when she fired a test arrow. She watched it fly through the air, land thunk on a pine tree bursting through a wall of bones.

"Yes," Mazi said, "Yes. I think this will do nicely. Don't you?"

The man they called Lens smiled and nodded his head quickly. This made Talia laugh and say, "It does, very nicely. Don't worry Lens, I don't think she'll try that on you, not unless you do something insanely stupid."

Lens laughed and it sounded more like a nervous cough. "No, hah, no. Not me. I am not a risk taker. Risks terrify me. Now, um, can we go? Let us move along a little more now. I did mention my brother was sick, didn't I? I did say he was dying and this little prezzie, which I went through so much trouble to retrieve for him, would be just the thing to cheer him up."

Mazi said nothing. She fired her bow one more time, the arrow going right above the last one. The bow sounded like someone sighing in both pleasure and pain when it was used. A haunting sound, that gave her chills, and brought back memories of dark things hunting her at night.

8

LENS LED THEM FURTHER AHEAD, walking towards the city on the hills in the distance. Tall towers rose out of the center of the city walls, reaching up towards a crimson sun that rested just beyond the hills. It outlined everything with a dim ochre glow. Her arm was twisted and angry now and was mostly wound. Echoes moved inside the gash, like ghosts wandering amongst her bones. Oh, no. She could see her bones. For a moment she felt fizzy with the promise of death. Her bandages all ripped to tatters. She tried moving her hand, and it was a clumsy distant thing. No, not again. She had been doing so much better.

"I don't think, Talia? I don't think... Talia?"

Talia was preoccupied, looking over towards the hills and the city. The sun rose a little more, just above those hills, and it was a strange red creature. From the city you could see a fog brooding about, with multi-colored lights flashing like gigantic fireflies. Talia stared at it, concentrating deeply. Mazi knew that look, she knew that intensity. The last time she saw Talia looking like that was during the ritual of fifteen hearts, her body spinning and her eyes fierce in the dark.

"Talia..."

The burns on her face seemed to glow in that morning light, burn red against the freckles on her cheeks. She let her hair fall, briskly over her eyes, covering those scars. "Huh," Talia said, and then turned to her friend. Lens was ahead of them both, surveying that city with a small, whirring telescope.

Talia's intensity drained away for a moment, and Mazi was worried. Did she really look that bad? She felt horrible. Her muscles ached and weakened. So hard to even stand upright. Everything tilted on its axis, and she said, "Talia, I, Talia I think..."

And then she was in the grass, her eyes wide open, looking towards something unseen floating above their heads. Talia leaned down over her, again, her movements slow and impeded with time, pulled up Mazi's body, held her close to her chest. "Oh, Mazi, Mazi, what is happening to you? What is happening?"

And then she looked down, and saw the wound. Her mouth closed to a slit, painfully tight, her eyes shaking, her face wet with a tear or two at the horror of the curse. "I can fix you, Mazi, I can fix you. Don't you go away on me, stay here, listen to my voice. Can you do that for me? I will fix you and I will make this better, just stay with us, listen to the sound of my voice, and don't fade away. Oh, by thunder and bone, please don't ever fade away..."

And then Talia undid the bandages, pulled out some ointment. The kind that smelled strange, mixed with ectoplasm milked from the hollow stones. She applied it down and Mazi didn't respond, her eyes still wide open. Her mouth twitched a little, and the curse moved away from Talia's fingers, fleeing. "It's grown so large... Mazi can you hear me dear? Can you me? Oh, please. Please tell me you can hear me in there..."

Talia jumped when a hand touched her shoulder and she almost dropped Mazi. She then turned her head, saw Lens above her. He seemed to come out of nowhere. Had she been that obsessed with helping Mazi that she lost track of everything else?

"That won't do," Lens said, one hand on her, the other on his precious package. The package twitched, moved.

"Is that alive?"

"Don't worry about that now, worry about it later. Your friend here, she needs help, proper help. I've seen the curse get like that, oh. It won't be long now..."

Talia gently placed Mazi down and turned. "Can you help her?"

"I only knew one person, oh. But they're not... they're not here right now, are they? No. Maybe we can do something. It will be ugly. Turn around."

"Turn around?"

Lens made a motion in the air, circular, spinning his fingers. She didn't trust him. She had to, well, trust him. She hated that she had no choice in the matter. Trust should be something you earned, not a price you paid for help.

She knelt down close to Mazi, leaned her head back up so they locked eyes. Those pupils still big, and full of tiny fires, her skin sucked of all color and left ashen and near dead. The curse was stronger than Talia. She would do as he said, for her friend. If nothing else, for her friend. "All right Lens, you have it. I won't look, just do what you need to do."

When Talia first came to the temple she was a shattered little girl of about nine. She could barely talk, her throat raspy and burnt raw from smoke. Her eyes were covered with rags, hiding the here scarred and burnt eyelids. She walked with a crutch for a bit, and had to keep her bandages wet and cool or else the pain would be too great. Mazi took an instant liking to her, and she became a mentor of sorts, teaching her every moment she could.

Everything was so bright when Talia finally removed the bandages from her eyes. Shadows and light, and then eventually forms and figures moving around in the light, and then people and then statues and trees and animals. Mazi was the first person she saw, the first face that bent towards hers in that blinding light. Her hands where the hands the snipped the bandages free, and her voice was the first voice welcoming Talia to the seers, to her new life.

"A life," she had explained, "Where no one will do that to you, never, ever again. I promise you that, we will keep you safe."

"You will?"

She nodded her head. "We are family here."

Talia wanted to cry but the tears burnt her face. That word brought back so many painful memories, the sound of her mother howling in pain, the image of her father's rage as he ran right into the fire to try and save them. He died, they all died, but not Talia. Why had she lived? She wasn't special, her life wasn't worth more than her father's or her sister's or her mother's. Why had she lived?

She asked Mazi that later and Mazi just said, "Who says

they are gone? They live through you. You lived so you could carry them inside of you, and every action you perform is an action that contains every aspect of them inside of it. Do you understand? You are the carrier of their ghosts, and this is a sacred honor. You will understand more later, when we show you the rituals and the oaths to the dead. Then you will understand what we owe to those we carry inside."

And she did, eventually, come to understand how her family now acted through her, how she had become a living memory. Each movement of her body was a rite, summoning them into reality. She took pride in this fact and vowed to become the best in everything. To honor them was to excel at all she did; anything less would be a failure, and a sin against their memories.

It wasn't easy. Her burns made even holding a bow a struggle. Her eyesight took a long time to heal completely, and even then, she learned to use her disadvantages to her advantage. The holes in her sight became possibilities of power. She pushed herself, so much harder than the other acolytes, so much so that Mazi came up to her a few times and asked her politely, nicely, to just slow down. Just a tiny bit, that was all.

And Talia laughed at her and kept going. Before long Mazi cheered her on, and brought her food and water, and helped her train as best she could. And they would stay up well into the evening hours, sharing bread and talking about their lives now, and the lives before the temple, and what the world outside the walls looked like. It had been too long since either of them had seen a real city, and they missed that life at odd hours with a hollow ache. Life was better here, yes. But the memories of the dead stuck around, and the yearning for what was never truly went away.

And now Mazi was cursed and on the ground. Maybe dying, maybe changing into some cursed creature that might kill Talia, if given the chance. And the only hope in this moment right now was Lens. For Mazi's sake. For the one woman who saw her, and saved her, and gave her life.

Talia wanted to turn around and see what he was doing, but did not dare disrupt him. Instead, she looked into Mazi's far away eyes, and saw her lip twitch and curl, and then her hand move in a strange way. Her fingers curled up in on themselves, then gestured in moon shapes and chaotic geometry. Whispers came from her lips, "Talia, I'm falling. I keep felling and I can't stop, I can't stop falling. Talia, catch me. Please catch me."

Talia grabbed her close. "I've got you," she whispered, "I've got you."

And then the sound of footsteps and Lens harsh voice, "I need room to get in there and apply this."

Talia moved back a little, just enough, still protective of her friend as Lens leaned down, a sliver of grey wriggling on his palm. It looked like hungry mercury. "What is that?"

He ignored her question, ripped Mazi's shirt open a little, revealing the spiral scar. Talia instinctively yanked Mazi's body away, and Lens held his hand up and spoke calmly. "I need to place this directly over her heart. It has to be done."

Talia nodded and then said, "Tell me what it is."

"A small piece of a ghost heart, just a sliver, just enough to help her."

He placed the writhing grey thing over her chest, and it dug down and spread out from her ventricles. Her eyes flickered and her pupils became normal again, and she started coughing. Talia held her friend close and said, "Where did you get that? The only people I know who harvest those..."

"Your friend, Naomi. She gave it to me. It's not much, and it wouldn't have done much for my brother anyway, not that little of a slice, not with how far his curse has advanced. He's beyond the help of such a trifle."

Talia nodded, holding Mazi as she made retching noises, and then a panicked whimpering sound. "You're going to be fine now, at least for a little," Talia said. And then she turned towards Lens. "Is that what you've been carrying, that you refused to show us?"

She hated being so accusatory, what with the help he just provided them and everything. But she still could not let go of this feeling that he was hiding something, something terrible, something dangerous. Something that would end up destroying all of them.

"No," Lens said without hesitation. "Not at all."

Talia was not completely satisfied. It felt like he was choosing his words too carefully. "Show it to me," she said, and gently moved away from Mazi. Mazi was able to sit up by herself now, and watched the two of them in a numbed silence. "Show it to me now!"

Lens shook his head, and slid the gauze wrapped item into a satchel. "No, I will not," and then he slung the satchel over his shoulder. "Just, please. All I ask is for honest trust right now. I trust you, and after all I've done for you so far, why can't you trust me?"

Talia moved forward, reached for an arrow. Mazi reached up to her, placed her palm against her hand, fingers wrapped around her wrist. "No, not now," Mazi said, "Not yet. He has done us no wrong that we know of. He's only tried to help us."

Talia leaned over, helped Mazi stand. Her legs wobbled, like a baby deer struggling to walk. She laughed. "I feel better, yes. I feel much better now. Thank you, Lens. And thank you Naomi, wherever you are, for giving him that slice. Look, look at this," she held up her arm, turned it over quickly. It still shook a little, but the wound had grown smaller and smaller still. "It's healed nicely. Maybe that will be enough for awhile, to keep me going, until we find Naomi."

9

AZI WAS RIGHT BEHIND TALIA. She moved as quick as she could, barely able to keep pace with her friend. She felt more whole than before, with only a tickling in her arm to remind her of the curse. There was a hope that eventually that would go away as well, that the small piece of the ghost heart had been enough. Maybe her curse was weak and her own heart was strong enough to fight it.

To the right and left of them she felt movement, and saw shadows waking up in the valley. Cursed forms, hunched over creatures, like whales on the land, scuttling about in enormous misery. They made low howling sounds, bellowing whale calls both beautiful and melancholy at the same time. The sound left a hollow ache in her chest.

"Keep going," Lens said from behind in a half whisper, "They haven't spotted us, yet."

A behemoth turned towards them and rumbled mournfully, as it slid along the grass, leaving a path of ruin in its wake.

The creature moved right past them, glancing their way only momentarily before continuing on. It was not interested in them in the least bit. Lens was right after all.

"I think they can sense the curse in you," Lens said, "That might just be our saving grace. I, I talked to my brother before I left. The curse had eaten away so much of him, it had replaced his consciousness with some kind of hive consciousness of the curse, if you can believe it. I asked it so many questions. It told me only one thing, over and over again. It wanted new bodies to change and make beautiful, it didn't want to touch those already cursed. Your curse will be our shield, Mazi."

They moved closer and closer now, the city within sight. It was just up ahead now, maybe a few hours walk and nothing more. A red rusted fog slouched around the building, filled with the multicolored lights. It was hard not to be drawn to the lights. They beckoned, hypnotized, pushed into a trance. Shadows moved in that fog, growling bent things, haunted and unknowing. Their shapes made no geometric sense. Each movement felt like a trick of the light, a visual hallucination. This couldn't be right. How could this be right? Mazi felt dizzy and sick with yearning.

"The whole city is... is... is cursed?" Talia's voice cracked in disbelief.

Nobody said a word. There was nothing else to say, the truth of her statement weighed against them heavily. Was this the right thing to do? How could Naomi be here? And if she was here...

What did that mean? Was she too far gone now, too far into the city, devoured by the world beyond the veil? And what did it mean for Mazi, being here. Constnatly taunted by a cuse that calls to her and wishes to drag her under its influence?

She didn't know the answers. She didn't want to know the answers. Her arm was doing better, the curse was asleep. She had to forget about these worries and move on.

One moment at a time, move on.

The tower stretched above them and dwarfed them, and the closer it got the more Mazi felt something waken inside of her. Was it the curse? Was it something else? It chilled her bones and made her stomach flip flop, and she felt like an orphan child seeing the temple for the first time. That sense of being so small and being so overwhelmed. And this couldn't be right, she rubbed her eyes, she had to be seeing things. From the center of the tower burst a bear. Before, it had been obscured by the fog and the city. Here, the closer they got, the more it came into focus. A real thing, meaty, fleshy. A bear bigger than any bear ever. The tower top crumbled around it, debris and broken stone tumbled earthward with each movement. The bear was not a normal bear, no. She rubbed her eyes again. This isn't right. This must be the curse.

And her heart flashed at the sight of it. Curse called to curse and she bit her lip. She would resist it. Her heart was stronger than the curse. She rubbed her eyes again. The deformity felt unreal, corrupted by the fog.

It had three skulls, skin pushed and molten, moving and warping against it. Chest struggled, arms still held tight inside of the tower. The sense of entrapment overwhelmed her. She could sense the bear's fear and frustration and pain. All three skulls had their jaws unhinged and mouths gaping wide. Fog poured out from those cavernous throats. Fog filled with lights and fire and the overwhelming sense of foreboding. *Doom, doom, doom* called the fog. This was the curse, spreading out in the air and corrupting everything.

"What..." Mazi said, unable to create words.

"This was what I feared when I left," said Lens, "The curse had just come to the city, riding in that body of a bear. Horrific thing, gigantic. I left quickly, knowing I needed to help my brother, so we could escape from whatever doom came to the city. Now I wonder if I'm too late. I only hope I can still move him, he might be too big, too burdened by the curse..."

"Your brother? Is that him up there, transformed into that bear *thing*?" Talia said, her words edging on hate and sarcasm.

"No. I'm sorry, you misunderstood. My brother will probably die soon, I want to get him away from the bear, from the city, from what is happening here. I've seen other cities fall like this, to other curses far lesser than this one. I don't want his last days to be filled with these horrors. What I have here is enough to get him out of the city, away from all of this madness."

"Oh I think I understand," Mazi spoke, pointing at the tri-skull bear, "And you say Naomi's here as well, you saw her enter the city? I guess we'll have to leave with you, then. If we're ever to escape the city with her intact and alive."

"No," Lens said, "I'm sorry, I can't risk it. I can help you as far as I can, but when me and my brother leave we're going alone. The bear, she's got eyes everywhere, followers all across the city. I've seen it all happen before, over and over again. Almost every city I've gone too, and I'm sorry, but I need to keep my brother safe. Safe from the bear, from her curse, from the vile promises she carries with her."

"She?"

And now both Mazi and Talia felt it, a sense of dread. They turned to look at Lens, but he was already moving on, walking ahead of them. He stopped for a moment, turned towards them. They glared at him with a gaze of confusion and distrust. Without missing a beat, he carefully reached down into his satchel, and Mazi's heart started to beat quick and lucid, now he will show us what he's been carrying this whole time. His gift for his brother.

Instead he pulled out three small black masks that squirmed in his hands like ginormous beetles. Blinking red and orange lights moved in tiny fires, and he tossed two of them at Mazi and Talia. They landed in a thunk in the grass in front of them. As he closed the satchel, slid a mask over his own face. It moved for a moment, wormed and squiggled like a larvae over his lips. Eventually it stopped moving, covering his mouth and nose completely, and when he spoke, his words came out in a wheeze and a robotic whisper.

"These were from the world before, I found them in the ruins over the sea, near the Isles of Rynsia. They said it was used to breathe the poisonous mist, when they had fought the curse centuries ago. I hope they'll still work now, they seem to, so far? Try them on, they always seem to move around just enough to fit. I know they can be... disturbing to touch, but this is a matter of staying sane and alive."

Mazi and Talia both slid them over their faces. They were cold blooded things, and they moved like insects against their lips. Each breath was a struggle to breathe, and the air tasted of burnt ashes and forest fires. For a moment, Mazi felt panic. How could she breathe like this? How could she survive like this? Her curse ached for a moment on her arm, a soft burning sensation as the muscles weakened. She would have to wear this, yes. She did not want to breathe in that foul stench. It could only make her curse worse, and she was just barely surviving even now.

"I know," Lens said, "It will take some getting used to, I'm sorry. I really wish these weren't necessary, but they are. Sadly, they are."

He began to walk forward, the satchel slung over his shoulder, his movements sluggish and slow. "Enough talking," he said, "We don't have much time." And they walked behind, two strange figures in the shadows. Mazi had left her shirt open still, not enough to reveal everything, but her spiral scar was naked and in full view. She did not want to hide it, and she hoped that Talia felt a comfort in seeing her own scars. As if they were connected by the wounds of their past, of the world before the Temple and all that came after.

"I had five masks originally," Lens spoke calmly as they walked. He now used a walking staff, something that he said was a relic from a place near the beaches nearby. He had pulled out what seemed to be a steel stick, and then snapped it forward and it grew, long and longer, until it was about his height. Out of the top snapped a cracked globe with fluttering moths trapped inside. The actual staff, much like their masks, looked aged and run down. Chipped bits of paint, cracked flickering lights. A patina of dirt and crusted muck covered the edges. "I gave my brother one, and then I... well. The other was misplaced in that damned bone labyrinth. And then there are these three."

Mazi wheezed and breathed and felt ick on her skin from

the mask moving against her face. She had no idea how she would ever get used to this. "Naomi," Mazi said, "Our friend. You said you saw her, did you give her one? Did she have one? You said she was going towards the city. Tell us. We need to know these things. Did you abandon our friend and leave her to die in this city?"

Lens stopped, and from even here, even with his mouth covered, Mazi could tell that he was visibly worried. His eyebrows twitched, and slid together, and a small sweat beaded up on his mottled head. "I... I..." and he turned to the city, the giant bear oppressing everything. "I did not have the time to help your friend. I am sorry."

Talia slid her mask up for a second, just so she could breathe a bit easier. "We're not near enough to the fog yet, right? It's safe that I do this?"

Lens shrugged in response. "I have no clue."

"You said that the fog wasn't there yet, the bear, not there yet. Did that tower grow overnight?"

"No, that tower was there, but taller and whole. The bear... see? She bursts through the top of it. Can't you see that?"

"I see," Mazi said calmly, detached. She kept her mask on, she didn't know if she could place it back on her mouth if she took it off. Better to just leave it on, then. "But you knew. You knew there would be fog. Or else you wouldn't have given your brother a mask, or else you wouldn't have brought the other masks with you. Why did you bring so many? What were you doing? And why didn't you take a second to help Naomi? It would've only taken you a single second!"

"I did not know, I promise," you could almost see the smirk inside of Lens eyes, his smile still hidden by the mask, "I left a mask there, as a precaution, in case he needed it. I only left him the one, since it was only him and no one else I'd left behind. That's all. I didn't take extra with me; I just did not leave extra behind. I carry all sorts of things in my satchel, all sorts of relics I've found looking, out looking..."

Talia slid the mask back down, hiding her own reactions to the conversation. "Looking for what? Tell us."

Lens turned, began walking back towards the city again. The giant cursed whale creatures howled and sang their cursed songs. "Nothing. I was looking for nothing."

Talia pulled her bow out, strung an arrow tight. "You don't travel the world looking for nothing. You don't leave your brother behind looking for nothing."

Lens stopped walking but did not turn around. His head slumped on his rags, and he looked like a doll, a plaything that would shatter if thrown against a wall. "I was looking for a cure. I went everywhere, searched in old books and maps. Listened to folk tales by the old, prying their words for hidden symbols that could tell me anything, anything at all! I decoded rites and rituals, I translated fragments of worm eaten scrolls. I swam into sunken cities, crawled into sleeping volcanoes, all looking for one thing. A cure for the curse, a way to bring my brother back to me. I miss him so much, and it had changed him. It turned him into a different thing all together."

He breathed, slowly, his body shaking, trembling, like an earthquake had ruptured his heart. Then? A violent movement, he slammed his staff into the ground. A pointless gesture. "But I am an idiot and a fool. There is no cure. I spent all that time looking and searching, and what for? For nothing. Pity me, if you must. But pity the cursed even more. Even you, new friend Mazi, even you will reach the point of no return and everything will change. There will be nothing left of you.

And you will not just die. No. Much worse than death. Much worse."

He shook his head, his body still trembling. Was that fear? Was that sorrow? Mazi could not tell. She was shook at what he said, and a fear took hold deep inside her heart. She was doomed, and now terrified of the future. What was to come of her?

"Nothing, nothing," he said again, "It's all pointless, all whispers in the dark. He's going to die, everyone's going to die. It doesn't matter anyway, I can't save anyone, I can't stop anything. The curse is entropy, it is the void of all things. It devours, and devours, and leaves only corruption in its wake. I went looking for the purpose of it all, the start and end, and all I found was nothing. Nothing."

Talia put her arrow back in her quiver, but kept her bow out. Mazi walked up to her, grabbed her shoulder, "Come on," she said, "Let's keep going." And when Mazi looked into her friends' eyes she saw the look of someone about ready to just stop existing. Not you too, she thought. Was there any hope for any of us? Would this be the end of everything?

More fear in the pit of her stomach at the thought of the curse. How could she die? How could the curse do this to her? That did not feel right or natural or even true. In her mind, she had always existed. From the moment of her birth until now, there she was, existing. If she died, then what? Would the world end? It felt like that was the case. That her death would be the end of all things.

A light snuffing out and leaving only dark in its wake. She couldn't let Talia see her fear. As usual, she had to be strong for the others. To hide her fear away and not give into weakness. And so she smiled meekly beneath her mask, as her eyes sparkled. "I know it seems difficult now, but Naomi is most likely doing all right."

"How can you... how can you say that?"

She pulled Talia close, put an arm over her friend, and then leaned her face up to her ear. She whispered closely, just enough, so that Talia could hear and no one else. "She is already cursed," Talia almost moved back in shock, "She has been for a long time now. She used the last of our ghost hearts decades ago, and I promised not to tell anyone. As long as she's still got that ghost heart? She'll be well. She's already cursed, so the curse won't touch her. We just need to find her, and bring her back home..."

Talia did not say anything in response, she just pushed her friend a little. Not enough, just a small nudge. Now untangled Talia walked a bit quicker and Mazi looked for a moment in awe at her friend. She almost shined in the fog, so bright was her inner light.

"You hid the truth from me."

Mazi hesitated for a moment. The sounds of the cursed leviathans drowning out all thoughts. "I made a promise to Naomi and I kept that promise a long time."

Lens did not turn around to see or hear this emotional complication. He only kept walking onward, forward, towards the changed and broken world that awaited them. After saying this Talia ran up, next to Lens, keeping stride with his stride but not talking to him. The silence was an accusatory weight that bound them together. And Mazi followed behind, her heart aching, as their bodies cut a triangle of shadows in the daylight.

They walked the rest of the way in silence.

10

THE FOG DRAPED OVER THE city. It turned buildings abstract. It made light into shadow prisms. And it occulted faces and transformed bodies into vague outlines, veiled by the curse. Even the foglights distorted everything. Patterns grew out of the multicolored illumination, casting strange images onto the eye. What was once a face would turn into a stone, and what was once a stone would turn into a bird, taking flight. Hallucinations? Probably. It all felt familiar to Mazi. Like the dizzy intense feeling of a rite or a ritual, when the ghosts made the unreal real, and the liminal spaces between life and death faded away.

She found herself hoping that Lens would walk far enough away to disappear completely. And this made her smile. She had such strange, mixed up feelings each time she saw him, even if it was just out of the corner of her eye. She had no words to explain such an emotion, but it was overwhelming. A sense of loss, a sense of being left behind. That feeling she felt almost all the time as a child, when her parents had died and she was left unmoored in the world, unraveling and falling apart.

A large shadow loomed over them, and with each step gained more and more solidity. A giant of darkness, solid still, and then it became a cliff of rocks unseen, and then it became a wall, human made, stones shoved together in a roughshod fashion. Shapes moved, bulged out, became bigger, smaller. Shadows on the wall swam through the fog and disappeared above their heads.

The sun peered through that miasma, a red eye in the sky. Cracked by the prism of the air-borne curse. Breathing was ragged; even the masks struggled to purify what they inhaled. The air that reached their lips was sweaty, moist air. It left a bad taste in her mouth. The world of the fog was claustrophobic. The mask added to this feeling, moving against her cheeks and lips. She had to resist the urge to throw it off and stomp on it, killing it like an invading insect.

Talia stopped by the front precipice, hand against the wall. Her eyes were wide. Her friend seemed terrified, and for the first time in forever, tears ran down her cheek. Her hand shook as she grasped the wall, her scars bright against her skin.

Mazi ran over to her friend, and said in that metal voice of the mask, "What happened? What happened?"

Talia pushed herself up right, "I thought I was dead," and she looked over to the distance, away from Mazi, towards the fog, "I thought that was it, that I was dead. I was dead. I swear it, I was dead."

"But, but you're not. Right? You're not dead?"

Talia shook her head no, no. She wasn't dead. She didn't say it, but she didn't have to. Mazi moved a bit closer, as if to get her friend back, to gain her confidence yet again. Talia moved a little bit further away. Not much. She didn't say anything, she didn't need to say anything. Even death could not right this wrong. Her friend still could not trust her.

"Please," Mazi said, "Let me take care of you like you took care of me."

Talia wiped her eyes. Her hands still shook, but it did not seem to matter. Her voice was hard, cold, a knife of ice in her friend's heart. "I'm not like you. I can take care of myself."

Lens was not paying attention to either of them. He walked up and down the front of the wall, muttering to himself. He pressed against it with the palms of his hands. "It was here. I swear it was here, right here. How could it have moved? It's been right in this very spot since I was a small boy, since I first grew up on these streets. And now? Now it's not. How could it have moved? Can a city be infected with the curse? Was that what happened here?"

His hands pushed the wall and he said, "It is solid, I can feel it, I can feel the solid wall, and the, oh. Oh. It's moving now, moving, oh," and he leaned over and dry heaved for a second, and then moved his hand from the wall. His skin drained of all color. He was a ghost in the fog. "It feels like flesh. No, not flesh. Like what is under the skin, the meat and sinewy and blood. It's pulsing, and throbbing, and wet and moving. Oh."

He held his hands up, stared at them. His eyes did not say a thing, he just looked at those hands, like he expected them to be stained or changed somehow, maybe even ripped apart or brutalized. Yet, they were normal. He looked over, and saw

Talia leaning with her back against the wall, staring off into the fog lights that flickered and moved in the shadows. And then next to her crouched Mazi, her eyes pleading with her friend.

"What's going on," Lens said, "Never mind. We need to find a way in."

Talia stormed away from Mazi, "Then let's do it. Let's find a way in."

And Mazi followed, meekly, shyly, feeling lost and estranged. "I thought," she said, "I thought you knew of the way in, that you grew up here. What happened? What changed?"

Lens looked down at his hands again, turned them over. He muttered, "Weren't you listening? No, it doesn't matter. The walls have changed, they've moved. They're living things. Look, feel," he placed his hand against the same spot earlier, and then yanked it back, visibly unsettled by his discovery. "See, right there, feel right there. This city is sick now, sick with the curse. How can a city get sick? It seems so impossible."

Talia walked past him, put her hand against the wall. She seemed unmoved. "I feel it," she said, "Yes. I can feel it," and then she moved her hands over and around, caressing it, touching it. "It's alive, I can feel it breathing," and then she stood up, hand still against the wall. "This is shaped like a door. Can't you feel that?"

Lens walked forward carefully, touched it with the tip of his finger. "A door, yes. This might be a door."

"Had it been a door before?"

"No, not really. Something larger was here, a gate. You understand? A gate. Not this, this human sized squishy thing." He pulled his hand back, unable and unwilling to touch it any longer.

Mazi walked towards the door. "Here, let me," and then

reached out to touch it. Talia moved back, moved away from her. Just a little, just enough to get the message across. *Your touch is not welcome here.* Mazi ignored it, as her hand went against the soft spot, and felt it. Moving, like warm water, like a muscle flexing, like heart beating. She ran her hand over it, and felt a connection, a spark. A fleeting memory, of the bear struggling forward, and something inside her chest. Someone so familiar.

She screamed and pulled on the muscle, ripping it from the wall in her hands, and then threw it on the ground. It moved and twitched, a raw open nerve, blood coating the earth beneath the fog. She was visibly burned by the incident, every muscle in her body tight like a fist. "No," she said, and spat on the twitching thing. "No!"

Lens walked past her, pushed against the wall, and his body disappeared for a moment in the fog. He pulled back, arm still in the wall, and then finally pulled that out. He seemed confused, a mixture of excitement and fear. Like he didn't know whether to laugh or to scream. "You made a hole," he said, his voice peppered with laughs, "You tore a hole right through it. It's not big enough to go in, not yet. But I felt it, pushed through it. It felt... so strange. So amazing. I wanted to be devoured by the wall! What a curious desire."

Talia stomped, pulled out a knife she carried in her boot. This one was used mostly for cleaning the kills after a hunt in the woods. "I can make the hole bigger," and she spoke with wooden words, words that carried no meaning in them. They were just words spoken and nothing more. She disappeared into the fog for a moment.

Mazi followed her into that rusted mist, while Lens stayed behind, waiting. Talia went up to the door, touched it, outlined the fleshy parts, and then yanked her knife through. She plunged it in, and the fog dissipated, as if the knife cut through the thick mist itself. The door was a horrific splendor to behold, like a portal made of meat. It vibrated, and tried to wiggle free of the sharp knife edges. But it could not move. Slick, snick, in went the knife, deep went the knife. The door writhed and a whimpering noise came from it, and Mazi wanted to run and go away from this. This was not right, this was sorrow, this was horrible, this was not a good thing.

Pushing all her weight on the blade Talia began to cut down. It seemed to move slowly, the muscle thick and sinewy and hard to cut. It made more whimpering noises as Talia reached the bottom, pulled her blade back out, and then went down the other side.

Eventually, the door stopped whimpering. Eventually, the door stopped moving. Eventually, a silence pervaded their thoughts. Talia kicked into it. Splash, the door collapsed and broke apart into a puddle of gore. "Come on, we're wasting precious time," Talia said, and climbed over the mess.

For a second she stood, struck by the cruelty of that moment. Was that something Talia always harbored inside of herself, waiting to come out? It was as if her friend ceased to be real, caring, individual, and became instead a force of destruction. Even when she said, "Come on," it felt cold and uncaring to Mazi. As if Mazi was the same as that wall of meat.

"Are you coming?"

"I'm, I think," she breathed slowly behind the mask, trying to calm down, "I think I'm going to tell Lens about the door being clear. I don't see him coming, he probably doesn't know yet."

Talia turned to look at her, her body and face occulted by the fog and by the scars and the mask. Her eyes held an intense sadness, a grim glare of betrayal. "Do what you need to do."

Mazi turned, then stared at her friend. "Please."

"Please what?"

"Please, don't do this."

Talia started to say something, but stopped. "I," she started again, her face struggling with things spoken and unspoken. "I still love you. As a friend, and yes. A sister, maybe, I know those words are fraught with so much meaning for us! But I feel it, and it is right. You are an older sister to me, and I love you. But..."

Mazi's heart fell down an infinite chasm.

"But I can't trust you. Not now. I don't know if I ever can. And that love makes it so much worse. Do you understand?" Her words hurt so much, pierced her heart with barbs, and they were even more painful coming through that mask.

A nod, neither yes or no, just something for her head to do right now. "I'm going, to get Lens. I guess."

And then she walked back into the fog, back through the door of flesh, back into the world outside the city. Separating the two of them, if only for a moment.

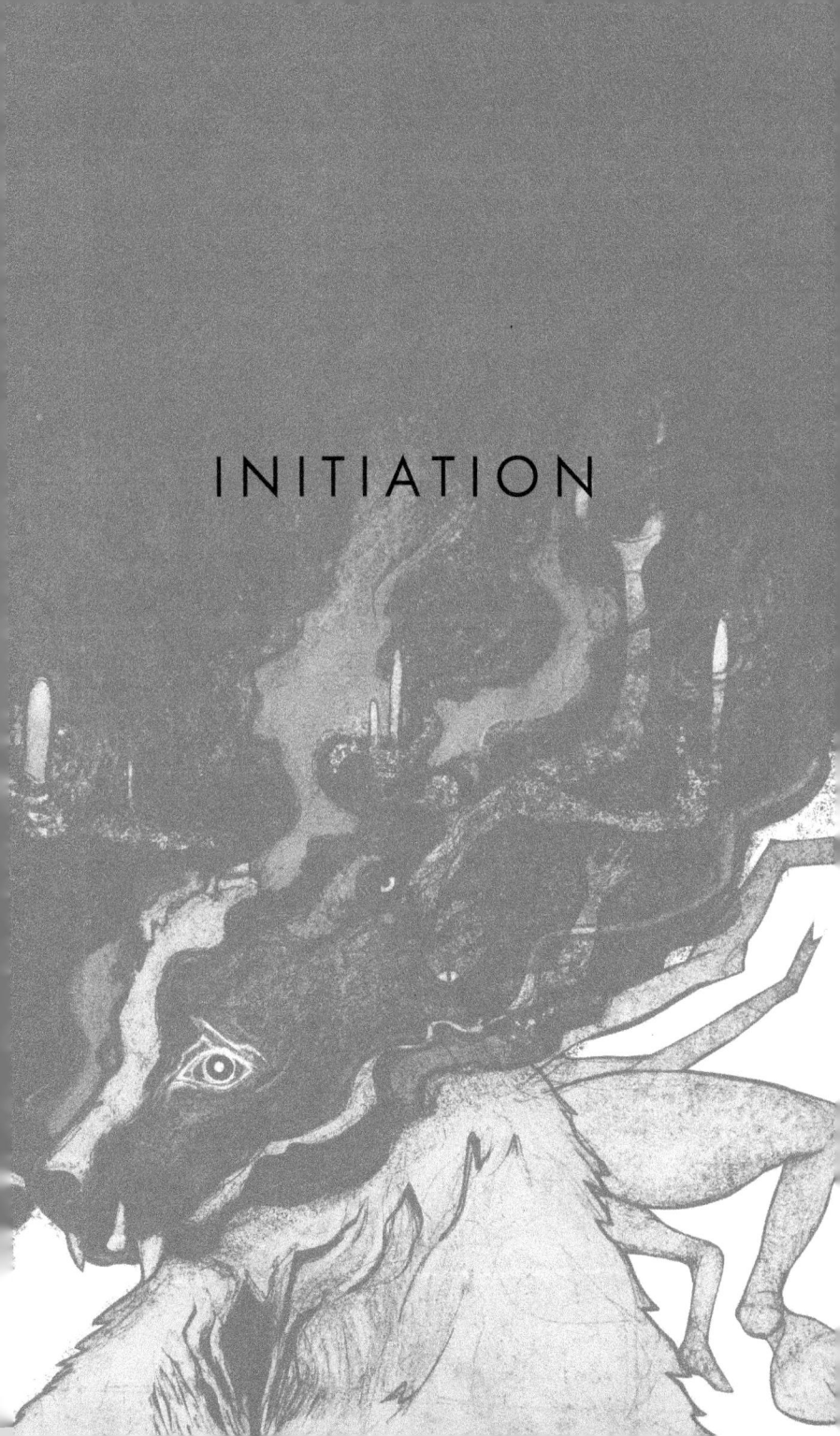

INITIATION

11

ZAGREUS REMEMBERED WHEN HE FIRST saw the Sata-Torun rising up towards the shining city on the hill. He was out in the valleys, weary and full of a yearning. He felt a need to serve a higher purpose, but nothing made itself known to him. It felt like he had one of his arms removed, and now it was a ghost limb that struggled to find meaning.

He tried to discuss this with the seers, who explained what they knew and it left him empty and confused. But they could do nothing to help him. He tried to talk to the whisperers on the cliffs near the sea, the ones who communicated with visions and mathematical fury with a being they called the Dzall. A being that they talked with in codes and images, who reported back to them with riddles and dreams. They did not know Dzall was a dyson sphere around a nearby sun, who reported to them through floating satellites. They only knew that once they drank the singing liquid in the hearts of the cave they could hear the Dzall speak, and it only spoke and responded to them in a wearying complex, mathematical manner.

And yes, Zagreus went and studied with the whisperers on the cliff near the sea, learned the symbols and functions that spoke to the Dzall. He drank the singing water, which burns still in his stomach and makes his skin feel electrified even now, even to this day. He called to the Dzall as he was taught to do, and his only response was silence. The great and terrible silence that greeted him everywhere.

This was the state of his mind when he first saw the great mother of the world, the Sata-Torun, the demon bear god. He moved through those valleys, his mind preoccupied by a combination of terror and loneliness. Nothing else existed in his world but the crushing fear of solitude.

He planned on getting lost out in the plains, far away from any known oasis or food. He would climb onto some rock or hollow stone, and leave himself in the sun to dry out and die. It would be, probably, a long slow painful death of starvation and dehydration. At this point in his life he would welcome that pain, that suffering. He knew that somehow, he might find meaning in his existence with this form of self-torture. After all, he'd heard the stories of the ancient mystics back before the start of time. The ones who had come to an empty rock and spent days near death and pondering existence. It was in their dreams that this world became alive.

Or so they say.

And then he saw it. The immense weight of the form shambling forward, the sparks and smoke and light around the head. Seeing it felt like lightning in his skeleton. This was his calling. This was the truth he'd been searching for. Here was the revelation of the infinite. Here was the meaning in the silence.

A million voices ricocheted around in his head in a chorus of code and symbol. It moved too fast for him to translate, and he knew this wasn't the Dzall who spoke to him like this. It was his new god. The demon beast before him, the curse, the Sara-Torun. He did not see a curse. What he saw instead was a promise of salvation. He watched the smoke and rust seep out of its head and change the deer in the valley. *Oh holy this transformation. Oh bright and beautiful and true.*

He trembled in awe at the sight of it, and in his head he heard growling, and then a voice saying, *pure pure pure pure i have made this pure pure pure pure so clean now and without the corruption of time, back to the start, ticktocktick. Back the start of all things...*

Zagreus knelt in supplication. He raised his hands up and lifted his head up. He knew the truth now.

The bear turned and looked towards the city. And on its chest was a woman, heartless naked and blind. And she held her body in the same form of supplication as Zagreus held his body now. They were mirrors, reflections, and he felt a surge of fear. The bear saw him, and he felt something probing his thoughts. And Zagreus knew that he should hide his thoughts, so he put up the mental walls, as they had taught him on the beaches when conversing with the Dzall. The bear glanced again, and then thought with the force of a shout, an explosion, a thundercrack, his mental wall exploding...

"I am Sata-Torun. I am the mother of the world. I have slept in bodies ancient and dreaming, and I have moved from form to form, slumbering in lesser minds. I wake now, I have come to purge the corruption of time from my creations. Come to me, I will change you. I will make you clean. This world was once a barren rock, and I made it breathe with life. I am the only one who can save this world from a slow unwinding death. See the sun? That is a dead sun. But I can evolve you, perfect you, make it so you can survive even here, even after the sun has died."

He moved forward on his knees, the gravel digging in and stinging with each shuffle. He raised his hands out and cried in ecstasy. He had purpose! He had calling! He had something greater than himself reach and she choose him! Destiny! Desire! The great will of the universe unfolding!

The fog slipped into his body through ears and eyes and pores. It moved around, and then the Dzall snake in his stomach hissed. He spat lightning and watched as Sata-Torun recoiled with a look of shock and dread. Zagreus collapsed, twitching on the ground, a small epileptic fit.

When he woke the bear stood above him. He noticed that she had three heads, triskull; all these eyes and sight looking out. The body of the blind and mute woman dangled on the chest, seeming to writhe and push out for a moment, and then she went still. The bear spoke through the voice of the woman on its chest. It spoke with pain and suffering.

"I cannot remake you. You will die when the sun dies."

"I swear," Zagreus said, "To you, to whatever you want. I promise, I promise, please. Save me, change me."

"There is something inside that keeps you broken."

His stomach burned and felt alive, and his whole body was vibrant and the hair stood up on end, every inch of him electrified. "I know, I am not worthy of your sight, of your... purification. I have debased myself, destroyed myself."

"No," she said, "Rise up. You have done nothing wrong, instead something wrong has been done to you. And to others too, I assume. I want you to promise me this, to promise me silence. You understand? What I tell you, what I show you? You do not speak it; you do not think it. You keep this quiet. Erase all of your mind. Become emptiness. Be my vessel. Will you help me spread the change?"

Zagreus's heart was heavy in his chest. "I cannot. Can I? I cannot."

"No, you cannot change. But, that is a meek thing, you are more important. You are the message. Not just a messenger. The symbol is the sign. Go to that city on the hill, and prepare them for my coming. And bring me to a place where I can plant my cathedral."

This was too much, all too much. Everything he'd wanted pushed into him. He was special, he was chosen, so he had purpose. Yet, it didn't feel like how he dreamed it would feel. For a brief flickering moment of despair, he realized that he missed his emptiness, and he missed the freedom that came with anxiety and uncertainty. If this was the truth, if the mother of the world spoke to him with such keen understanding, then he had no choice in anything at all. He had to follow. All of his life he wanted to follow. And now that he was called to follow, he entertained so many second thoughts, but they were all meaningless.

He felt a tickling in his skull and realized his mind shield was down. His thoughts were black suns, sucking in everything and spitting out no light.

"I can devour you. I cannot change you, but I can devour you."

Zagreus could not say anything at all, she had read his

thoughts naked and burning in his mind. He supplicated himself again. "No, no, I am sorry I doubted you, I will do as you ask. I am your servant, your hopeless fire, I am your hierophant."

The bear shuddered over towards him, and he could now take in the full sight of her. The body was an incredible ruin, patches of fur missing, the body covered in small fungi, vines, clumps of earth, and other detritus of time, and massive, powerful. The black, steel claws drank in light. Two of the three bear heads had large clumps of skin and meat missing, leaving only bone and eye sockets. Other parts had small branches sticking out, like she was part oak tree. The human body dangled down on her chest was sunk in and mixing with fur and skin and claw. Human parts, wrapped up in those vines of fur and flesh and vegetation, all mixed up on her human body. Her eyes looked like two blind suns, and her mouth was open in an unheard prayer. Not wide enough for a scream, too subtle for a whisper. These lips moved in a ritual perfected long ago. With each step closer a strange smell washed over of forest and machine.

"Rise," she said, "Rise. You can shield your mind, I know you can. I can feel it. From this point on, place that wall up high. You understand me? Do not let another inside, not anyone, not even me. No one must see what you've seen unless they see it in skin and stone. I want only the voice to send my sorrow to the world, your voice, my message dressed in flesh. Keep your mind closed off and empty to all who want to peer inside of it. Let them only see a wild stream, the waves of the ocean, water, water, nothing else but water."

And that's when Zagreus understood. She did not want the Dzall to know of her existence. He was more than happy to follow. The Dzall never spoke to him, only gave him hopelessness and silence. He could easily return the favor and give them the same.

He grabbed his hat, said, "Yes, of course, nothing more, nothing less. Just the sound of waves will they hear," and then stood nervously in the shadow of the bear. Waves of fog rushed out from her body, obscuring the worl. She walked forward.

"Go now. Spread the word, so I can give them life beyond the death of this world."

And with that Zagreus ran along, out from the shadow of the bear. Clouds raced overhead in dark iron that forced themselves over the sun. He moved towards the gates, babbling about the amazing world that was to come, soon, soon. The guards did not believe him at first, not until the bear lumbered up the hills and the valleys. Then they saw, and it was too late. Everything was changing.

12

THE DOOR THROBBED AROUND MAZI as she walked through it. The ribs and meat undulated against her shoulders, breathing. Each step it felt like the wall lengthened, grew longer, eventually became a tunnel of muscle shoving them out. When they reached the other side it closed quick behind them, sealing itself off. Not even a shadow in the mist, the wall became a memory, a whisper. Something they knew was there but could not see.

Mazi knelt the minute she came back through, caught her breath, tried to grasp the reality of her surroundings. Lens stood right behind her, leaning on his staff, both of them struggling with the insect masks on their faces.

"Where is she? I thought you said she was here."

Long tall slender things moved in the dark of the red sun shadow. "She was. I swear she was right here, and now she's not. Let's go. Find your brother; find our Naomi. I don't know. It's..."

Lens moved forward, blocking her sight for a moment. "It's not pointless, if that's what you're trying to say. I think it's easy to think that, but it's not a true thing. Pointlessness and meaning are matters of perspective. What is your perspective? What is your need? How do you desire, and *what* do you desire? Those are what give us meaning, that is how life matters."

Mazi wanted to knock him over, pull an arrow out and put it through his head. She didn't know why, but his pontification irritated her. It felt too simple, like it boiled everything down to the individual, isolated and alone. The thought of the world being this lonely, random place where each person existed as a collection of desires frustrated her. It made her so angry, and she knew it was a pointless anger. Yet, she felt it still the same. With that anger, she wanted to murder Lens. Steal whatever it was he held so dear and use it to save Naomi. And maybe, yes, even to save Talia

Talia. If she were dead, Mazi would destroy the world. She had to stop, hold herself still and dizzy. She wanted to give into it, embrace her anger and let the curse change her. The curse could make her powerful. It could give her the might to burn everything to the ground, starting with Lens.

And with that thought, she remembered Noami's face the day before she disappeared, bath water still fresh on her cheeks, a small smile and a trusting laugh. Mazi could not betray Naomi by causing sorrow, even if it would feel good and right. She had already betrayed one person close to her; she couldn't betray two. Especially if her gut instinct was right, and Naomi was probably dead or transformed or she did not want to think what else. No, no thoughts like that. This was not the time for thoughts like that. The curse throbbed, begging for more anger. She would not feed it today. Even if it caused her more pain and made her disabilities worse.

A spark in the dark and then lights shattered bits of fog and flung the shadow away. A fizzle of illumination, and then a lantern swung through the dark. At first Mazi thought it was a foglight. Then she saw a hand, and the mist peeled back gave way to Talia, standing there, scarred face and bow across her back. She was crouched still, her hand cupping the lantern, keeping the flame alive while she closed the glass around it. She didn't smile. She just stood.

"Let's go, Mazi. Naomi's somewhere close. Your brother, too."

The light cut through the fog in a halo of revelation. Lens walked forward, using the staff as a crutch of sorts. He seemed to almost limp a bit, but then straightened out, walked a bit smoother. "Certainly, certainly, of course my dear. I remember where my brother is, and if this city hasn't changed too much it won't be long to find him. And hopefully, along the way, we can get some information as to what happened to your friend."

He walked ahead of Talia, out of the range of the light, a shadow in the smog. Talia followed close behind, the light moving with her, a circumference of radiance, slowly dissipating into the haze. Mazi had no choice. She was pulled along again, in other directions, towards some common unseen goal.

Without Talia, without that light, she was nothingness. Emptiness. No Naomi, and Talia ignoring her, and then Lens making her feel lost and empty and broken. She just wanted to cease, to stop, to not exist anymore. A shadow corrupted her heart, put out the flames in her mind. She felt grey and rainslick. She wanted to be nothingness.

The circle of light shone forward again. It was just enough to let Talia's head through, just enough to shine a fire on her hands holding the lantern, the rest of her obscured by swirling mists. "You coming? Come on, I can't go on without you. You know that."

And that was enough. Mazi dried an eye with her wrist and nodded. She said nothing, just darted up behind the two of them, following close but not too close, their shadows still a triangle in the fog.

There were noises in the dark. The sound of stone scraping on stone, of wires scurrying like rats across the city floor, and the electrical hum of flash lanterns. There were moments when the moving city got caught in the lantern light, as the buildings grew, like trees branching out at highspeed. Organic structures would sometimes spiral out, then burst into fractals of stained glass windows, or become overrun with fast growing vines, choking stone and ceilings alike.

From time to time the shadows turned to people, clusters of them on street corners. Some of them changed, cursed, broken and bent. Others were still human all over, wandering around the mist lost and lonesome. Their eyes like vacant rooms, faces gibbering in muted terror. They wore no masks for breathing, so they were changing. The fog made certain.

Other times people walked by, or rode past on old machines that squeaked with rust. Some would wander on changed carriages, gulping dinosaur things, and others would try to tame cursed horses with long lizard tails and multifocal insect eyes. When they walked past with lantern light the doomed city ignored them, or turned away to pretend it couldn't see. In the eyes of the cursed, the three of them did not exist, all thanks to Mazi's throbbing wound.

It had gotten worse. She felt it, and with that came that terror and anxiety of dying all over again. It was one thing to know you may one day die, but it was another thing all together to know exactly what will kill you in the end. She couldn't help it: She looked down at her wound, and saw the curse spread out against her arm.

"Wait, wait," she muttered and tried to get the gauze out of her satchel. Her fingers clumsy again, the cursing corrupting her muscles and nerves. The wound looked like a crack on a porcelain doll, not a thing of skin and meat. "I need to... I need to..." and she tried to get the bandages out, but she spilled everything out on the ground. She couldn't help her clumsy fingers. Mazi got down on her knees and sobbed. She hated her curse and hated her arm and hated the fact that the world had been so cruel to her. No ghosts would save her now. She was doomed to a slow, rotting death. Maybe she should return to the temple and let the seers set her on fire. It would be better than being destoroyed and devoured and transformed into a shell of the curse. Anything would be better than that.

Talia turned back, walked over towards her. The lantern was bright sharp and poignant, and the light of it hurt Mazi, and she winced visibly. Talia knelt down next to her, picked up the gauze and said, "Let me," in a voice that bordered on humane again. She wrapped it tight, pinching the skin.

"Thank you."

Talia said nothing else, just stood and turned. Concern for her friend leaked through, past the chasm of hurt that had opened up between them. Mazi felt a sting of relief, and knew that this wasn't enough to patch the distrust that rose between them. It was a start.

They walked through a spiral of people, standing in line at the base of a maze. These doomed strangers were dressed in pilgrim clothes, with wide black hats and white gauze over their eyes. Their bodies were claustrophobic close, raw skin and limbs brushing up against Mazi, pushing against her. For a moment, she worried she would get lost in the throng and commotion. Her heart almost stopped. The curse called to her, told her to move towards the tower. She ignored it, and tried to keep Talia and Lens in sight. Any moment now and she could be lost in the sea of the spiral crowd, drowning. She hated it. Too many people. Too many. She wanted this to be over already. And her curse ached again.

Oh temple and song, don't grow, don't grow any bigger. Stay small curse, stay small and delicate. Resist the call of the tower, resist the changes.

A person walked amongst them, dragging people to the front followed by cheers and shouts. "Another chosen!" They shouted. "Another to feed the changes!" And with that they started dancing, and Mazi was dizzy and off kilter. For a moment she sunk into the bodies, the spiral pulling her down. Breathless. The way they danced was ecstatic and wild. It reminded her of the dances they did at the temple, the ritualized steps to summon the ghosts. What were they summoning here?

She pushed herself out of the crowd, caught sight of Lens

almost disappearing into the distance. She had to keep going. She couldn't succumb to this curse. She bit on her cheek, felt pain blossom between her teeth, and kept moving. The crowd shouted.

The key! The crown! The mirror! The sword!

Over and over again. It stuck in the thoughts, brought images of a black mirror crossed with sword and key. The crown in the center a plain and painful thing, wooden and symbolic. She wanted to shake these images from her mind. She could not shake them from her mind. It felt like a code, wakening something dark in her memories: the desires to do terrible things to people.

And then, she sensed a presence emanating from the tower in the center. She knew that presence; it was Naomi. It was unmistakable. Such a strong, vibrant sense of being. And then a voice from her curse, into her mind. It flowed through her thoughts in Naomi's voice. It had to be her voice! She wanted to show her something, something so amazing and beautiful it would make the awe she had felt at the temple like a simple thing. No. She broke from the trance. Naomi would never use that analogy. That could not be Naomi calling out from the tower. It must be something else. Something that borrowed her shape and haunted her voice. This terrified Mazi more than anything else. Could the curse take their very identity, and use it for their own purposes?

And if so, what does that mean for Naomi? She couldn't think that now. She needed to believe that Naomi could still be saved. She believed that with every bone in her body.

Mazi walked picked up the pace. Someone reached out, grabbed her by the curse. A sharp pain corrupted her thoughts, and she had to stop, almost fell to the ground. She felt that, a connection, a corruption, a reflection. She grabbed the hand back, looked up, saw a small boy, probably no older than ten, with wild staring eyes.

His lower body was a mixture of machine and spider and skin. Intestines snaked out to an octagon of needle legs, his head and arms placed onto it like doll parts. "What is that," he said, his voice a mockery of a little boy's voice. "Tell me, tell, what is that," and then he jabbed a finger at the mask on her face.

Blink, blink, the lights flickered and the mask started to squirm. Mazi couldn't respond to the boy's question. She was too busy pushing the mask back onto her face. It clicked and fluttered, and the mandibles slid against her cheeks. No, no, she thought, I've changed enough. I can't breathe in the corruption and change even more. Stay on my face, mask. Keep me whole.

The child laughed. It was an oddly innocent sound coming out of that mouth. The face even glowed a little, more of friendly playfulness than inarticulate malice that she felt a second ago. Eventually the insect mask calmed down and she stood up, breathing shallow breaths, panic under her skin making her pulse run rampant.

"I need it."

The little boy laughed again and said, "Some day we will fill you with fire and grief," and then scuttled off into the line again, standing with the rest. After a moment of bringing her frightened breathing calm again, she turned and saw shapes turning into shadows. Lens was out of sight. Talia was out of sight. Even the lamp was swallowed by the fog. Mazi was lost. She would change soon. She couldn't help it, it was going to happen. A pit opened up in her stomach and she wanted to scream. She couldn't lose them. She ran, her breath heavy and thudding inside of her lungs.

And then, up ahead, that lantern flickering amongst the crowd. The spiral of bodies still danced, moving quicker and quicker. Something was going to happen soon, a violent energy stifled the air with sweat and anger. Lens head peeked above the crowd. Talia's arm held up the lantern, halo bright.

Almost there, Mazi just had to keep moving. She had to catch up. The bodies moved quicker and quicker and quicker, shoving her, pushing her. She screamed, pushed through, choking on dust and the scent of raw human sweat. There. Almost there. She reached out, grabbed Lens's shoulder.

"Oh, there you are. We thought we'd lost you."

Mazi nodded. Talia seemed worried and relieved at the same time. She chewed on her lip, and her eyes had that look of fear and joy. "I know, I'm sorry. There are too many people; I feel like I'm drowning. Is it much further?"

"Up there. Don't worry, we're almost there," Lens said. He pointed. They saw the destination twisting in the air. Two buildings, gently emerged in the amber lamp glow. Between the two buildings danced a ramshackle bridge, groaning with each twist and bend. The buildings and the bridge were industrial forged, made from a corruption of rust and stone and glass. They were also organic and changed, covered in leaves and roots and fleshy muscle. It was a living thing, like all things in the shining city. It moved and breathed, an elegy of sounds and motion, bringing the world into focus.

They all paused, all three of them in a perfect triangle. Each line equal to the last, and the lamplight a circle around them. " I hope he's still there." His voice carried a soft tragedy with it. For a moment, Mazi felt sorrow fill the air between them. Her training as a seer took over, and she no longer felt estranged or distrustful towards him, but instead a kinship with another suffering human in a world full of suffering. There was a fear there, an innocence there. And once more she felt that she knew him from her own past...

The déjà vu was a splinter in her mind, digging in, pestering her with no relief.

13

THEY CLIMBED STAIRS THAT SPIRALED up the side of the building, with Lens in the front and Talia in the back. Her lantern light a circle of amber around their ascending bodies. As they walked, Lens pulled on his hair, gently tugging on it as they moved higher and higher. Mazi wondered if this was a nervous reaction, his hair mostly molted out in tufts. Was that caused by his anxiety? What did he have to be anxious over? Maybe this had been a mistake. Maybe following him would lead to their doom.

The steps were a wash of stone and ochre, and it shifted with each movement. Subtle changes, obscured by the haze. The changes so gradual, it seemed like a trick to the eye. Doors appeared, some opened leading to vacant rooms. Others slammed shut with bodies beside them, watching the three of them as they walked higher and higher. Mazi noticed something strange, unlike the rest of the city. Most of the bodies here in this building remained unchanged so far. She still did not risk removing her mask.

The cursed air drained these unchanged people in such a visible way. Gaunt long things, stretched out and stretched taut. Skin like drums on bones. Eyes shallow sunken things, teeth jutting out mostly gums and lips sneering back. Hair on their heads were delicate, wiry clumps. They eyed the strangers as they walked past with suspicious gazes. Mazi knew that look. The same fear of the cursed that had haunted her since she was a child. They had best be careful here. These were the kind of people who burned the curse out of fear for their own lives.

If they could sense the curse in Mazi, the three seekers might be doomed.

They walked in silence. Mazi felt the silence weigh on her. The silence was an accusation from Talia, a wordless assault of indifference. She thought of breaking this silence with a question, or maybe a hand on her sister's shoulder, but when she did her foot slipped and gravel fell and she caught herself, heart afire and thunderpulsed, unable to think about anything other than *not falling, surviving.*

They eventually made it to the bridge, the abstract scaffolding hung over the expanse between the two buildings. It moved and changed, faded in and out of the real. Parts became stained glass, others steel. Lens walked forward, stood on the edge and looked across.

The sun blistered over their heads, the heat magnified by the cursed fog. Mazi wiped some sweat from her forehead. It stung her eyes, and each droplet made her mask squirm uncomfortably on her face.

"He's just over that way," Lens said, "Not much farther now, until we see him. Oh, my brother, my brother."

Talia grabbed his shoulder. "After this, after all of this. You will help us find her, correct? You will help us find Naomi?"

Mazi stayed back, stayed near the wall. She wanted to find Naomi as well, but her mind struggled once again with the black pit of despair that snaked around her thoughts. Naomi. She was dead. Oh. Mazi knew it now. Naomi was dead, there was no other reasoning, no other truth at all. She slid down against the side of the wall. *Dead, dead, dead, dead.*

Lens spoke calmly, yet his voice seemed unsure. "Yes, of course. I can help, I think. I mean, I know she came to the city, that's for sure. And I guess I know this, I know this, I mean, this whole place, I know it. Even though it is changing every second, every moment, somehow a truth of the reality stays. And because of that, I can be your guide."

Talia seemed satisfied and let go of his shoulder. Mazi grabbed her knees and put her head over them, resting her ear against her leg. "She's dead," was all she could say. Not even loud enough for it to matter, just loud enough for Talia to hear.

"Maybe, maybe not," was her response, "We've come too far to just leave it as a riddle. Her life, her death, we must see it with our own eyes. Otherwise, we wonder until our own deaths. We owe it to her to either find her alive or find her corpse. You know it's true."

Could Mazi take that, actually seeing Naomi's corpse? It would wreck her. Her curse wore on her, and the hopelessness of the moment ate at her mind. She was a fool. Her strength was all bluster, all fear wearing a mask. This had all been a mistake. Her muscles ached and twitched. Her arm felt useless once again. She was too terrified to look down and see the wound spreading.

Not again. They have no more ghost heart. Not again.

She leaned her head forward, and saw in the mist a giant shadow moving towards them. It seemed to walk across the bridge with an innate prescience on what portions would be real and which portions would move or change. As if it spoke to the curse of the city, communicated with it on some preternatural level.

This startled Mazi out of her stupor, and she stood tall. Clumsily she grabbed her bow and armed it with an arrow. The damned curse made this harder than it should be. Numb wooden fingers holding the arrow. Aching shoulder muscles made everything feel a million pounds heavier. But she would do this. She would not die here, in a cursed city, by some monsterous shadow.

Lens held out his hand behind his body, the universal sign to stop. That this was a moment to reflect, not to assault. Mazi let out a strangled laugh, no longer certain of anything anymore. Talia lifted her lantern up, forcing the light to widen out and turn that shadow into a real thing.

"My brother..." Lens whispered painfully, biting on his knuckles, "Oh my brother. What has it done to you? Look how it has changed you. Look, look. Even the mask couldn't keep you safe. That curse was inside you already, has been there for decades on decades. Growing, growing. Oh, sweet love, oh blood kinship. I should have never left you. Look at what I reaped! See this world! See this corruption! All because I could not let you slide into sickness again and again. Yet here you are, like all the others. I could do nothing. Nothing. I could do nothing but leave you."

He fell to his knees and sobbed, as the shadow moved forward into the light. Horns burst out from his brother's skin, and spread out into branches and antlers. Tentacles ripped through the air, and wiggled and stretched, reaching out for human contact. A sextet of human arms scraped the bridge as it walked, and two long legs strode forward, moving perfectly across the bridge, never falling once. This city spoke to him, the curse whispering of what was safe and what was dangerous.

And yet its face. And yet that face. And yet there it was, sunken amidst the oozing parallel transfigurations: that face. A beautiful, beatific, perfectly human face. It was angelic in that mess of corruption. Perfect cheek bones propping up perfect features. Eyes that sparkled like blue lakes. Those thick angelic lips carved into the sides of temples, as it muttered incoherently. Mazi felt like it was the language of the ghosts, yet more bestial. The face was lit by some unseen light, as if his insides were torches, illuminating his features.

And then below that face, his chest had a huge hole ripped into it, right where a heart should be. Lens saw it at the same time everyone else did. His hand went to his face, hiding his features.

"His heart, his ghost heart..."

Mazi snapped forward. "Ghost heart?"

"He devoured his own ghost heart. It was burning up. I saw that when I left. I knew he didn't have much time left. But not like this. I thought—maybe—I could stop it, if I moved fast enough, I could stop it. I might be able to. I might. Be able to. I'm too late, oh temple and song, oh brother, please, please forgive me. I am too late."

Mazi reached a hand across and grabbed him, harsh,

knuckles red. She felt his bones like a lightning bolt through her body. "Where did you get a ghost heart from?"

"You don't remember, do you? I guess it's for the best."

The figure moved closer and it howled. Unlike the other cursed and changed, this one seemed different. His face was passive and angelic, while his body spoke of violence in the way it moved. Talia budged Mazi aside, handed her the lantern, and then pulled out her own bow and arrow. "I don't think this one will just leave us be. He is unlike the others. Can't you see it? There is a hatred that burns inside of him when he sees us. The light that glows around him, it burns when you glance at it. Can't you see it? He will murder us."

"It cannot be. It must not be. I did not break our promise!"

Lens stepped forward on the bridge, the wind whipping his rags around, his hand tight on his staff like it was the only thing that kept him alive. "I was gone for too long, yes. And I did something, something horrible, yes. I know it, I look around and I see it. But I did not break our promise! You understand me? I kept the oath I swore to you! I may have done wrong, but I have had the best intentions. Always, always, the best intentions."

The wind made the lantern dance in Mazi's hand. She steadied it and dropped her bow. She needed to keep the light focused on the shadow in the fog. Talia needed a clean shot at Lens's brother, and she was the best person here to do it. Mazi would light her way and give her arrow a clear shot to his brother's face...

And that face felt so familiar. It was that same déjà vu she felt when she'd first met Lens. He was older now, yes, aged by decades. She had been a child. Her memory tickled a little; it came back slip by slip. Something to do with Naomi. Her childhood, and Naomi, and the ghost heart.

And so, She shouted through the wind, "Where did he get the ghost heart?"

Lens ignored her, reached down into his satchel. "Here, let me show you! I do not lie. I have it for you, right here. I hope I'm not too late. No, I can see your face, I can feel your love still behind your eyes. It's not too late, it can't be too late..." As he rummaged through that sack, looking for what he'd brought all this way, his brother thundered forward.

Its human mouth opened wide and wider, a tunnel of flesh and muscle, teeth sharp bones under his lips. He was over Lens in a split second, the angelic face split wide by mouth and muscle. He was about to devour his brother. Talia fired three shots. The arrows lit up bright and luminescent, reflecting the lantern glow like shooting stars. The bow string thrummed when she struck it, a concrete orchestral note.

Two hit. Pain scored across its face, mouth howling. It stumbled back, and almost fell, the tentacles grasping onto the edge of the bridge as it pulled itself back up. It clambered forward in a blind rage, arrows stuck up out of the shoulder blades like the remnants of ripped off wings. The face was still beatific, calm, otherworldly in its transgressive bliss.

Oblivious, Lens still rummaged around inside of that small bag. His hands moved things around, and Mazi wondered if the bag was infinite on the inside. The creature stepped back, moved back away from him a little, just a little. Fear in the glance, looking over at Talia, at her arrows and her bow.

Lens shouted triumphantly, screamed "Yes, yes, finally, yes," and grabbed the bandaged up precious thing he had been carrying with him all this time. He turned around and looked at his brother, the two of them still and silent.

"See?" he said, "Do you see? I promised you and here it is, just as I said. I had destroyed this city, changed and murdered so many! But it's worth it now, here it is. Do you understand? Here it is."

He held it out in front of him, and it seemed to whisper and glisten in the palm of his hand. Grey dust fluttered down, creating shadows in the lamplight on the bridge. The dust moved away from him, the wind rustling his hair and rags. "See?" he said as he walked. "See? A promise. An oath. I love you, you understand? I love you. Brother to brother, I have saved you."

He moved forward, and the creature stayed still, uncertain. The human face smiled in tiny nostalgia. Lens walked, foot after foot, toe to toe, his eyes staring only ahead, the lantern light behind him flickering and sparking and fizzing. He unwrapped the bandages. Still, the face smiled, pained yet trusting.

Mazi knew that face when it smiled like that, she knew that smile! She remembered now, that face weeping in a bed, bandaged, a young adult face, a little younger than Talia is now. He was in their temple. Lens was there as well, sitting next to him, reading. It all came at her, trumpeting in her thoughts at once.

She said it out loud now, shouting. "I know you! I remember you!"

And then she saw it, the item in the bandage, and felt rage, immense intense rage. "You lied!" she howled, it burned her throat and her eyes, "You lied to me, Lens!"

She felt red felt everything red beyond the rust and fog and beyond the blood inside her veins. There was an intense hatred and everything inside of her burned up, her rage a fever in her skin. Talia moved her bow down and said, "What? What are you talking about? Mazi, what are you talking about?"

A whisper. "Is this how you felt? When you realized I lied to you, kept things from you? Was this how you felt?"

Talia nodded. "Tell me now..."

Mazi pointed forward, pointed at the thing he held in his hand as he approached his brother. "Don't you see it?" and then again, her body so tense with anger, every part of her a bullet of frustration and betrayal, "I remember! You! You! I remember you!"

14

THE LAST TIME MAZI HAD met the brothers she was naked and running with the other acolytes. They were barely out of their first decade, and still years away from the rites of the seer. The rain pelted the ceiling and the stairs, and they heard the thunder moan and shake the world. A rough crack like a whip at random moments, and they would squeal in mock fear and run through the darkened hallways, up long steep stairs into the libraries and hollow ritual chambers. The rooms were darkened, the candles unlit in the daytime. Yet the rain clouds overhead blocked the sun and created a mock night.

Rain poured down like small waterfalls to the left and right, streaming in from cracks in the roof overhead. Talia was not born yet, and would not come to the temple for a few more years. Mazi had hardly any friends amongst the other acolytes. She felt stranded and different, and even now, when she ran naked and laughing she felt like any minute, any second and she would slip and be caught as a stranger in their midst. Alone, even in a crowd of people. She knew this fear was a silly thing, but it was there, still there, every second, every moment.

They reached the top of the steps, a gaggle of little girls laughing and shoving each other. One with a crop of red curls bent under a waterfall, lifted her mouth up, and drank the rainwater. She spat it out, said it tasted like mud, and then dared the others to drink. "Go ahead," she said, "Go on, drink."

No one moved forward. To the left, they heard footsteps in the library, coming their way. Everyone was silent in anticipation. Mazi steeled herself, tightening her fists and her gaze, biting down on her lip. She was going to do it. The others were cowards. Mud. So what? It would taste like mud. She walked over, lifted her head up, opened her lips, and felt it. The water rushed in, and it was lightning, not mud. It rippled with electricity and lit her heart on fire.

"Children, children!"

A scolding voice as an elder stormed through. It was Sophia, her hair tamed into a top bun, her eyes calm and yet stern. Her outfit was an elder's uniform: blue dappled robes spun down simply around her body. "We have visitors in the sleep rooms. Go, get dressed, go! They are outsiders and they are boys, so you must grab some clothes right now. Quickly, quickly. Naomi is stalling them, but I'm not sure for how much longer. Go on, get dressed!"

The murder of girls laughed, some uproariously, others quiet sad giggles they tried to hide. Even in their laughter they moved down the stairs, heading back to the basement and their cells below the ground, where they left their clothes neat and tidy on their beds. Folded just so, in case one of the seers came down or the elders and thought something was awry.

The silly, inane freedom of running naked, playing tag, slipping on rain water and drinking thunder from the sky. For a little while they were allowed to be *children*, innocents in a world that swallowed innocence alive.

Mazi quickly got dressed. She pulled her dingy grey robes over her head, tying them shut with a rope for a sash. She didn't have a weapon yet, not even a knife for rituals. That would come later and in due time. This was a time when she was expected to be protected, by the elders. It was a time when she was supposed to feel safe. Yet, here she was, not feeling safe. The others were getting changed too, but she felt a mob mentality flicker between them. Mazi had just come here not long before, and she still spent most night's sleeping in Naomi's bed. The other girls teased her, and one day even threw stones at her when the seer's weren't looking.

She didn't tell any of the elders why she had bruises over her body. She feared more retaliation, so she said nothing at all. Sometimes, she reasoned, it was best to keep quiet. Silence was the only way to survive amongst a crowd of children like that, especially if you were an outsider amongst outsiders.

The others were moving now, gathering close together in a circle, all dressed and talking amongst themselves. Mazi didn't mind. She stayed outside of their circle, walked past the rows and rows of beds. "Where are you going?" one said, and she was startled but tried not to show it. "I'm going back upstairs, in case they need our help?"

"How did the water taste? Like mud?"

She shook her head no and realized that was the wrong answer. The others laughed and the other girl who drank said, "Oh you just like the taste of mud. Go on, get out of here. This is our own ritual. It's one we worked out for ourselves. Kitua brought her village's ghosts with her, so she's haunted. We're going to get rid of them, and we don't need you here messing it up."

Mazi nodded and said nothing. Silence was the best response, yet again. She then started to walk up the steep stone steps leading back to the first floor. Vines crept and covered the ceiling. Roots dangled down with crunchy leaves and sour berries. Berries the elders told the girls not to eat, but there were always a few that did so anyway. The fever the berries brought were thick and dangerous, and sadly there were always a few who died.

Mazi thought about those dead little girls often. She understood that appeal of the berries. Look at them, ripe like red jewels. They seemed to pulse in the sunlight, begging you to pluck them from the vine and slip them over your tongue. How sweet that would feel...

And then she thought of the ghosts and the empty shells and what it would feel like to die so painfully, and she pushed the thought out of her mind. Sometimes she wondered why the elders kept the berries here at all. Later, she would find out that it they were used in some of the more dangerous rituals, to bring them close to the land of death so they could talk with the ghosts directly.

Eventually she reached the top of the stairs, glanced back down and saw them talking in muted tones, their whispers barely audible. They seemed to speak gibberish, and pass a needle back and forth. She couldn't watch this part, so instead she walked through the great hall, towards the entranceway. Large stone heads dotted every other passage, their mouths opening up as doorways to other halls. Between those were cracked stained glass, and far overhead, in the giant arches that seemed to be infinite in height, she heard the rustling of feathers as birds flew from perch to perch.

That was when she realized the truth of the matter. There were strangers here. Strangers, in their temple. She remembered the outside world, remembered the man who tried to carve her insides out, leaving the spiral scar on her chest. Her mouth was dry, her head woozy and strung out on shadows. Someone was here. Boys from the outside.

She pinched herself and cried out. It brought her back to her senses, a trick Naomi taught her when she first came to the temple, terrified of everything and everyone. The pinch reminded her that this was real, this moment was real, and she was not to let her mind run away from her. She had to go and see who these strangers were. She would keep to the back, watch from the corners of the world, just in case, just in case they were him, and he was back to get what was his. She had to see, she had to make sure she was safe.

They were just boys, children like her, nothing more. Certainly, the one was only about a year older then her, and the other? About four or five years older than her. The older boy had started to grow a thin bit of stubble under his nose. A sad attempt at a moustache, but nothing more than that. He was barely a teenager. That made everything so much worse.

He twisted on a stretcher, his head up to the sky. He moaned and rolled about, and then screamed a little. His eyes were slammed shut, his hands writhing in knots all twisted up and bent in strange formations. *They almost look like rituals*, Mazi thought, *they seem like tiny spells*.

His knees were bent up, and she saw tatters of his pants and gasped a little, hiding her hand to her mouth to keep the sound as quiet as possible. His legs were ripped and shredded. Holes dotted along his knees and shins. Black ichor oozing from them, like tiny voids against his skin. The curse. It had been so long since she'd seen the curse in person. It took her breath away with all the awful memories it held. And his face, it was perfect and angelic. This was the face she would recall so many years later.

The other little boy was his brother, a man she will come to call Lens. Although at this point he called himself Etun. Mazi would never find out which name was his true name. Lens, Etun, it wouldn't really matter in the long run.

This little boy, just a year older than her, knelt on the floor, head pointed up, his hands in his brother's hair. He began petting it gently, and making soft cooing sounds to try and help heal his pain. This made her heart ache. The little boy was beautiful with long hair in curls and his eyes a hazy grey.

No wonder she would not recognize him later. He would become scarred and bruised and broken. His perfect nose mushed into his face, his mouth now marked with still raw cuts, and his hair pulled out leaving stress marks and baldspots.

But, here he was angelic. Yet his brother's face, beatific and calm even now, would be the one she could remembered all those years later. He seemed to have an inner tranquility that so conflicted with his brother's intense beauty.

She moved quickly, hiding in the shadows of the room, like a small lizard leaping from branch to branch. This was the large alcove, to the left of the entrance, with lots of shadows on the walls caused by the storm raging outside. A candle flickered in Naomi's hand, and the other seers paced the room. Some glanced out the cracked windows, looking for others in the pine trees beyond.

"I think we should just let them go. The last of his kind we let in here wreaked such havoc."

Naomi walked forward, palming the light. It reflected on her face and danced the shadows around the room. "I think that's cruel. You speak as if they're not right here, not listening to our every word. Can't you see this? He suffers from the curse. We cannot turn away suffering, do you not remember our vows? They are sacred and binding in the silence."

The seer stomped up to Naomi, her face in a warm grimace. "I speak in front of them because their kind *does not* care about us. You remember what they did to Loa! The poor girl can barely speak, her words were cut right from her mouth. They don't see us as people; they don't care what they do. Not until they need our help. And then what happens? We help them, they destroy us. Helping the likes of them is not worth the pain they will cause our sisterhood."

Naomi did not raise her voice. She moved her hand away from the flame, and touched her warm palm to the sister's face. "I know you've been hurt. I've been hurt too; we've all been hurt. But we can't let that stop us from doing the right thing. When you reached the inner caves near the stones, and you swore an oath to the ghosts, what did you say?"

A mutter of words, and then she said, "You do what you need to do, but I will be out, watching the acolytes, keeping them safe. Just, whatever you do, don't use the ghost heart. We only have two left, and who knows when the next reaping will be? It could be months, years, decades. Just, please, promise me that."

Naomi leaned forward, placed her forehead against the other seer's forehead. "Go now in peace. I will do what needs to be done."

They nodded their heads, and moved away, pulling back. The other seer walked past the doorway, out into the great hall beyond. Already the rain slowed. Pretty soon it was just a mist, and the sun broke through the clouds and into the stained glass windows, sending a prism of light across the floor. Naomi blew out her candle, and walked over to set it down, and caught sight of Mazi.

Mazi, who was now exposed by the sudden burst of daylight.

"Come here," Naomi said, "Come here love. There is nothing to be afraid of, nothing at all. It's only a little curse and that's all. You can help me, do you want to help me?"

Mazi nodded in response and crept over, moving slowly and uncertainly. The air tightened, and her skin prickled with goosebumps. There was an ill sense to all of this, something whispering of future horrors to come. She ignored it. It was probably the curse, or maybe just her own anxiety of her past surrounding her and begging to run away. Her spiral scar ached, and she thought yes, that must be it.

15

THEY HAD TAKEN HIM THROUGH the halls, up the stairs and into the whispering chambers, where the ghosts of the recent dead sit and wait. These were the forbidden places, and Mazi nearly dropped her end of the stretcher in shock. Thankfully, the younger brother, Eten, picked up her end quickly and they all stopped for a moment. She dry-heaved a little and looked around in a panic. She shouldn't be here. This was not her place. This was off limits.

She couldn't even look at Naomi, the one who had brought her here. Had she assumed the archetype of the trespasser now? One whose feet burned on sacred soil? The one who had come to steal the skull of a god and use it as a lantern in the underworld? The rituals did not lie, that was her now; she was the Trespasser. And when they caught the Trespasser in all the stories and rituals, they hung him upside down and cut him open, let the guts spill out. He hung there for days until he died. He did not scream, he did not complain. He only smiled, each moment each day, even at the fires of night, he smiled. She knew this story so well, it terrified her, and kept her away from forbidden areas like this one.

"You are not the Trespasser," Naomi said briefly. "Someday you will learn that those archetypes are just words, passed around, spoken in brief fear. But that is it, just language and stories, concepts, useful in only the abstract. I know what we've taught you, but those are only steps. Minor steps, at that. You will understand this more, later on, when you accept the mantel of seer."

Mazi nodded but she still could not look at anyone, she only stared at the walls covered in scrolls and books. The air smelled of glue and leather and mold. It was the scene of someplace holy, and she felt her feet burning. This was the sacred center of the temple itself, known to acolytes and sees alike as the Lotus Lyceum. The room was a hexagon, like the cell of a beehive.

"We need your help Mazi, please."

A grunt of a weary voice and she nodded, snapping Mazi out of her trance. She turned and ran back towards them, reached over and helped her carry the body out into the granite skull outside. They laid him down on the moss-covered stone head, and then turned and walked towards him. Birds fluttered all around them, taking off into the air and towards the sun setting over the hills in the distance. It was so beautiful up here. She had never been here before, and her heart ached at the scenes spilling out around them.

And then a rancid smell rose from the boy's body, as a red haze surrounded him, changing the features of his face. Later, she would smell that, when they were walking towards the shining city on the hill, before they placed the living masks on their faces. She would later come to know of that smell as the scent of the curse, itself.

She couldn't help it. She visibly twitched, and leaned back and retched, walking away. The boy could not be offended at this point. Both his eyes were closed, slick shut, and his mouth muttered nonsense. "The key, the crown, the mirror, the sword," he kept saying over and over again. The words scorched the images into her mind, only to resurface later when she would walk passed the spiral of bodies near the bear tower.

She tried to stop retching, just enough, but every time she walked over, she had to turn around again. The smell was too much. She was on her knees now, her lungs and stomach and throat all in pain. She dry heaved a few more times, her mind a swirl of just wanting it to stop, to just stop already. She felt something, Naomi trying to hand her a small bit of gauze.

"Wrap this over your mouth and nose. It might not kill the smell completely, but it should be enough."

She did just that, keeping it loose enough to breathe. The smell was still there, but not strong enough to turn her stomach inside out again. She stood up, turned around, and said, "How can I help you?"

Naomi was over the boy's body, gently closing his mouth, to keep him from muttering those words. Now his mouth just made clicking noises, and she could still hear those words reverberating around in her mind. Each click translated into the correct symbol. Click. Key. Click. Crown. Click. Mirror. Click. Sword. Over and over again.

Naomi reached into her satchel, pulled out a beaten brown book, with a black star on the front. After that she pulled out a roll of gauze, some knives of varying sizes, a small phial filled with butterfly wings, and a large glass tube filled with two chalk colored hearts. The hearts seemed like jewels, delicate, flickering in the sunset. "Come over, and be careful. The curse spreads easily, but I've never caught it. If you do as I do, I'm sure we'll both be safe."

Little Lens was over at the edge of the stretcher, nervously moving about near his brother's feet. There was fear in his eyes, and Mazi swore she had never seen anyone so scared before in her life. "We had to cross the bone labyrinth to get here," he said. His voice was cold, numb. "I, I just. He was, and there was, there was so much."

"I know," Mazi said, "I know. You came without our invitation, so you faced a labyrinth with teeth. The maze has many faces. On one hand, it is a place of great spiritual purification. On the other hand, it is a trap, testing those who go through it."

"I... I don't know if I can ever forget..."

Naomi sighed, looked down at her tools, and then looked back at Lens' brother with a worried look. He twitched, eyes closed, mouth clicking, his wounds writhed and sputtered, threatening to start changing the boy's body at any moment. "Stay over there, please? Just stay over there, and don't look at what we're about to do."

"I... I want to see, he's my brother."

Naomi picked up a pair of tweezers, reached into the phial and pulled out a butterfly. It didn't move, it was probably dead. With her other hand she pulled up a small knife covered in circles and lines. The lines glowed gold and the circles flickered and hummed. "Stay over there," she said, "And do not look. You do not want to look."

Lens turned around and stared off into the city and pines. Naomi nodded and looked at Mazi and said, "Are you ready?"

And Mazi said, "Yes."

Long hours of working on the poor boy's wounds, and now it was night. Their only sources of light were a loose group of candles spread in a triangle around his body, and those ghost hearts flickering with a dim, ashen light. So far, they'd kept the curse under control. He hadn't changed yet, and they were constantly fighting the wounds, making sure they did not spread any further. Naomi was weary, and her eyes sunk and her skin scratched like paper against the Mazi's when they touched, just barely. Her hair looked thinner now, too, and her hands seemed to shake a little.

"Are you all right?"

Naomi wrapped fresh gauze around a small area where the curse had receded a little on the brother's arm. The tatters of his legs and stomach, and the shadows that crawled in the wound were unchanged. " Don't worry about me. How are you feeling?"

"I feel the same as before," and Mazi pulled on the gauze around her mouth. It had slipped a little, and she could feel that retching feeling rolling around behind her lips and in her throat. Even a small exposure to the mist and the curse set her heart racing, with sweat trickling down her back and leaving wet spots against her robes.

For a second Mazi looked away as Naomi cut another small slit in the brother's stomach, and slid another butterfly under the flap of skin. Lens had curled up and fallen asleep under the tree at the edge of the granite skull. His body was outlined in a glimmer, and he seemed almost like a ghost in that dim light. Was he cursed as well? He seemed to be fading, and she worried any minute now he would turn to mist and disappear.

Naomi did not need her help. She was stitching the wound shut, the butterfly coming to life the minute it touched the cursed blood.

Mazi walked over, her bare feet silent on the moss, her robes billowing behind her in the eastern wind. She sucked in a breath, reached a hand out, hoping against hope that he wasn't cursed like his brother. She didn't want to risk it, yet she couldn't leave him here. So faint, so ghostly under the moonlight. People had turned to ghosts all the time in the temple, it was considered the greatest gift a seer could have. They just shook off their skin, and becamse a bright and shimmering spirit, their flesh in a loose puddle on the floor.

She didn't want that to happen to him, not yet. His spirit had not been prepared. The gift would destroy him. Her hand grasped his shoulder, and it felt warm against her palm. The boy smelled like boy smells, sweat and dirt and musky leaves. Why did all boy smell like the earth on a storm drenched day?

And yet, still, that was a good sign. He did not reek like his brother, he was not cursed.

His body moved, and she jumped back in shock. He wasn't a ghost after all. Groggily he said, "Is it done? Did you help him? Could you cure him? They wanted to burn his body, and scatter his ashes in the cliffs by the sea. The whisperers on the cliff insisted, saying otherwise he would change and corrupt everything in his path. They said the curse was an ageless hunger, and there was no cure. It was better to just kill him now and get it over with, to decrease the suffering in the world."

"She's still working on it," Mazi said and tried to smile.

"Oh. Why did you wake me?"

She had no response for that at all. She couldn't tell him that she'd thought he was turning into a ghost. She realized how silly that would sound if she'd said it out loud. Instead, she turned her head, really quick, to see if Naomi needed help. Her friend looked like a wraith by the candle glow. She finished the stitches and reached for the last butterfly. If she came over and offered help to Naomi now, she knew she would only be interrupting. So instead, Mazi turned back to Lens, and said, "What did you see in the labyrinth?"

He was pensive for a second, as if he wasn't certain if he should tell anyone anything. His eyes spoke secrets. Finally, he said, "We were hunted by wolves the size of bears. They had... oh. They had... oh. They had human skulls for faces. No eyes, just teeth, like wolf teeth placed in a human mouth. They had an amber flame from their bodies, and they skulked, searching, as they sniffed the air. They could not see us. They were blind, so we hid. But they searched, and they could smell the curse. They were coming for us, to remove us from the world, itself."

Mazi had heard of these creatures. They had been created by the seers over a century ago, during one of the bad plague years when the curse got out of hand. They were lucky they'd survived. Usually, when the inzai start hunting a member of the cursed, they do not stop until they rip them to shreds.

A horrible thought. She shivered, and pushed some hair behind her ear. She felt strangely vulnerable now, as if he revealed something about her. Like he had seen something inside of her in that maze, that the wolves were a part of her. It was a strange feeling, and it made her feel more exposed than she had been earlier, running naked and drinking lightning from the sky. She knew that the wolves really weren't connected to her, but she could not shake that feeling. Maybe, they were. She had dreams at night of hunting in the labyrinth.

Maybe a part of their souls were taken at the temple during a ritual, and placed in the inzai, and then they would hunt during the dreaming hours unwillingly.

She pressed on, moving past her unease.

"How did you survive?"

His voice was a ghost voice. "I'm not sure we did."

The night grew on, flew through the hours as they sat and talked. Every once in awhile Mazi would go back, check on Naomi. Poor worn out, exhausted, Naomi. She begged to help, asked to help. Naomi waved her off, said what she was doing now was too much for Mazi. It would kill her, she didn't have the strength nor the training yet. Just keep that boy company, she'd said, it would be more than enough help right now.

And so she did, she kept him company and they talked of their lives and everything. She never mentioned the spiral scar, or the time a man had wanted to steal her insides for himself. That was a secret that she would only let Naomi know. No one else would know such things. Not even here, at the roof of the world, with the boy sharing every horrible last detail of his sad life.

An in the whee hours of morning, Naomi eventually called her over, and said, "I've done so much, and it's still not enough."

He was quiet now, no longer clicking or talking. His mouth was bubbling with the drool of those fast asleep. His hands were in tight fists, and you could see cracks and black ichor along his knuckles. No more large gaping wounds. Just bandages and slits of sewn skin that fluttered with caught wings.

Naomi bent over, opened one of his eyelids with a cautious hand. It did not resist, it just let her fingers pull open, pry apart. The eye behind were black and ink and swirled around in his head like a starless night. Mazi caught her breath, keeping in her shock. He was still far gone. The curse had its hooks in him, and he would not last much longer at all.

Naomi sighed, and reached down. "I was worried it would come to this," and she touched the tube of hearts. "We only have two," she said. "Only two."

Mazi walked up and hugged her. Naomi's body was all bones and angles, her skin barely clinging onto muscle. She'd lost weight in the few hours of working on the boy's wounds. The curse had taken its toll on her. Mazi hugged her even more, squeezing her, hoping to fill her up with love and make her whole again. She tried not to cry, and only barely succeeded.

They stayed like that for a moment. Mazi holding the woman who had treated her so kindly since she wandered to the temple. Her new mother, in a way. A bond so strong that it broke blood. And there was nothing she could do to help her. She could only watch as her friend wasted away from helping a stranger in need, and it broke her heart. She wanted to save her. She wanted to save all of them from all the sorrows in the world.

"I tried, so hard," she said, her mouth against Mazi's shoulder, "It feels futile sometimes. I know the curse can only be cured by burning. But, I can't murder. I can't. And I can't let him go about, spreading this. There are only two left, and it's not a cure. It will only buy him some time..."

"How much time?"

They turned and looked at Lens. Everything else was a dark blue shadow, accenting his body in the dim morning dark.

Morning fog rolled through the hills down below, as Naomi stepped forward on the granite skull, her hands clutched close to her chest, as if she were deep in prayer.

"It depends on his heart. This could either kill him, or buy him a few years, tops."

"Oh," he said, "Oh."

"Some people, they say, have an iron heart. They can go their whole lives without the curse waking once again. They are the rare sorts, those who have an intense love of everything in life. They might not even need a ghost heart, or say it is said in old books and rumors. I've never seen it happen myself, I've only watched the curse destroy and devour."

"Like today," he said.

"Yes, like today."

He walked forward as the rising sun crested behind the hills, and outlined his body in rays of light. "But you can stop it. You said so, you have two of the hearts, use one, please. Use one! Even if you can only buy us two or three years, it's more than enough. I can't do this alone, I can't live in a world like this alone. Not with what I've seen."

Mazi leaned her head down. She knew that feeling, she understood it. When that man held her down, began to cut her open, she thought the same thing. And even here, even now, she had moments surrounded by people and still felt alone. It was a bitter, angry feeling, one that suffocated you and left you under the weight of your frustration.

"Help him," Mazi said.

"We've only had two hearts for thirty years. It's so hard to find one, the ghosts who leave them behind have to be happy in death, and so few ghosts are like that. Most are hungry, or they are jealous, or angry. Few are melancholy, but all of them despise the dead and regret the living. I'm not sure if we'll ever find another one, not in my lifetime."

His brother started thrashing and screaming on the stretcher. He grabbed at his stitches and ripped them open, and butterflies flew out from under his skin, dying once they hit the air. The three of them gathered around, held him down and Naomi laughed. A fearful, haunting sound.

"We'll do it," she said. She looked at both of them, all of their hands holding his body down, keeping him from ripping himself wide open and letting the curse run free. "I'm going to need your help. Both of you. Can you handle this?"

They nodded, as Naomi reached down and grabbed a knife. It glinted in the early dawnlight, as she sucked in her breath. "It's time," she said, "Now. It's time."

And she began to cut.

16

YEARS LATER, DURING THE HARSHEST winter the seers had ever known, there came a harrowing knock-knock that echoed through great halls like the dead calling for help from the living. The outside was a blizzard, and the sky was filled with short sparks of lightning. Thundersnow. Some of the more mystical minded of the elders said it was a good omen. Others said it was a bad omen. Still, the knocking continued, growing fainter with each rap, until there was only silence.

Defiant, Mazi came forward and pulled on the large gates, the wind and snow blustering in. Outside the pine trees were shadows in the dark. Snow transformed the world into a whisper. It had only been a year since Mazi had walked the runes, called to the hollows, and took the oath of seer and stone. The elders didn't like her brazen questioning of all things they considered true and at the heart of all rituals. Her hot temper and maddening questions were what made Naomi proud, so she hushed, held the other elders back as the gates opened, asking them to just wait and see. She trusted Mazi, and they all should, too.

There was a bundle in the snow. It looked like a bag of sticks, and then it moved, just a little. Not conscious, it had collapsed out of weary exhaustion and now twitched half frozen almost dead in the dark cold. Mazi picked up the body, a little girl, of about four or five. Bone cold wrapped in bandages, stick thin and lips blue. When she brought her in, some of the acolytes closed the gates and began to sweep the snow away. A cold followed her, a cold that carried with it the burn of a fire.

She walked. The girl inside the bandages pulled free, and revealed horrible burns under the dingy gauze. Recent scars, they still looked raw and red and infected. Later they would learn of the fire that took her family, and some think that maybe the snow and the cold where the only things that saved her from dying. They checked for the curse, and found that she had not contracted it at all. No one argued with taking the girl in; they could not leave such a sad thing outside, to die of exposure in the harshest winter they'd had in years.

Mazi saw to it personally, remembering what Naomi had done for her. The two of them even started to work together, helping Talia to come out of her shell, to no longer fear every second of the day. It took her a long time to even talk. She was mute for the first year she was there, communicating only with hand gestures and body language.

Eventually, she began opening up. The first person she spoke to was Mazi. And after that, Naomi. And finally, by her third year at the temple, she was laughing and joking around with the other acolytes. Mazi saw a mirror reflection in this young Talia. Someone who had been torn apart by the world, and who sought comfort from their own loneliness.

What she never told anyone, not even Talia, not even Naomi, was the reason why she had brazenly opened that door. She had hoped, *hoped*, that it would be Lens on the other side of that door. Every time, she expected him to be there, as if nothing had happened, ever. The same boy who came to them for help, his older brother dying, his whole being vulnerable and wounded. And so she waited, year after year. Looking, waiting, hoping. Her heart hungered for this boy, and she had no idea why. They had made a connection, certainly. They'd spent all night talking to each other. Surely, it had touched him as much as it had touched her. He would be back any day now to say hello, or even just thank you.

Yet, the years went on. She played those moments over and over again. She drew pictures of his face, but they yellowed and aged with time. Eventually she started to forget, little by little, what he looked like. She tried to imagine him older, and each time she did, she felt a frustration. Her mind was unable to pin each feature exactly. Soon, she forgot even what he had been wearing.

She retraced their steps some days, going all the way up to the top of the granite head, and stared at the sunrise. She ran through all the corridors in the same ways they did, once, over and over again. After some time, she started to remember less and less, and the boy felt unimportant. They had bigger rituals that felt so much more than her desire for friendship with some stranger they had helped all those years ago. When Talia arrived, Mazi found a new purpose, someone who needed her just like Mazi had needed Naomi when she first came to these halls. The boy turned into a lost echo in her mind.

On some rare nights, she still dreamt of him, and woke up with her heart beating rapidly. Sweat caked her, stuck the blanket to her skin, and she could not place why she felt so lonely. Each time she woke up after these dreams she felt a loss of something important. The past was never a closed book; it moved forward, projected outward. It kept pace with the present, just out of reach, a hologram of what was projected over the day to day moments of the now.

She wandered the halls at night during these hours, and sometimes Talia would wake with her, unable to sleep herself. Nightmares of burning and hearing her sister screaming, just an infant, unable to save her. They comforted each other in those hours. And Mazi, not knowing why, would lead them both up to the granite skull to watch the sunrise. It was forbidden, but that didn't bother either of them any longer. This was more important than rules and rituals. There was a connection there. She knew it between her dreams and the real. But the memory had long since faded, and she just had this overwhelming emotion in its place. She knew that something important had happened when she was a child. She could not say what. She could only feel a powerful emotion hidden behind a cloud of memory. One that she blamed on the sunrise and the beauty of it on the hills. Anyone, she reasoned, would feel the same feeling she had felt at such a landscape under the stars at night.

Later on, when Talia was older and becoming more brazen and talented herself, she waited for Mazi on the granite skull, knowing exactly what she needed, even if Mazi herself did not realize these things. Talia had a hot ceramic mug of tea, with a small chip on the corner. She handed it to Mazi, and they passed it back and forth, and sat on the giant stone skull and looked out across the pines. Even on cold mornings, when it was all ice, they salted and shoveled, and made room for a warm blanket, and carried out this very personal ritual.

It was a ritual of two. Mazi once tried to invite Naomi up, but Naomi always refused. Bad memories, she said. And Mazi tried to reason with her, but after a while Naomi just said no. She had realized that Mazi forgot it all, forgot them being up there, and the ghost heart going into the dying boy.

All that fire and light, and the world changed. It became a grey world in a flash of an instant. Naomi pushed the heart into the screaming boy, while Lens and Mazi held him down. His limbs thrashed, his teeth nipped at the air.

Eventually he stopped moving, the heart pushed deep into his ribs. He floated for a moment, glowing just a bit. His skin changed, his wounds closed, and the curse seemed to be a distant thing, but not gone completely. Naomi hit the ground before they could celebrate, her eyes wide open and unmoving. Her hair had turned bleach white in a few moments, completely removing the grey and black that had been her hair before. And on her side they saw blood, soaking through her robes—her blood.

Mazi rushed over and bandaged her, almost tripping on the loose stones. The sky was full of clouds, and she pushed Lens, almost knocking him over and off the skull. She leaned over her friend, moving fast. Her medical training kicked in right away, and it was over in an instant. The wound, she thought. The wound was worse than it looked. It was always that way, right? All that blood confused things, made things more complicated.

When she was done she helped Naomi sit upright, her body covered in cold chills, trembling, hands up to lips. Her eyes were wide and like two stars in her skull. Her lips where a chalky grey color.

"It's nothing," Naomi's teeth chattered, "Just a normal thing, after all this."

Lens's brother sat up on his knees behind them. He looked at his hands, at his stomach, at everything. He stood up, his legs wobbling, and he almost fell over. Lens walked over to him, his shoulder a crutch to the stumbling body. "How is it?" Lens said.

"Been worse. Way worse."

And he motioned with his head, over at Mazi, who was still holding Naomi in the morning light. The two brothers walked together, moving as one creature. "Thank you, so much," Lens said, and his brother nodded, and said, "Yes. Thank you." His voice was rough and worn down, the words barely words at all.

"You cannot leave, yet," Naomi said, her words shaky, her teeth still chattering, making it hard to speak. "You need to rest. Go downstairs, all the way downstairs, to the first floor. We will be down shortly."

The brothers nodded, did not speak another word, and turned around. They walked up to the giant old archway that led back inside. It was covered in small faces, tiny figures expressing words in a language no one alive understood. They moved through the dangling vines, parting them like a veil, and entered into the stained glass hallways beyond.

After they had left, Naomi closed her eyes for a moment, and then breathed ragged and raspy gulps of air. Before Mazi knew what was going on, Naomi began to cry. At first small tears, barely noticeable on her cheeks. And then eventually into whole-body, soul-wracking sobs. Mazi pulled her close, kept her body wrapped around Naomi's.

They did this in silence. Eventually, Naomi stopped for a moment, and spoke with a ragged voice. "I thought I'd died," and then she laughed. After the laughter came choking gasps, she paused and said, "I really thought I'd died. I saw my death so many times this morning. It enveloped me, chased me and hunted me. I did not think I was going to make it, and then I saw an opening. Like a gate in his chest, I pushed the heart in. I pushed it further into him, deeper than any heart should go. And I thought I had gone too far. I felt jaws wrapped around me, biting down. They weren't his jaws. The jaws of his ribe, maybe? No, the jaws were something else. Something else biting into me."

A pause and Mazi knew she had to ask the question, but did not want to. Not asking would not avoid the situation. The question was already in the air, hovering around them, waiting. She closed her eyes. "Was it the curse?"

Naomi pushed Mazi away gently, a moving apart of their two bodies. She stood up, still shivering with an internal cold. She walked like her feet were broken glass. "Let's not talk about that now. Come. I'm not sure the others will be as kind to him as we are. He desperately needs that right now."

Mazi bent over, started packing up the supplies. She hurriedly put them all together, and then said, "Will we tell the others about the ghost heart?"

Naomi did not turn around. She kept her back to Mazi, her

features hidden, keeping her reactions a riddle. "No, and you won't tell them anything about what happened tonight."

"But they'll find out, won't they? One ghost heart is missing?"

The two walked together, side by side, Mazi about half of Naomi's height still. Naomi kept her face hidden with her hair and the shadows of the room. It unsettled Mazi, she wanted to see her friend's emotions, to be able to tell what her friend had been feeling. Like all children, she wanted her new mother to be safe and well. Not knowing gave her a stress that burned at her. "We will have more important things to worry about, all of us will. Much more important than a single heart going missing."

"Naomi? Is there something you're not telling me."

In response she reached out and grabbed Mazi's hand, and squeezed gently. The two of them walked like that, holding hands and in silence, all the way down the stairs and into the great hall, where the acolytes waited for them.

17

NAOMI SAID HE NEEDED TO rest, to let the heart do its work and fill his body with ghostfire. The other seers grumbled and some avoided Naomi from that day on, barely speaking to her. Even when she became the high priestess years later, after Sophia died and told her to take the dreams, to take the light, to make something of the sisterhood in her wake. Even then, they still did not speak to her. To them she was a bad omen, the whole temple tainted by her actions.

The elders were the worst. While the boys were there, the elders clustered in attic rooms, read books in the libraries or performed private rituals in the hollow chambers of the skull. They had acolytes bring them small bits of food, nothing important. Just bread with some salt, and maybe some water. They were fasting while the boys remained, not in protest, but in ritual, to keep the curse away from their halls.

The brothers were given a room on the first floor. Past the gardens, now rich in spring blossom, the flowers drinking in the rain and light. It was humid enough that it felt like walking through water. Mazi led them about those first days, showing them where they could go, what they could do.

They walked through a few long halls, and then into open spaces with green limbs breaking through windows, showering leaves across the floor. And then they walked into the room of relics, with limbs of saints frozen in strange tubes filled with blue light, and a few heads floating, hung from ceiling rings. The heads circled in the dark, the only room kept without windows, without light: the room of the saints.

They walked quickly through this room. It made Mazi feel peculiar. Something felt *uncanny*.

They went through another hall or two and finally came to the lost places people barely went anymore. They said that twenty-five years ago an earthquake shook everything, leveled a mountain, made the seas swell and created a massive wave that wiped out the shining city on the hill. It ruined this portion of the temple, but left the rest of the place mostly intact.

Here, though, it was a ruin. Messy stone blocks, the ceiling collapsed in some areas, and still intact in others. There was a pillar crumbled, and another slanted sideways. Nature grew wild and starving in these rooms, reclaiming as much as it could. Grass spines poked out from cracks in paved floors. Vines hung down with sour fruits bursting from leaves. Clusters of mushrooms crept along the edges of the walls. They wiggled when the three of them walked passed, as if sensing their presence. At night they glowed, and it gave them their nickname: Little Lamps.

Their room was squat in the center of this mess. An enclave, mostly intact. It might have been a monk's cell, centuries ago, when they spoke of a cloister living here, before the seers took it over. No one knew exactly what had happened to these monks, but they had died, for certain. All wiped out at the same time. It is said that their ghosts are the ones that haunt the hollow stones.

Mazi was in the front, and she pushed aside the spider-webs. The two brothers seemed unperturbed that this would be their sleeping quarters. On the floor were two makeshift beds. The room was half destroyed, exposed to the elements. It also let in a fair amount of sunshine, reflecting on the murals painted across the room.

"Here you are," she said, and she walked the pace of the room. "You won't be here for long, but if it does rain, feel free to go into the main hall for some shelter. I'll be here a few times during the day, to check on you, and bring you food."

The older brother hobbled in, and collapsed on a makeshift bed. He rolled over briefly and then began to sleep. It was as if the exhaustion ripped at him, dragged him down to slumber without even a spare thought.

Lens walked in after him. "Thank you. I'll read for now, and don't worry, we'll keep out of your hair. I know the others aren't too happy about this arrangement."

Mazi nodded and said, "It's nothing," and then started to walk out. He reached over, grabbed her hand. She turned, and behind him the trees outside of their stone shell moved gently in the spring breeze.

"No, I mean it," he said. "Thank you for everything. Tell, tell your friend? The one who saved my brother. Tell her thank you, over and over again. I cannot tell you how much this means to me. I almost lost him. I don't know what I would do if I ever actually lost him. Tell her this for me, please?"

Mazi pulled her hand back, nodded shyly, and then walked out the door, back into the halls beyond. She ran through the rest of the building, back to the places that felt more familiar, more like home. The temple was big enough that the less explored sections felt almost like a foreign world, and it was easy to get lost.

They say that that when young acolytes explored too much of the ruins, a shadow chases them, and they never return again. It's just a story, just a thing they say to keep everyone safe. But Mazi had a feeling that there was a truth to this story, and it bothered her. The boys would be safe. That curse would probably keep them safe. After all, the curse made them the most dangerous thing in the temple right now, shadows or no shadows.

After she'd shown them the way, Mazi immediately went back to Naomi's room. She climbed the countless steps, and found the head priestess Sophia sitting by the bed, her head on Naomi's lap. When she saw Mazi enter the room, she moved her head back, stood up and nodded. "I'll leave you two alone for a moment," she said, and scuttled out of the room, hiding the tears on her face with the palm of her hand. She closed the door behind her, and Mazi came forward.

The room was a circle. The walls lined with shelves and shelves of books and different tools: tools for healing, tools for night; Tools for scrying, for singing the oaths to the ghosts;

tools that had lost all meaning and function, yet slept still on the shelves, blinking blue and orange lights. Between the arch of shelves was a huge picture window, looking out to the pines. The grass swayed with an unseen breeze. Naomi's bed was in front of the window. She laid on it in a half sitting position, her back up against the shelves, her knees bunched up to her chest. After Sophia had left, Naomi had pulled her knees up, and leaned her head down.

Mazi took it all in, and gasped. She held her hand to her mouth, trying to hide her expression, and failing miserably. Naomi was thinner now, even thinner than before. It had only been a few hours. Her face had a hollow look to it, and she was pale and wan and trembling. "Come over here, please," her voice sounded even worse than before, a delicate, broken sound.

Mazi walked with hesitating steps, her hand still over her mouth. She wanted to cry. She didn't want to cry. Seeing someone she loved change so fast, so horribly. It was too much.

"You have to keep a secret, all right? If I show this to you, you need to promise me you will tell no one. Promise me."

Mazi shook her head, then said, "Promise." She pulled her hand back for a brief moment, just a split second. She then sat down in the wicker chair right next to the bed. The chair that Sophia had ignored earlier. "Does Sophia know?"

Naomi nodded. "Yes, she's the one... the one who noticed. I thought maybe just a fever. Wounds can do that sometimes, and people survive it. We have root and words to help a person come out of a death trance caused by infection."

A heaving, heavy exhalation of breath. What was about to be said next seemed to take effort, and Mazi feared the worse. She leaned forward, leaned in, her hands making knots in her robes.

"Look," Naomi said, "Look. Don't look away. Look."

Her hands parted the still strung tatters of her robes, revealing the wound from before. Bound up still, with gauze. "You did a good job patching this up," Naomi said. A strange series of stains were along the gauze, like splotches of spilled dirt rubbed in. "Such a good job," and she pulled at one of the threads, and unwrapped the bandaging from her side, revealing the eroding skin, and the wound like night spreading. Stars beneath the wound, and bones, and a whisper of strange words coming from the wound itself. She poked a finger against it, and the finger seemed to blink in and out, flickering in the world. She wrapped it back up, breathing heavily.

Mazi had not moved at all. Her hands made knots in her robes, her body leaned forward, and her eyes were wide, her mouth trembling. The lips couldn't stay still, so she moved a hand up, closed her eyes. A small tear, she wiped it away. "The curse."

"Yes," Naomi croaked, "It's inside of me now. No one must know, and no one must know what I am about to ask of you."

Mazi nodded. She had this feeling, she knew what was going to happen next, and she was fine with it. She would keep the secrets, she would do the deed, and she will hide her silence. If it were to keep Naomi whole, to keep her with them even another year? She would do anything.

"I want you to," and she coughed a bit. A retched sound.

Mazi leaned forward, put her hand on Naomi's cheek, holding her face while Naomi coughed. She said, "You don't have to say it. Hold your breath, keep it safe in those lungs. You don't have to even ask, do you? No. I know what you want, you want me to go and get that other ghost heart, and bring it to you."

Naomi nodded, the coughs slowly dying out, regular breathing ragged but unfiltered. "Thank you."

"Does Sophia know? What must be done."

"Yes. She cannot do it herself. She actually... she requested you be the one who perform the action. You have less eyes on you. You are still new here. She knows that I care for you."

Mazi stood straight, tall. Beams of sunlight came in through the large window. The sun was over the pines, directly over the crescent of the window pane. The light landed on her body, lighting her in the shadows. She didn't say anything else, she could not, she leaned in, hugged her friend, her almost-mother. She wanted to tell her that the bond she felt, it felt larger than the both of them. It was almost as if Naomi had given birth to her years ago, and left her with some false mother, who watched over her until she came here, came to this place and found her real mother.

"Thank you," Naomi said, as they parted. Mazi walked over to the door, did not turn around, did not look at Naomi resting in the bed. She couldn't stand to see her like this, slowly changing.

She opened the door and walked into the great hall. Sophia stood there, and she looked at Mazi, inquisitive, yet unable to ask. In response, Mazi only nodded and walked on towards the relic room, where they had kept such things as the ghost hearts, hidden amongst the treasures beyond time. Sophia watched her walk past, and after she was far down the great hall, only then did she go back inside and quickly close the door behind her.

Mazi moved through the various halls and rooms. She was nervous, and she moved nervously, a child both determined and frightened. She cracked half smiles of anxiety at anyone who walked near her, almost certain, always certain, that she would be found out. No one seemed to think anything was amiss except for her, but that didn't assuage her guilt. She knew what she was doing was wrong. The elders would be so angry if they found out, banishment would be the lightest punishment she would face.

And yet, she could not watch Naomi quickly fade and die, or throw her in the pyre to cleanse the curse.

She walked down the stairs that they had just been playing tag on the other day. It felt like a million years ago, and she felt so much older now, even though it had been barely any time at all. She walked passed the puddles that still lay dormant on the floor, the only memories of those waterfalls from the other day. She moved through backrooms, laughed, joked with some other acolytes, the jokes of the nervous.

She finally got close to the ruins, close to the closed off sections where the boys were resting the day away. Maybe, she thought, maybe I should see how they were doing? No. Both Sophia and Naomi trusted her with this. She needed to do it. Naomi needed to get better.

She found the saint room, and went through the relics. She knew that it was here. It had to be here. But the satchel in the corner that had held the hearts and other instruments of curing the cursed was missing.

She heard footsteps. Soft, scattered things. She turned around, thinking to hide in the shadows, but realizing it was too late. Lens opened the door, walked in, shedding light in the room. He had the satchel in his arms. Their eyes met for a moment, a recognition that neither of them should be there, not now, not at this moment. They were both trespassing in the dark.

"I'm... I'm sorry. I couldn't do it. I wanted to do it, and I almost did it, but I couldn't do it."

He placed the satchel on the dirt. She could hear the ghost heart beating inside of it.

"Why?"

He edged towards the exit. "They said it couldn't last forever, that the curse would come back, and it would be worse than this time. I had to... I felt like I had to take it, to keep him safe. I know it's wrong, I'm sorry."

He turned, started walking away, not closing the door. His shadow moved out into the light, and Mazi walked forward and picked up the satchel. "Thank you," she said, "You don't have to leave yet, come back."

He stopped. "I need to be with my brother. I need to help him recover. The minute he's better, we'll leave you alone and you won't have to worry about us anymore."

"Oh," and she wanted to tell him about Naomi being sick, about needing this to help her, and that she understood what he had done, even if it was wrong. What she was about to do now, that was wrong too. But she had sworn to Naomi she wouldn't tell, and so she didn't. She just slung the satchel over her shoulder, and started the long dash back to Naomi's room.

18

I T FELT LIKE FOREVER, RUNNING through the maze of passages, darting in and out of rooms connected by large stone faces, the sunbeams glittering to either side of her body. The center of the halls were long shadows, the stone ceilings like mock tree branches far overhead, filled with the tittering of sparrows and the stray shaft of light pushing through a crack or two. The moments stretched, and the faster she moved, the slower time bound to her, creating an infinity of seconds between each step. The people were a blur around her, heads turning and looking at her running past, but not saying a thing.

This was a dangerous thing she carried with her. If anyone found out that she took the last ghost heart for Naomi... For her, for Naomi, for all of them. She felt like she was being rude, moving aside, darting between bodies like a fish, the crowd of seers like a stream moving around her. A few shouted out hey, another asked where she was going so fast, and yet she ignored them.If they caught her, all was lost.

Mazi'd already lost one mother, she couldn't lose another. Was she crying? No. Stop! She couldn't be crying. She rand around the corner, slid, and almost fell. She held the satchel aloft, keeping it from tumbling and breaking. Those hearts seemed so fragile, constructed out of such tender crystal. She bumped into an acolyte who pushed her a bit. But instead of arguing, or trying to hide, Mazi just picked up speed again and kept on running. The voice behind her yelled and shouted, but Mazi didn't care. Naomi had to keep going. The curse couldn't take root in her, it just couldn't.

She knew that Naomi had a strong heart. That this ghost heart would save her and she would be good for decades, yes. She would live a long and healthy life. That's what people like Naomi deserved, a long and healthy life.

Now was the evening hour, with low purple light of a sun just set filtering into Naomi's room. Sophia was there, standing by the door, waiting for her. Naomi was on the bed, her mouth shut, the pain of the curse visible on her face. She moved on the bed, possessed. Her wound was much larger, devouring her with shadows. She growled, and her hand changed for a brief second to bear paws, and then back to human knuckles tightened around the bedsheets. For a moment she had three heads, then two, then three heads again. The changes were coming fast, she'd only come just in time.

Mazi ran over, quickly, handed the satchel to Sophia. While Sophia rummaged around for the hearts, Mazi walked back to the door, closing it shut, quickly. In the distance she heard some people talking, maybe moving forward. Mazi paced a bit, her mind whirring with a million fears. They saw her. They watched her run. They figured it out. They put the pieces together. They were going to come in now, and banish them all, and they would wander the pines and the cities while the curse burned and changed Naomi, eventually destroying them all.

Sophia pulled the tube out, breathed heavily. Mazi stopped pacing for a moment, watching, needing to watch. She had to see this whole thing through. She could not hide her eyes. She's seen so much now, so many things a child her age should never see. This would be just one more thing, in the litany of sorrow that was her life.

One, two, three. Mazi held her breath, watched as Sophia cut into Naomi's chest. The scalpel sharp, digging in quick. There was blood. There were screams. The chest seemed to move, elongate and change. The rib bones twisted about like bone tentacles, looking for a way to rip into Sophia's skin and stop her. But Sophia would not stop. Not even for a moment. Mazi watched the whole scene in awe. Even breathing would break the silence and cast a pallor over everything.

Sophia's hands pushed forward, shoved the heart into Naomi's body. Naomi screamed, loudly, horribly, her breath ragged and tattered, her limbs moving, trying to push with knees and hands, to get Sophia off of her, to take the heart away. The curse was in control. Mazi stopped gawking and ran over, she knew that her help was required now. She knew what to do, and held Naomi's twisted body down. Naomi's skin felt hot to the touch, and Mazi almost pulled her hand back, it burned so much. It left scars on her palms that would take years to heal.

She pushed back down, arms and legs, holding them still.

Like a scarab on her back, kicking out, trying to push out, as Sophia pushed the heart deeper and deeper. Blinding light shot out of the body, flickering reality, like a strobe of fire, and then smoke. In the smoke the body relaxed a little. For a moment, Mazi saw something she would later forget. Naomi was a bear goddess, with three heads, her heart a bursting flame on her chest. She spoke half words, half growls. Then the smoke thinned out, the fire evaporated. The room smelled like roses and wine spilled on the stones.

They caught their breaths and looked down at Naomi. She was covered up now, with a blood-stained grey blanket, her skin clammy and a little cold, but not too cold. Her breathing was ragged, and the wound from earlier was now a small flap of skin, nothing more. Subtle, different. Yet it might be enough. It might keep the curse sleeping for decades, or for maybe all of Naomi's life. Mazi was not crying any longer. She'd spent the last of her tears on the run over here.

"She has a strong heart," Sophia said, " This will be it, I think. I think this will be it."

A knock-knock on the door, and a familiar voice, one of the elders. "There is some concern. We saw, oh. Is everything all right? We heard, we saw..."

Sophia looked over at Mazi, held a finger to her lips. *Shhh.* An image that burned into her brain. That finger, that silence it spoke. She then started bandaging Naomi's body, making it seem like that was all that was required. "Open the door but let me talk. I want you to keep yourself free of any lies. If anyone asks you later, change the subject."

"I understand, I promise," and then Mazi walked over and opened the door. A murder of elders huddled in, with the acolytes in the hall beyond, looking in, trying to get a peek at what all the commotion was about. This would be the subject of gossip, later.

"A fever, a terrible fever," Sophia said, "It gave her nightmares, the way she screamed. But I got it in time, I think the infection is cured, at least for now."

"Infection?" one of the elders warbled, "Infection. From that boy you brought in no doubt. Let's take a look, see if there's a bit of the curse in her."

They came forward en masse, moving like an ink blob over the floorboards of Naomi's room. A claw shaped hand pawed at Naomi's head. "Cool, cool. But that stench of sick, and the skin is slick with after-fever sweat. Hmm. Let us look at this, shall we? Let us peak behind those careful bandages."

"Wait," Sophia said, "Don't... I mean, I just got her fever down."

"Oh don't worry, don't worry," cluck, cluck, cluck, "We've fixed so many a broken body in our years. We just want to see, you see? Cursed or not? We can't let that devil of a thing in our homes. Cursed or not. Let's see here. Let's see."

Fingers tapped at bandages, pulled them up strand by careful strand. It was like watching someone knit in reverse, pulling the threads apart instead of pulling them back together again. Fingers probed the open flap of the wound, tried pulling it apart and open. Poked at it, felt it, rubbed it, sniffed their fingers, licked the palms of their hands. Satisfied, they put the bandages back the way they found it, quickly, moving fast.

"Hmm. Yes. Hmm," they said, their voices interchangeable, their words moving from body to body. It was as if they all had a same mind, congealed together through the ages. "It seems as though everything is all fine and good and no one is cursed. I feel something is amiss, though. I can't place my finger on it, but something is definitely off," they pointed at Mazi, "You, little one, yes, you. Come here. Why were you running through the halls?"

Mazi walked forward, and knew she had to answer, and knew she had to lie. Even though Sophia did not want her to lie, she knew she had to do it. "Naomi had left her herbs, salves, and ointments for treating infection downstairs, with the boys she'd treated earlier. I ran because she was so bad, the fever burning away her wits. I knew that such infections can kill if they're not treated with root and stone. Naomi had told me as much when they treated that sick boy."

A few *ahems*, and a few *yes, yes*. And then, "You were there; you saw it. How did she get this wound?"

Another lie. She bit her lower lip, but continued. "He was mad with fever and pain. We had to hold him down while she stitched him up, and he was in so much hurt, he bit out, tearing into her side."

Mazi bit on the inside of her cheek, hoping that the pain would keep her anxiety away. Her thoughts swam, her vision burned. Her whole body was a rigid steel bar. They clucked their tongues, the mass of elders, they nodded, and then said. "Yes, of course. Yes. We will talk to her in the next day, after she rests and recovers. We just want to make sure, you understand. We just need to make sure."

And they scuttled back out of the room, an oozing clump of bodies, shutting the door quick behind them with a mess of fingers and palms. Naomi was still out, still asleep, turning, muttering to herself. "You should go, maybe check on those boys. It's getting to be dinner time, and they might be hungry. I'll keep a good eye on her. No need to worry."

Mazi walked forward, placed a hand on Naomi. She stayed there for a moment, palm against the clammy slick of her skin. She didn't want to leave here her alone, but she knew Sophia was right. The boys needed food, and maybe a kind eye. Pretty soon the elders will want to talk to them, and that could change everything.

She went back down, through the halls, towards the ruins. It was getting dark, and she carried a lantern with her, the flickering lights of the candle spreading shadows through the halls. Everything was empty, everyone was up in the mess hall, eating food and laughing and hanging out. She enjoyed being outside of the crowd, seeing it from the outside. There was something nice to that, like she was a part of the crowd and yet still distanced away from it. It was hard to explain why this brought her comfort, but it did.

Eventually, she found her way to the monk's cells near the end of the ruins, walked through the relic room, and came to the small area where the brothers stayed. The night air was crisp, and overhead the stars blinked through the crescent ruin of a ceiling. No moons in the sky tonight, just stars and a whisper of clouds. They were sitting on the floor, around a hololamp placed on the ground. It sparked blue light, and Mazi had seen these before. Probably something passed down from family to family, or maybe discovered on accident in the junk mounds south of the city.

Some say there are even islands of garbage, floating in the sea filled with relics from centuries ago, back when the world was lit by lightning. Not by fire, not by candle, but by lightning.

The older brother was still asleep. His breath was rapid, but other than that he appeared to be normal. Lens sat squat on the floor, staring up to the stars beyond. He seemed to not hear her arrive, nor see the change in shadows caused by her lantern.

She sat down next to him, looked up at the stars through the ruin of the ceiling, and then pushed a bit of stray hair behind her ear, and nudged his body with hers, trying to get him to at least say something, to acknowledge her existence.

Finally, he said, "Don't lie to me," all while still looking at those stars.

Shocked. "I wouldn't, what is it?"

"He'll be fine. Right? I mean, for a while at least. I ask because he hasn't woken yet, not in a little bit. I keep trying to wake him up. I shook him, I yelled. All he did was grin and roll over. Sometimes I wonder if he's messing with me, or something else."

"He will be fine. You know that, if they ask... he was just sick. Right? Not cursed, just sick."

"Yeah. We went over all of this so many times. I will lie. I promise I will lie to everyone for you. Is that enough? I wonder."

"Are you hungry?"

"No. I'm not sure. No. Are you?"

She shook her head no.

"Oh. Why?"

"It's dinner time, they're all eating upstairs. I was just wondering if you wanted something."

"No, no."

She leaned back, took in the entire sky. So many stars. On a night with no other light, the sky seemed infinite. She'd never seen them like this, so many of them. A crowd inside the heavens, blocking out the void between them.

"You can go, and eat with the others, if you want."

"That's all right," she said. "I feel fine here."

A sigh. And then. "It's your friend, the one who helped us, isn't it? She's not doing well. That's why you were in that room, why you were looking for that satchel. She needed it."

Mazi put her hands over her heart, felt them clench into two fists. She wanted to scream and run around and kick and destroy everything. Instead she blew out both of the lights, leaving them in darkness. "See?" she said, calmly, without the fear she felt grasping at her insides, pulling her apart. "There are so many stars in the sky, even more now with those silly lights off. Have you ever seen so many before? I don't think I have. It might be because I never actually looked before. And now, I'm looking. I'm staring at it, and it's overwhelming."

She felt the shadow of his body slide down, laying next to hers. They just spent the hours there, worried about their friends, unsure if either will make it. It was a night of fear and companionship, the two of them staring at the sky, sleepless and moonless, a cold comfort in the dim glitter of starshine. Eventually the sun rose, the world filled with a slow mist, and Mazi excused herself. She went upstairs, all the way up to the granite skull. And she watched a new day, and wept silently to herself, bound up in the worries that haunted her. Sitting there, at that place, were everything had changed.

Later, when she went downstairs and back to the ruins, she discovered that they had left without saying a word. No one had stopped them. Naomi was still recovering and could barely move. Sophia was by her side, helping her. The rest of the temple didn't want the boys there anyway, so they had let them leave. Even though his brother was still recovering as well, they had let them leave. She couldn't blame them for leaving. They must have felt the stares and hatred of everyone in the temple, and knew that they were not wanted.

19

SHE RECOGNIZED LENS AND HIS brother now. All of the emotions and feelings bottled up from the last few decades came rushing back all at once, flooding her with so many complex emotions. The four of them on a bridge, surrounded by mist and a cursed reality. She saw the past and present at the same time, his face both changed and unchanged. Now that she saw it, she couldn't take the thoughts away, that feeling of falling now, that feeling of drowning now, the realization a claustrophobic fear. She almost screamed when she realized everything. A sense of overwhelming betrayal clouded her thoughts, and then she saw the ghost heart in his hand...

Mazi had laid her head against that heart so often, dreamt of that heart, it had burned into her mind, and she recognized it the minute she saw it. Naomi's heart. She'd dreamt of that heart, daydreamed about that heart, and knew it like the back of her hand. Naomi's ghost heart. He had pried that from her body, and lied to them. She'd felt connected to him all those years ago. They could've been best friends. And now, he had led them all the way here, to her brother with Naomi's stolen heart. Ripped from her chest, the curse left to consume her.

Mazi screamed incoherently and everything turned red, all she saw was red, and she tried to pick up her bow and ready an arrow, to stop him, to just stop him, but her hands were clumsy anger hands, and they didn't seem to want to work and the pain grew, like her curse was now feeding on her anger, growing and pulsating and devouring that hatred for strength. Oh, temple and song, not now, please not now. Ghosts, come to me, help me, save me from this curse. Let me get revenge for the one we loved.

Time was a frozen droplet, movement slowed down mist slow, crawling across the real, everything moving snailpace. His hand lifted up, slow and liquid, the heart unwrapped now, the hand pushing it into the brotherbeast.

"He had stolen her heart! That's Naomi's heart! He has stolen her heart!"

He didn't even turn, didn't even move, it was like he could not hear her, that he existed in some space between space, where sound waves would not permeate. His fist shoved that heart, moved it into the gaping chest hole, pushed it in. The brother thrashed the air, no longer calm, howling hungry angry, all those limbs thrashing and tentacles lashing whip-crack in the silence, in the air.

"What do you mean? Naomi's heart? She's... oh. You said she was cursed? Is that her ghost heart? The one you had used on her? Tell me, Mazi! Is that what you see?"

Mazi had no time to respond to Talia's questioning. She moved quick liquid anger and pulled up her bow, yanked it back, arrow strung and holy, and then let it fly. The bone-bow made a sound like whispering thunder, and the arrow was a shooting star, parting the mist. It thrummed in the air, a vibrating string, oscillating on an unheard frequency, tearing at the world around it. It struck into Lens' hand, and he fumbled, pulled back, that heart sliding out of the cursed brother's chest with a slick thick slump, slurp, floating out, hitting the ground. It did not break, but instead rolled for a bit, threatening to shatter to pieces. The light was a dim glow, throbbing in that mist. She had to get it now, before it breaks, before Lens has another chance to use it.

Time sped up resumed normal time and Lens turned around, fire in his face, his palm broken apart with arrow shaft. He pointed at her with the arrow and said, "Why? What? Why? You remember me now, don't you! Do you know what I did? I guess you must know, by that look on your face."

And his face was calm and he smiled. He just said, "I understand. I do. I hope you understand, what I did, and why I had to do it. You know how this curse destroys. I see it on your face. We will do anything to keep our loved ones safe. Even if it means our own destruction, and even if it means the destruction of the entire world."

He bent to pick up that ghost heart, and Mazi yanked back the bow, arrow at the ready, aiming for his head. Talia reached out, grabbed the arrow and snapped it in half. "No. You don't want to kill him."

"Oh," Mazi said, "But I do."

"No. Trust me, you will thank me when this is over, and I saved you from murdering someone you knew, sometime, maybe a long time ago. But someone you knew."

He couldn't pick up the heart, he tried, and tried, and over and over again, grasped out, slipped through his fingers, his palms unable to grasp it because of the arrow sticking out of him. He stood up, grabbed the shaft of it, and bent it down, breaking it off. He screamed in pain, grabbed his hand, howled for a moment more. He then flexed his fingers, and then bent over and tried to grasp at the heart again. Tears of suffering filled his eyes with pain.

But his brother moved faster.

As he struggled with the arrow in his hand, she remembered that night, staring at the stars, laying side by side. They did not speak, only had silence between them. A silence informed by a common understanding. That they would do anything they could to save the ones they'd loved from being destroyed by the curse. She would do anything for Naomi, he would do anything for his brother.

Those scars, his broken face, how long had he searched the world for another ghost heart? He had found strange items, been all over the world, looking for a cure, probably. Maybe something to fix him, to change him. And all the while she had stayed inside the temple, stayed with Naomi. She felt meek in comparison to Lens, the man who had searched everything and everywhere, all looking for the truth to it all. And here she had stayed, looking past the riddles, searching for each moment of each day and nothing more. She had grown compliant, passive.

He had done the unspeakable. Would she have done the same for Naomi? Perhaps, but perhaps not. And then she realized that Lens must have stood over Naomi's body and cut out her heart. A chilled feeling spread over Mazi's body. She remembered the man standing over her own body, cutting a spiral scar into her skin, looking to remove her own heart. Lens had done that. The world had burned that little boy away and left a monster.

She watched him struggle, and rushed forward herself to go towards the heart. Time froze. She saw his brother move like liquid fire and an intense fear shook her body.

His brother's face still calm and beatific. His brother's mouth wide and wider still, like a snake unhinging its jaws to swallow a rat. There wasn't even enough time to scream as the mass of limbs and tentacles surrounded Lens, the jaw wide open, tongue whipping about and around his neck. The brother grinned the whole time. A horrific, sadistic grin, the tongue tightening into a thick noose. Lens's eyes swelled out. His face was purple like a bruise.

Mazi felt trapped. She could only watch in horror. The two brothers who cared for each other so much, devouring each other in front of her. She wanted to feel vindicated after what Lens had done to Naomi. Instead, she only felt empty and sad and numb.

The tongue yanked Lens into his brother's lips. The mouth shut down, slurping noises assaulted the air. Time froze into a jewel around them, each moment endless, as Talia knelt on the ground and fired off a few arrows. They pierced the mist and shadows, landing on the cursed demon's face and eyes. It let Lens drop, screamed, howled.

It was all too late. Lens' face was gone, replaced with a

slurry of skin and blood. His corpse slumped over, a rotten sack of a body that tumbled over the edge of the bridge, and fell down through the mist into the nothingness below.

Mazi ran forward while Talia fired, her eyes focused completely on the ghost heart, Naomi's one saving grace. If she was still alive somewhere, she would need it. Mazi slid without thought, acting only on instinct in this moment of terror, as the face and head chomped down. It bit into pavement, just barely missing her, and coughing up stone dust and broken teeth. She grabbed the heart, and spun around, holding it close and dear, while Talia pummeled the creature with a flurry of arrows.

The cursed brother stomped after them, arrows sticking out of various limbs and body parts, the head now strange, sunken, no longer looking human but more like a wax face melting in the summer. The eyes flickered, grew out on stalks, and searched around and found them and followed. It dragged the dead limbs behind. Its body slouched towards them. It whined as it moved, a terrible sound that would haunt them forever after this moment.

The two of them ran. Talia fired arrows back. Their bodies climbed and scrambled across the changing bridge and buildings around them. They had seen the fate of Lens. They did not want to repeat it. Stairs would appear and disappear, parts of the bridge fading in and out of existence. Doors would pop in front of them and lead to nowhere. And the cursed brother beast behind them seemed immune to the shifting reality. It did not need to be cautious or careful, instead it seemed to dance with the changes.

Talia shot another arrow, and this one landed right into his eye stalk. The wound blistered and smoked. Somehow that gave them hope, that maybe this was the disease devouring itself. They'd all heard tales of the weak hearted burning up, the curse destroying the host. Maybe this was about to happen, maybe they could hasten it with their violence.

Mazi looked at her hands as she ran. The ghost heart beat arrhythmically, skipping and then tripling beats. This was not good. Had Lens damaged the heart when he took it from Naomi's body? She hoped not. She reached down to the bandage on her own wound and ripped it free, and, as she ran, wrapped it around the heart. Hopefully, that would help for a little while.

They leapt, slid, moved further. Talia fired some more arrows, and almost fell when a floor went missing, but she was able to grab, and climb up, and then they saw it. The cursed beast had stopped moving. Not all at once, but it slowed down, and then stilled. The body was now leaking smoke everywhere, the face a puddle of features, no longer resembling anything remotely human anymore. It flickered for a brief moment, and then caught fire. The body crumbled against the flames, like a building burning down to the ground. Ashes spit out into the wind, floated around them and left black smears of ash against their hands and arms.

They stopped and watched, catching their wind once again, their bodies screaming out in pain. Lack of sleep, too much movement, too much of everything, it caught up to them, wearing them down. Everything hurt and Mazi felt this overcoming need to sleep. But she would resist, and watched as it slowly burned away into nothingness. There was no relief here, only a soft pain in the heart from everything they'd witnessed.

Mazi felt sad, and grabbed Talia's hand, and gripped it tightly. She never wanted to let go. For so long she'd wanted to see Lens once again, only to be betrayed and watch him die in front of her. There was such an ache inside her chest, it was overpowering. Had her heart weakened in sadness? Will the curse devour her completely now?

"That was..."

Mazi nodded. "Too much. All too much."

"Yes. Right."

She held the heart close, felt it still alive, beating stronger now. A good heart. A heart that could probably last another hundred years. If only they could get it to Naomi in time.

"Is that the ghost heart?"

"Yes."

"The one that Naomi had used."

"I would know it anywhere."

They walked on in silence. The world stopped shifting for a bit, as if the death of the cursed brother beast had reset it. The two of them no longer conspired against the two women. The bridge disappeared behind them, overcome by the mist and the fog. The building up ahead opened up to them, spreading stones like arms. They paused right before it, and Talia turned to her and said,"Do you think?"

"Think what?"

"Do you think that she's dead?"

"No, Talia. I know she's alive."

"How can you be so sure?"

The heart called to Naomi against the palm of her hand. It wanted to be with her, and moved like a compass against her fingertips. "I'm sure of it," she said, not going into detail. Would she even believe her, if she told her how the heart moved and throbbed and called out? "She's alive."

"Oh. You're cursed, too."

"I know."

"You can do it, right? Use it on yourself. Naomi had her time, she lived longer than anyone else probably could, just on that heart alone. Now it's your turn."

"I..."

She couldn't do that. She looked at the heart as they climbed down, felt it in her hands. This heartbeat was one she hard in her dreams all the time. It was Naomi's and only Naomi's. It had lived with her for so long, it had ceased to be a ghost heart anymore, and now fully and truly belonged to another. She could not do it. Even if the heart was not tied to Naomi in some way, she could not do it. She didn't have it in herself to deny Naomi this redemption. She could wrestle with her own curse, but she couldn't see someone she loves suffer.

"No," she said, finally. "I can't do that."

"Oh," was all Talia could say in response.

And it broke Mazi's heart to hear her say that. She must have felt the same way as Mazi.

20

FTER HOURS OF MOVING THROUGH building after mutated building, they finally found stairs that led them down to the outside world once again. Fog obscured the streets beneath their feet, and Mazi could not wait to get away from this place, and return to a solid world once again.

The sun had set not long ago, and night spread quickly through the city. The only light was the shy light of a candle that Mazi held in her hands. The stray wax dripped over her knuckles.

Talia bent down in the cone of light, and rummaged around in her filthy burlap sack. After a few moments, she pulled out their lantern, opened the glass door. "Here," she said.

Mazi leaned in, bent the candle to the wick, and watched the flame sputter to life. She then blew out the candle and threw it to the ground, swallowed up by the mist. Everything changed around them. The lantern revealed a city that was more threatening than it was in the daylight. Mazi held her breath in disbelief, as the city destroyed itself, turning into basic shapes and reconfiguring into something else. Those blocks floated past them, danced around them, and whizzed over their heads. They had to duck and move out of the wa. The stones reconstructed themselves. They changed into walls, and passages, and corridors, and doorways. Everything felt strange, and neither of them spoke. The sound of the city was a deafening roar of stone and granite.

They tried to orient themselves in the evershifting landscape, to find a way that pointed back towards the temple, and home. A maze, a labyrinth, that's what this was, this was turning into a scrambling, spiraling labyrinth that led them by eye and fist towards the center.

A heretical mockery of the Bone Labyrinth.

Even in the fog and the dark they could see the tower at the center of the city. It was the only thing that was not reconfiguring itself into the maze. It stood straight and violent, pointing towards the sky. Mazi wished she could see the moon in the sky above their heads. But the fog was so thick, it obscured everything. No stars, no moon, no night sky to speak of. Instead of a moon, there was a halo at the top of the tower, around the trifold head of the bear. That was where the maze led. All paths led them straight towards the bear, and its blue halo glow.

There was a dizzy sick thing inside of Mazi's stomach. This was a realization. Something she did not want to come to grips with. It wasn't the curse; it wasn't any of the other wounds and aches that she'd gained along this quest, either. This was the pit of the world dropping out.

But she didn't want it to be true. *Oh, please, Naomi, do not let it be true.* This couldn't be right. It had to be wrong. Yet, there it was.

The bear was Naomi. She laughed at first, then almost vomited, then steadied her body, using her bow to balance herself. The bones of the bow dug into her hand a little. A hand already covered in wax burns, numbed slightly from the curse waking up.

The heart in her hands started to thumpthump, wanting to return to her former owner. She held the heart up, towards the triface of the bear demon. It began to beat faster. She pointed it away from the creature, and it began to beat slower. *No, no, no. Please, oh no. Not her. Don't let that be her.*

"What is it?" Talia asked.

A cough, and then Mazi slung her bow back over her shoulder. She didn't want to move on. She had to move on. There was no going back now. There was no other choice.

"The heart, it wants to go there. See?"

She pointed it at the bear, and again it beat rapidfast.

"Oh. Are you certain? It could be the opposite, you know. It could be beating fast because it wants to go away, to return away from there."

"No," Mazi held the heart close to her chest for a moment. "It needs to go there. That's Naomi."

"The bear."

Mazi nodded in the dim light. The world still moved around them, twitching in the shadows. Those maze walls now a living thing. It looked exactly like the Bone Labyrinth, the pathways the same. The only difference was what it used to construct itself. The bones of a city, rather than the bones of the dead.

"Naomi is the bear, connected as one. I'm sure of it."

A flash in her mind, an echo back to something else,

something that happened so long ago. When they had placed the ghost heart inside of Naomi, she had seen a flicker of a bear's muzzle. This bear's muzzle. A reflection of what was to come.

"Mazi, something horrible and terrible, larger than both of us is happening. Will this be worth it? What happens if we free Naomi, and she's herself for a little while longer? What will happen to this city, to the curse? What will happen in ten, twenty years from now, when the curse wakes once more? How will we save her? How will we save you? Listen to me. Use that ghost heart on yourself and let's go back, and tell the sisters what we've seen. Maybe they can help us, maybe they can help Naomi... Maybe they can help you."

"No." It was a whisper. "No. Don't ask me again."

The idea ate at her, but she knew this was the correct answer. There would be no world without Naomi. Her death would be the end to everything, she had to save her. Even if it meant giving into her own curse and dying.

...from above, far above, through the occulting fog the shape of the labyrinth moved like skin pulsating, a spiral through a circle, through a triangle, through a square, a sacred geometry of time and space leading all paths inwards, towards that center tower, that sacred stone, that navel of the stars, and the strange head sticking out, and remember, remember, what some had said, that the first labyrinths were based on intestines, that inside of our bodies we carry such tools for awakening of the self, that all mazes are constructed out of light, and they carry illuminations in our guts, in each of us, this path burning inside of all of us, and that the curse is a path, the light is a path, that the shadows are the paths between stars, and the stars are the paths between galaxies, that to walk the path was to carry a torch or lantern or candle, and that She was called Torchbearer and She was Called Tzani, and She was called the Lady of the Labyrinth, the whisper of the maze, and that she died and was reborn in the center of the stomach, in the navel of the space, that connected inwards, into our own internal labyrinths, and that Mazi had a spiral of scars on her chest, where someone tried to open her and release her own labyrinth into the air, and her scars traced into stone mirrored this maze here, the newly formed maze leading towards that center tower, and it would reflect that bone labyrinth from before, where this all started, and it reflected that internal intestinal system of passages we all contain, she just wore hers on her skin, a labyrinth of scar and bone...

Mazi walked, following the heart, letting its beats be her guide through the restless winding passageways. Her scar itched uncontrollably, a disturbance that seemed to follow her through the labyrinth. With each step further, the itching moved up the spiral scar, closer and closer to her own infected heart. She felt an echo and an ache at the center of her scar. It called out in ripples towards that tower, that bear, to where Naomi waited for her.

The shadows moved briefly around the two of them, growing long in front of her body, light cutting against her back. She paused, holding the heart close to her chest. It wormed against her own skin, sensing the curse she carried as well. The fog swirled and moved in a sudden disturbance, like the swirling waves of the sea around the prow of a boat.

"I am not going to let you commit suicide."

Talia's voice, a knife to the silence.

"Oh?"

"I'm here. I'll always have your back."

"Oh."

Talia didn't have a spiral scar on her chest. Her scars where all things of the past, and they stayed there, in the past. While Mazi's scars where of the present moment, speaking to her now, the maze around them a mirror to her own suffering. She needed this in a way Talia could never understand. Curse to curse, scar to scar. Heartless now, both Mazi and Naomi, carrying labyrinths on their skin.

She wanted this scar to have meaning, so much meaning and truth. But she couldn't say that to Talia. She couldn't deny her friend, her sister, this revelation she was about to experience.

Talia walked up, the lantern splitting Mazi's shadow into spokes around her body, a wheel of night rising up from the light. "I am only here to help you, I promise. Let's find Naomi. Please."

"Oh." Mazi's words felt far away from her own voice. That hopeless, cruel, dark cloud drifted over her heart and mind. She sat on the ground and didn't want to move, couldn't move, her whole world spun around. The heart beat weaker in her hands. She felt it struggling, the muscle struggling to move. Did it still want to be with Naomi?

Was the ghost heart dying without a host?

"Mazi, Mazi? Let me see your arm... that arm, the cursed arm."

She held it out, numb and broken. Talia inspected the curse, touched the gauze, poked at it, peeled it back and saw the small crevice under the skin. It had only grown a little.

"You're doing better than I thought." Talia paused. "That heart, it's getting weaker. How much time do we have left? Before it's useless..."

"Oh," was all Mazi could say. She repeated it a few more times. She wanted to push past this grey veil that suffocated her. She wanted to climb up, stand up, move forward, getting that heart to beat properly once again. She felt a weight against her body, pushing her down. A weight of sorrow, of everything in the world crushing apart. Talia was right. What would happen next? They can't cure everyone, they couldn't save everything. The curse had taken on a vicious new life, it spread and destroyed and changed. It corrupted everything. Even if they'd saved Naomi...

Then what? The world was still doomed. She took off her mask. Talia looked down at her, glared at her.

"Why did you take the mask off?"

It fluttered out of her hands, and took off into the fog and dark beyond. There was no going after it. It was free now.

"I'm cursed, it's already happened to me. The fog cannot do any worse. I breathe it in, see, I breathe it in and I'm fine, the wound is the same, I feel like... it would only disrupt me if I were uninfected. But I am infected. I'm doomed, don't you see? The mask doesn't matter, none of this matters."

She breathed the fog in, sucked in those shadows into her lungs. The scar spun, and ached, and then leapt to life once again. It began to blaze after a moment, a holy light against her skin. She looked down, saw that dim blue glow. That was where they were. The cursed air was talking to her scar now, showing her the way. Would it be worth it, now? If her curse got worse? Would it be worth it to save Naomi and give her the ghost heart?

Of course it would be.

The despair lifted inside of her. The sadness moved away, and not the ghost heart began to beat rhythmically against her palm once again. They were connected now, all of them. They were going to do it. They were going to save Naomi.

"She calls to us, Talia. Can't you hear it?"

"No, I don't think I can. Mazi, Mazi, look at me. I don't think that was a good idea. You seem... different now. Different somehow. We should hunt down your mask and put it back on, you know it's the right thing to do."

"How is that? Tell me? But first, take off your own mask and look into my eyes with your own eyes. Breathe it in, it is wonderful, come on Talia. It will show you the light of our path! How right and true this whole journey has been."

Talia stepped away from her.

"No, I can't. You seem more animated, yet it's a hollow animation. Like a scarecrow set on fire."

Mazi was offended in that moment. "Take off that mask. You will understand, the curse can be a blessing sometimes. It gives me such instinct, such insight. I can see beyond the actual, in the real beyond the real."

Talia stepped back some more, her lantern swinging in her hands. "Why don't you carry the lantern as well? Just in case."

"Of course," and she stepped forward and grabbed the lantern with one hand, holding the ghost heart with the other. Talia slid her bow out, armed it with arrow, and walked cautiously behind her friend. She kept to the shadows, just out of light. her hand quivering on the bow as they walked further, moving onward, closer to the center of the maze.

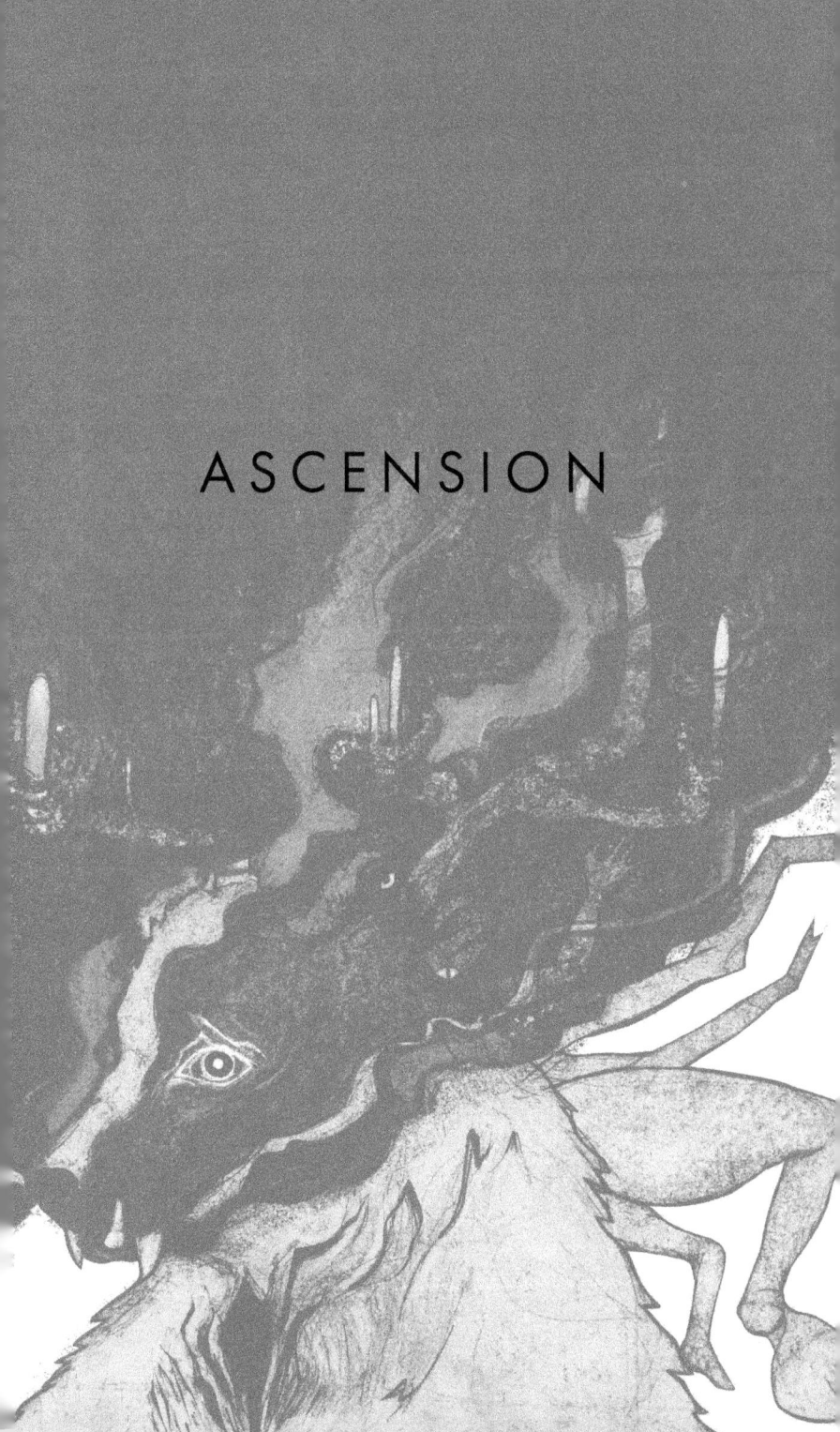

ASCENSION

21

HAVE YOU EVER WONDERED WHY there was an end to your body, why there was a wall keeping your thoughts from spreading out from your head and into the world? Why couldn't you feel what I felt, why couldn't you see what I saw? Why did my touch become your touch and turn back into my touch? Where did your body end? Where did our bodies begin? When you entered her, did you cease to exist? Did you melt into her body? Did she show you the deep secrets of this world, and the puzzle to our lonely existence?

We are all more connected than we could ever understand. My words the ocean waves. Your words the sunrise on a beach. And her growl, the earthquake that woke entire worlds.

You inhaled and you could hear her thoughts. You exhaled and understood her desires. There was no more ego, no more thought, no more person or place or thing. There was only everything, existing in the infinite womb of the Sata-Torun. This had become the messy sea of existence, where thoughts were not thoughts and where being ceased to be being and became something else altogether.

Noami struggled in darkness. Everything was noise around her. She heard loose crowd of voices praying and performing rituals. They reminded her of the rituals of the temple, and for a brief moment her ego flared up once more, like a butterfly on fire. She wanted to be whole again, and separate from the Sata-Toran again. She struggled against her flesh that had merged with the curse. She was stuck. Web of body, web of skin. She forced herself to remember all those little details that made up the concept of who she was, before the curse took over.

That time, so long ago, when she was a separate entity entirely. When she had been loved at the temple. Mazi needed her. She remembered the last moment, when she had been free of the curse. Her body on the ground, held down. A bandaged man screaming over her, demanding the ghost heart. His hands scrambled as the ripped at her skin, digging into her chest. There was such pain on his face. And she remembered him. She remembered his brother.

She wanted to forget that; it hurt her so much. But that memory was a skeleton key to everything else. It unlocked more complex aspects of herself. Pieces she had thought lost to the curse. Every time she went back to that memory, it hurt. But in the distance she saw other memories flashing out of the corner of her mind's eye. She fished for them, her return to pain was a bait on the hook of her swimming memories.

She wanted to remember her wife's name. That was

something she would keep for herself, hidden away from the Sata-Torun. So, she passed through this fire once again, and she remembered. She was tangled in the roots of the silver tree, dreaming a sacred dream. She dreamt of that tree, and from the branches dangled ghost hearts like apples. She reached into the shadows, and heard the call of a trumpet blaring out. She startled, looked up and saw only that tree. Nothing else, only that tree. The dream was a memory. When she was a little girl, very little, they had come through the bone labyrinth. They had all walked in a spiral a line of seers and acolytes and elders. It was a haunted winter evening, and the air was crisp, and the bones were dusted with snow. It was that twilight hour, when the world was a purple bruise of shadows.

The tree glowed in her memory, and it glowed in her dream. They all held baskets out and went through, picking the hearts from the branches. Each seer performed a ritual, bowing, whispering, taking. A kiss of hand to head, thanking the tree. So many ghost hearts, burning up on the branches. When a ghost burned up, burned bright, they took the ashes to the tree, and then spread the ashes around the tangled roots. The rituals were very specific, a clockwork of limbs, and symbols, and hand motions.

But the memory was shattered by horn and howl, and a familiar looking bandaged man. Was that Lens? The little boy who she'd helped all those years ago? The scars, the bruises, his eyes like thunder in her head. He kept demanding the heart, her heart. She hadn't eaten in two days, just sips of water, it was all part of the ritual, and it left her light headed and foggy. Nothing seemed right. Nothing seemed real. How could this be real? How could this be happening?

Her bow. It was on the other side of the tree, and she had to get to it, quickly. She stood, and wobbled as she walked, lightheaded from hunger. The tree glowed, flickered at her touch. "What?" she said.

He demanded it, and said it again, and said he knew that they had more hearts, and that the temple and the seers were being greedy with them. His brother needed it. He had to get it for him. If she wouldn't bring him a heart, he would have to take it. He growled, and looked terribly sad and, said if she had nothing to give him, then she should run.

This part hurt. She knew him. She knew he had good inside of him, and yet he still felt driven to this action. Maybe she could stop him; maybe she could save him. Oh, it hurt to look back on this part of the memory, her own empathy had poisoned her actions. Not that she would change anything. She would never give up her empathy, even when it was the cause of her own deathless death. It was all she had in this world, her ability to care and heal for others.

It was all so inevitable. She would not change; he would not change. The world burns on in indifference to either of them.

She walked across the tree, slowly for her bow. She saw something glint like a smile in the dark. What was that? And then a movement, a knife in the air. He stabbed down, and she scrambled, kicked, pushed him back. She reached, tried to grab the bow as she fell. Instead, she tumbled on top of it and snapped it in half with her weight. She cursed, stood up and he leapt again, knife plunging into lung and back. She coughed blood, wheezed, hurt to breathe. Had to breathe. She remembered being in pain, but could not remember the pain of the moment. Here, the pain was only betrayal.

She tried to crawl forward. Something inside of her collapsed as she moved towards the world outside. Why was her stomach so wet? Was that her blood? She wished she could remember that pain, the physical burning ache of knife wounds riddling her body. It would dull the pain of betrayal.

Don't stop remembering. Your wife's name is on the other side of this, see it flickering there? A fish, caught in the deep of memory. Swim towards it, and remember.

And he was on her again, his boot in her back as he kicked her over. She head butted him and he clumsily jerked away for a moment. She tried to crawl forward some more, but he was on top of her again. He seemed bestial with need, and he cut a spiral into her, and pulled out the heart. It was still sinewy and bloody and then she felt something inside of her change.

Her curse had woken once more.

She felt the spiral of wounds burning through her, a labyrinth tearing through skin and muscle. He ran away, and she wanted to stop remembering again. This was the moment everything changed. The curse split her open, and she knew it had been painful, but her memories were numb to it all. It was as if the physical sensation had been wiped away when the bear had burst through her spine.

And then it all came back to her. Sophia. That was her wife's name. Sophia, running her hands over her face, quick kisses on her forehead and a laughter they'd shared together. Sophia. And then came the other memories, rushing through her mind. Poor Mazi, and her struggle to fit in with life at the temple. She stuck out, and they loved her for it, and they hated her for it. Naomi felt a smile on her cheeks and it burned at the memory of Mazi. She was a daughter to her, in so many ways. Maybe, in another life, she had carried another Mazi inside of her womb, and they were still connected all these lifetimes later. An echo of an umbilical cord tying them together.

And sweet, powerful Talia, who rose up and shone so bright... her two favorites. The two that reminded her that love could exist, that family could exist, even after Sophia's death.

That death. That difficult death.

No death was ever easy, was it? And yet, Sophia's death seemed to hit her the hardest. But no, her memories were disrupted yet again. The flashing light out of the corner of her eye drifted away, and she returned to the horrible here and now. She wanted to scream out Sophia's name, but could not. The curse had taken control of her mouth. At least she would remember her name, for now. It was something to hold onto. Something to keep her going in the most horrible of moments.

The grey shadow of a man in robes to her left, and a grey shadow of a woman in robes to her right. Both of them stood with arms raised in a symbolic gesture. Somewhere, someone shouted, and a roomful of people cheered. Long lines stretched out of the tower and into the cursed city beyond. Everyone here felt warped, changed, broken. They yearned for something else, something to burn bright inside of them. She felt it, that lost missing feeling that each of them felt. They craved revelation, and to be a part of something far more important than themselves.

And they walked up, touched her open wounds, and drank her blood. She watched them do it, and watched them twitch and scream and shout words incomprehensible words. The pain was a numb and distant thing. She wanted them to stop. That was her blood. She needed them to stop. Her sight was still just shadows and grey things walking around in the dark.

For a brief moment, her sight came back. Full color, burning bright. Was this her sight, or the sight of the curse? She could not tell the difference, but she let herself get caught up in the colors of the world. Each person drinking from her wounds now had a bright fire dancing around their heads. Shafts of light sifted in through the cracked holes of the ceiling, and it reminded her of the temple for a brief moment. And this made her sad. Her home, where they'd buried Sophia's body. Where she'd lived so many lives amongst the seers and the shadows.

This was her eyesight after all, wasn't it? She saw the tower from the inside, and the curse's trifold head was still outside, crashed through the ceiling. She forced herself to move forward, to pull her body from the bear's body. It was thick, sticky, like tar, and it ripped her skin as she tried to yank herself free.

But it was no use. And in a blink, her sight was gone once again. Only grey shadows and human shapes and nothing more. She sobbed and screamed and could hear them all just ignoring her, keeping on with their ritual. They had wanted to change, like her, and she wished she could give it to them. The curse was slowly eating away at her sense of self, and soon there would be nothing left but an empty echo.

22

TALIA AND MAZI FIRST LEFT the temple. The massive doors just swung shut, and the noise startled the choir, silencing them midsong, as everyone rushed towards the door. They had not had a chance to say goodbye. It had all happened too soon. First, Mazi and Talia were here, and then before the acolytes knew it, they were gone, just like Naomi before them. The sorrow felt never ending. How many would perish to the curse?

A rush of girls pawed at the door, mostly younger women, still new to the temple. They all wanted to run out, to see them leaving, in order to make the feeling of loss less painful, in some paradoxical way. There were so many of them, a tight ball of bodies crammed together, trying to open that door and see if they could still see them.

Someone coughed, and they all turned to see sister Sash. She had one eye gone, with a delicate patch covering the strange white globe that sucked out her sight. On the patch was a gold etching of a key. Her other eye was green, darting about, her red hair in a messy pile of curls stacked and bound with pins on top of her head. She had been the one, decades ago, who had drank the sky water and said it tasted of mud. She had been the one who had bullied Mazi, and had created the ritual of blood for Katua's ghosts, and had led the girls through the dark. No one really speaks of that day, and she regrets it so much. They had lost Katua, then, and Sister Sash had lost her eye. But no one had even noticed for a week or so, since they were too obsessed with the two boys in their care. When their attention had returned to Sash and the missing Katua, it had been too late.

The ghosts in the dark were dangerous things.

She felt guilt for bullying Mazi, and tried to support her as best she could these days. She even spoke up for her, after Mazi had left with Talia. *Speed through the dark*, she had prayed. Now she had to clean up the mess Mazi had left behind. She'd seen worse and been through worse. All she needed was her confidence.

She sucked in air, made herself feel larger and larger still. Confidence, strength, an interior wall of flame. It wasn't an easy thing, building up this feeling, it had been more and more difficult since the losing her eye. Though, she'd gained a friend in Mazi, the tribulations of that day still haunts her.

She impatiently tapped her foot on the ground, and the acolytes turned and looked. They scrambled all around her, the door open only a tiny crack, as it let the light of the rising sun slash through the halls. Sash knew they respected her out of fear. She knew of the whispers behind her back. It was the one-eye. It terrified them. That and the gossip of what had happened. There were rumors that Sash had given her eye to the ghosts. Rumors that she had given Katua in sacrifice to the ghosts.

No such thing had ever happened. But she didn't speak of it. Speaking of what had happened would open a wound too great. And she owed it to the sisterhood, to Katua, to the ghosts, to keep on living.

"Quiet. Stop acting like this is the end of the world. They'll both be back soon enough and you'll feel silly for getting worked up."

The girls nodded in a loose unison, their heads slightly out of sync as they bobbed up and down. Sash thought this was fairly entertaining, and for a moment she'd forgotten her own sadness at Mazi leaving them. "Time to get back to choir practice. We need your voices pitch perfect for this evening. A few of you are making your debut to the ghosts, and you want to make a wonderful first impression. Trust me on that one."

There was a cry out, and another girl laughed. Someone else moaned in faux agony, and the laughter rose up again for a moment. She had to get them under control, a disruption like this could ruin the evening if she let it. She stared at them with her one good eye, and then spoke solemnly. "Listen here, we cannot set aside our duties out of sadness for our kin. So many have died in these last few days, and so many more will follow. We owe it to them to keep going strong, and do our duties to the dead." She stamped her bow on the stone floor, to emphasize her words. "Tonight is more important than our friends leaving us. Tonight is even more important than the curse, or even death itself. This ritual is for those beyond death, whose doorways we can only glimpse out of the corners of our eyes. Much like this crack in the temple gates, and the light of the sun that lay beyond it."

For a moment they stood in awe. Some twisted at their robes, nervously. Others giggled, and then held their hands over their mouths, to hide their glee at the absurdity of the moment. Sash let them have their mirth for a moment. She waited, letting the weight in the air build the silence. Once everyone was completely quiet, she scratched her chin and said, "All right now. Go. I'm not going to repeat myself."

This ritual only happened once every ten years, so it was important to get the days right, the hours right, everything right. She watched them running up to practice, and remembered that day all those years ago, when the rain slicked down in waterfalls, and they ran like giggling animals through the halls. Just like that, just like that. She didn't want to remember. But she had to. Things that are shadows inside built up, and spilled out.

At this memory, she got a harsh chill, and balled her hands into fists. Why was this memory coming to her now? The two brothers. Her eye. Katua. Was this all connected? She hoped not.

Her stomach was in knots, and the air had that coppery taste to it, like a thunderstorm right before the downpour. They might not survive the ritual tonight. So many bodies, so much death. The ghosts were restless, and everything was weighted with the promise of silence.

Beams of light broke through ceiling cracks and surrounded her with the fluttering of dust motes. For a moment she was alone. Where had all the girls gone? Had she blacked out during that memory, and too much time had passed? That image struck her again, that little boy and his sick brother. This was lightning in her heart, sending shockwaves through her body. This whole thing was connected to those boys, to her eye, and to the greedy ghosts on the dark night. The girls were gone, so none of them would see this.

She walked over to the giant door, slid it carefully open. Her hand almost slipped on the moss that grew against it. Out beyond where the fields, and the pine trees that surrounded them. She stepped the the door and looked around. Everything was wrong. The sun set now, and stars were just beginning to sparkle. In the distance, she saw the city, far off, the city on the hills, and she felt that the storm in her bones came from that city.

Her dream. This was all just like her dream.

The night she'd lost her eye and Katua to the ghosts, she'd had this nightmare vision. Nightmares left in daylight. This was stronger, more resilient, it clung to her memories when she woke. For the next week after her eye went missing and Kutua vanished, she dreamt this same dream, and always woke the same way. Completely drenched in sweat and her body feverish with terror. Eventually, the dreams left, but the feeling stayed in her bones, waiting to wake up.

Today was the day it woke up.

She never told anyone about this. They barely believed her about the disappearance of Katua, and the sacrifice of her eye. She almost felt silly that she believed in this nightmare so strongly, and that she felt worse about leading Katua and her sister into the darkness, where the hungry ghosts lay in wait.

The loop started with the boy and his brother. The boy carried his brother's head in his hands, and the head was constantly screaming. The boy then pointed at a mirror, and inside of the mirror was Mazi, burning. Her whole body was fire, yet the reflection did not seem to be in pain. She seemed, rather, to be blissful and aware of the fire.

Then there was a flash, and she stood outside, like she stood now. On the hill there was a red cloud surrounding the city. Next, there was a child, running from the bone labyrinth, screaming. Loud, strange, horrid screams. And the child was naked, but without any gender. The child was terrified of all things. And the child begged her to come inside, to let her become a seer at the temple.

And her dream loop ended with her slamming the door shut. Then she opened it, starting the loop over and over and over again. Repeating, constantly, never ending, for weeks when she was young.

When she woke, she still had that loop in her mind, and when she tried to sleep again the loop played and played. One morning twilight, she wrote the dream down on a small scrap of parchment. Only after that, after writing the dream down, did it finally fell still.

Until today.

She stared at the bone labyrinth and the city on the hill. For a brief moment she actually expected a naked child to come running out towards her, and was sad when it didn't happen. What had her dream tried to tell her all those years ago? She felt like it was trying to get her to do something

After a moment of waiting, she decided to just shut the door and get on with the evening. There was so much to prepare for, after all. Some rituals cannot wait, and tonight's was a very important one.

She inhaled, exhaled, and tried to center herself. No good. There was no center anymore, only the electrical anticipation of some horrible premonition. She leaned against the door, as the sound of the choir filled the air. Bells tinkled, and footsteps skid down stairs and long hallways. Closer, and closer the voices came. She puffed out her chest, held her head high. They must not know of her worries.

She let the sound engulf her entirely for now. She needed that, the whole feeling of the world disappearing behind those uncluttered voices. A smile. This would be a good ritual tonight, she felt it. They would take a few of the others with them, people who weren't exactly part of the rite, but who could stand as a lookout, protecting them from any attacks.

Maybe, her nightmares were nothing. Maybe this feeling in her bones was just sadness at Mazi going out and looking for Naomi.

And then she remembered something, from a lifetime ago, and wondered why she remembered this now. She had run away from the Whisperers on the Cliffs. She shouldn't be remembering this now. And yet...

It hurts to think about this. Her parents had sold her when she was very little, barely old enough to walk. They had taken her to the whisperers on the cliff and sold into servitude there. She didn't like to think about these memories. They were harsh unkind things. Years of servitude, of torture, of pain. They had taught her so much, but they had taken so much from her. That glow of youth, stolen, and replaced with oracular eyes. It had been a long time since she had communicated with the Dzall, a longer time still since they deprived her of light and sound, and suspended her in a dark far from the light. They forced her to drink the singing water, and learn the coded language that spoke in the symbols of her mind. Those same symbols, she realized, were like the cards they used to play with in the city. Back when she saw them, strange things, with simple iconography for memorization and gambling.

A skull with wings, a key and a heart. She remembered, it became a complex code, a fractured language, one she had to study over and over again, just so she could speak with the Dzall. She learned the symbol language before she could even speak properly, and still now it seems like she has a secret that others would never understand. How could anyone understand the language of the Dzall? No one could.

Why was she remembering this now?

Her dream. The night she lost her eye and Katua. This all felt like something she had seen in a vision from the Dzall when she was so little. It came back to her, in fits and starts. The well. The cards in her mind. Those potent images that clung to her skin.

Her stomach felt electric. Could she still access the water inside of her? The water that gave her visions, and life, and the ability to speak to the Dzall?

Yet, there it was, coming back to her in this moment. The acolytes sang and moved around her, and she was a million miles away. The nightmare played out in a loop in her head. Over and over again, as if it were trying to tell her something important. And she remembered that well, that darkness, and the water that stung her insides. There were more important things to do now, and she was no longer a servant to the Dzall and their cruel religion. She was a seer, and the ghosts needed her.

She snapped out of it, and the girls saw her return to them and laughed. "It's time now, girls," she said. And she turned around, woozy form not eating much today at all. She hadn't even moved from this spot since this morning, had she? She'd been completely lost in memories and visions. It had been a long time since that had happened last, and since she'd lost time. She didn't like that feeling. She threw open the door, and got ready to go to the stones. The acolytes laughed and cheered, ready to move onto their next stage in the sisterhood, when they could care for the ghosts and worship with dance and song at the hollow stones.

The world felt empty. Was she alone again? The others were still here. They were just in sepia, and she felt so far away from everyone. This couldn't be happening. How could this be happening?

A little girl, there, bathed in moonlight. Her body curled up in a spiral, burnt rags clung to her body, and she wasn't even conscious. She looked so sick. She hadn't seen someone this bad since Talia had come to them. And it was just like in her dream. The same girl, the same rags, everything. It was exactly like she saw it in her dream. She couldn't believe this. The world felt far away and distant, and the thunder woke in her bones.

Everyone stood around the child in a large circle, with Sash in the center and the crumpled spiral child at her feet. She leaned down, and touched her, gently. Everyone else moved back, as if the child were a bomb and they didn't want to be in the fallout.

"I feel like I know you," Sash whispered as she brushed hair out of the child's forehead, hoping to wake her up. No such luck. "I do know you, somehow. You feel like a whisper of someone I had known, so long ago. I wish I understood why, and who you are, and what my dreams mean."

An elder walked forward, her body hunched over and her face covered in a map of scars. One and only one of the seers could be the sacred map bearer. A new one is designated only when the old map bearer dies. She spoke, her words carrying a weight to them, as if she was speaking more from her position in the community and less from her own design. "Go on, stay here, watch after that one. I can lead them through the forest, and lead them through the rituals. You keep to the temple, try and fix whatever is broken."

Sash reached down, her hand on a child's cheek. "If it wasn't for the breathing, I would think she was dead." And it did look like a little girl, even though the child in her dream was sexless. "Are you all sure you are all right? Doing the ritual is our sacred duty. Another can probably watch her..."

The map bearer grunted and said, "Just do as I say."

"Be safe," Sash said, and then she picked up that frail body, so tiny and weightless, and carried the child inside. She rubbed the curly hair on her head, and then wondered if this was right, if what she was doing was helping or hurting things. Was that dream a warning? Or was it a gift? Where was Sash's place in all of this? And what of the child?

What of the child?

23

SISTER SASH TRIED NOT TO think of the others, out in the woods, hunted by who knew what. The world had changed; everything was covered in teeth. She tried not to think about how alone she was in the temple. The only seers left behind where bedridden and sleeping upstairs. Instead, she forced herself to focus on one thing, the cold child, who was now barely awake. The child was eating slowly, drinking what she could. She had been mute in Sash's arms, unable to speak a single word. She only mewled, and twisted in her arms. Sash cooed her, and tried to coax words form her, to see if she could speak. So far, nothing.

What is your name? Are you from the city? Where is your home?

Each time, silence. Each time the child moved back, flinching, as if she was about to be struck. It broke her heart to see this happening.

She let the questions rest, and worked on bringing the child back to waking life. It took a bit longer than she expected, and for a moment she worried that the child would never wake, and instead slip into a coma. For some reason, she knew that this would not be the case. It was a gut instinct. She needed this child awake. This child had answers.

Later on, she would regret some of the things she did. But these were acts of desperation, and she felt like she had no other choice. She had to wake her. And so, she shook the child, and yelled, and banged pans and jumped around. Nothing worked. She was sobbing and near tears, and decided to heat something up. She hadn't eaten all day. Maybe the child's stomach could rouse her from slumber. Sash brought the child into the kitchen, laid her down on top of one of the cluttered tables, and started to make some tea and warm some of the leftovers.

It didn't take long. Once the smell of roasted vegetables filled the air, the child rolled about, stretched, and sat up at a crooked angle. Her eyes were still closed, and she held a hand to her mouth, signaling that she was hungry.

Sash asked her, "Are you hungry? Would you like some?" And the child looked like she was going to say something. Instead, she flinched back. It was a motion Sash had seen a lot through the years. So many abused children fled to the sisterhood's doorstep.

"I understand. You don't have to speak. Not to me, not to anyone here." Sash walked over to the child, who was still flinching, and hugged her close, head against head. That was when she noticed how cold the child was in her arms. Like hugging a block of ice. She hurried up, ran to the sleeping quarters, the cells, and other various places in the temple, collecting armfuls of clothing and blankets and pillows.

Sash wrapped the child up so tightly, trying to force the warmth into her bones. She was still ice to the touch. She stared into the child's eyes, looking for some sign of discomfort or cold. Her face was flush with colors, and she was not shivering or seeking out heat in any way at all.

"Are you still cold? You feel cold, but you look fine. Do you want me to get any more blankets?"

No response. The cold child didn't smile or frown, she simply pointed at her mouth, and made more mewling sounds. That was when Sash smelled a burning smell in the air, and knew it had been her food. Cursing under her breath, she ran over and began to scrape the plate to throw it out.

But the child cried out in pain, and kept motioning to her mouth, Sash took off as much of the burnt bits as she could, and rushed over and held the child, and fed her carefully. She made sure not to let her eat too fast, lest she would choke or vomit, and just watched and helped as best as she could. The child was ravenous, and even though she was so light and tiny, she was obviously older than her frame. Malnourishment, abuse, and starvation would do that to a child like her.

Sash knew. The whisperers on the cliffs had done the same thing to her. How horrible she must've looked when she first arrived at the temple, all those years ago.

Later, after the child was done eating, sister Sash brought her a cup of warm tea in a bulbous circular mug. They both nursed their teas slowly, and Sash decided to talk a bit about her own life. These were things she never told anyone else, but somehow knew that this child would understand. She talked about the whisperers on the cliff, about the life here, in the temple. About what they do every day, each day, with their rituals and sacred dances that fed the ghosts.

The child listened. Steam from the cup drifted up her cheeks.

Eventually they all came back in the morning. They were surprisingly cheery and singing as they walked through the front door, a loose line of acolytes stretched back to the pines beyond. Some were bandaged, but most appeared to be unhurt. The door swung open, and there was a strange color to the sky, a deep iron grey that almost blocked out all light. This was an unnerving sight for this time of year. A bad omen, if she'd ever seen one. Combined with the storm feeling in her bones, and the arrival of this strange girl from her dreams, she was unsettled as to what could happen, and what this could all mean. Sash did a rough count, and figured that none of their party were missing. She had not slept the night before. Like most people in the last few weeks, she barely slept at all.

They sung as they wandered in, and Sash helped them shut the door, making sure not to wake the bedridden elders upstairs with too much noise. She walked up to Madeline, the seer who had gone with her into the darkness, who had seen the horrors she had seen. "You didn't lose anyone, did you?"

Madeline leaned against her bow, a look of weary exhaustion spreading across her face. "We got attacked, but this time we were ready. Our archers made quick sport of the cursed, that was for certain. Although, things are different now, aren't they? Can't you feel the change in the air? Something has changed."

"Yes," Sash said, her stomach fluttering as she remembered her dream yet again. "Yes. The girl's upstairs right now. She's awake, and she's reading over the acolyte's book of rites and songs."

"Oh. She wants to join us?"

"I don't know. She isn't very talkative, but it's not like we haven't dealt with that before. Just give her time."

"I'm sure you're right. Should we come and meet this strange girl?"

Sash shook her head, "Yes, but we should be careful. She's very skittish. Almost as bad as Talia was when she first came to us."

The acolytes were still singing, and a few started dancing, repeating the ritual they had performed earlier in the woods, out by the hollow stones. There were moments of clapping, then shouting, then an uproarious, joyful laughter. They were experiencing that after ritual joy, that brilliant release of pent up emotions. It was done, and they had survived both the oath and the attack. Everything was vibrant for them, and they all felt invincible. Sash knew that feeling. She wished she had gone with them and felt that for herself. Still, there were more important things going on now. Joy can wait.

For a moment, Sash wondered if any of those poor wounded girls had been cursed. All of those questions, the inspections, the keeping them safe, and away from the others. That would all happen, eventually, and did not need to happen right this second. She would let them have this moment. Things would get bad later. She knew it in her gut. Best to let them enjoy these moments while they could, so they could have something to hold onto in the dark.

Madeline clapped her hands loudly. The acolytes all fell quiet in a quick rush of silence. "We're going to have some breakfast, and there is a girl we want you to meet. She will probably be joining us soon, as an acolyte. She needs us, and we need her, and she is scared and frightened. Rememeber back to when you first came to us, and you were scared and frightened. Treat her the same way, with kindness. With love. With hope."

No one said anything for a moment. They all understood the seriousness of this moment, and let the after-ritual joy slide away for one moment. "Good," Madeline said, "She's been through so much, but now she's here with us, and it will all be for the best. We finished the rite, survived the cursed in the pines, and now have a new sister in our broken, dysfunctional family."

Madeline moved forward, the group following her loosely behind. Most of the chatter had stopped, and instead they started to chant again, this time something more solemn. A song to welcome the child to her new home. Sash knew this song, she had sung it on many a winter's eve, when the sun seemed to be perpetually gone, and the world was blanketed in moonlight and shadows. It was a song of the lonely hours, and of death calling for life. It fit this moment perfectly, even though it was not winter, and no one had died. It instead slid in like a jigsaw to the mood, evoking a powerful sensations that burned inside their veins. Was this a fugue for the world? Was the world dying? Was that what they all felt?

But still, still, they sang:

with our silence
your skin is broken
marked our bones
with this verse
the book of letters
lay unopened
a dormant hunger
a bleeding thirst

Sash watched them leave, motionless in the alcove. She listened as they walked off, into the hallways beyond, all those children, singing. They were shepherded by the elders and the ancient seers, moving them towards the stairs and the mess hall that lay beyond. Their bodies a beautiful chaotic swirl, and above them an owl hooted and darted from rafter to rafter.

Sash waited, just a minute more, she did not want them to see her crying. Her tears burned her one blind eye, but still, she couldn't help it. These were tears for what was coming.

After a few days, and Mazi and Talia still had not come back. Sash paced and tried to get rid of this bad feeling that still twisted around inside of her. It seemed to get worse with each passing day. Her only reprieve was spending time with the new girl, El. That was the name she gave them, writing it down on a loose scrap of paper and handing to Sash one dreary, heartbroken day. She still wasn't speaking, and Sash wondered if she could speak anymore.

There was one who came to them years ago whose tongue had been ripped from her mouth. Eventually, the wound where her tongue was had become infected, and they were unable to cure her. Sash hoped El was more like Talia, and her silence was one of trauma, not imminent death.

She wasn't sure if El communicating via the written word was better or worse. She could be doing it because it's easier, and creates a wall between her and everyone else. Or, she could be doing it because her tongue was a swollen infected mess and she would die soon enough on her own...

One thing that really bothered Sash were the days El drew something *other than words*. On these days she would only draw loose clusters of symbols. The first time Sash saw her do this, the lightning worked in her bones once again, and her tongue tasted of copper and the promise of a storm. The omens, again. Those same symbols she'd seen in her visions when communicating with the Dzall all those years ago. She had to fight back the fear these symbols brought to her mind.

She still recalled the language of the Dzall. It burned in her stomach. Maybe she could try and communicate with her that way. "El, my little one, come here. I have something to show you, all right? I write, and you tell me if you know what these mean."

She drew some symbols from her own visions, ones that El had not drawn herself just yet. Circle with a sword in the center, three triangles spinning around a square. Crosses, hatches, and a crude representation of a hand, and a flame, and then a hand again.

El looked at her and laughed a hoarse sound. That was new, she'd never laughed before, and it brought light to Sash's heart to hear it. She smiled, and El smiled back at her. Another thing she'd noticed in that moment—El's tongue was okay. No infection there. "So you don't recognize these at all?"

And the girl shrugged and started drawing different symbols. This time a series of spirals and a leaping figure. Sash did not understand these, and so she said nothing and just let the child finish her art. There was nothing there, was there? No connection to the Dzall at all. She had imagined such things.

Later, she made the mistake of asking her about her past, and what led her here, to this spot. And El ran and hid, under tables, under blankets. When Sash tried to help to her, El ran farther away, panting, breathless, constantly hiding. Eventually, Sash found her asleep in some cubbyhole in the ruins at the edge of the temple. The same ruins where the boy and his sick brother had stayed all those years ago. The connections, all these connections, gave her rough and vivid dreams every night.

Until one night, she realized, sleepless, her mind buzzing with everything that was happening all around her, that she had to try and do this again. She had to try and communicate with the Dzall. The very thought of it made her angry and nervous and terrified. But she had to do it, to figure out the connection to El, and her own visions, and the disappearance of Naomi, Mazi, and Talia. They all felt connected somehow, she just had to untie the strings and see where they led.

Even if the very thought of doing this again brought back the worse of all her memories. Starved, naked, dying of thirst deep underground. Suspended over the dark, and the Dzall in her mind, feeding her visions. She swore she would never do this again. But now there was no choice in the matter. She'd stood by while others had died and disappeared and she would not do the same again. Losing an eye was nothing compared to losing her friend, Katua.

She made sure El was still asleep, and that the others would not know where to look for her. No one could know what she was about to do. No one. She could not be disrupted, she'd heard of people who had disrupted midtrance, when they spoke to the Dzall. Most had died from heart attacks or simple strokes. Such was the way of the Dzall.

She went to the ruins near the edge of the temple, where she had found El, where the brothers had spent the night decades ago. She walked past what used to be the ritual room, which was now half flooded after the riverwaters rose in the forest. There were still leaves floating in it, and a skim of muck that clung to the bottoms of her robes. There, in that dark ancient place, she blindfolded herself. There was no well to hang upside down in, nothing to drown out the sounds or the sights of the world but herself.

She only hoped that her meditation would be enough. She knelt down, the gravel biting into her knees, her head bowed. She opened her mind, focused on a series of images. A key, a door, a lamp. These images she had been taught over and over again, that concentrating on just this series, was a code, a key, a way of opening the communications channel to the Dzall.

It happened so fast, the minute she finished the imaging sequence she felt a hallway of thoughts spread wide, filled with clouds and endless static. Soon, the images came as well, waves of them rising inside. She collapsed to the ground. She could no longer concentrate on her limbs; she could only become a receptive vessel, her whole mind retrieving everything they sent her and unable to do anything else.

For a moment she couldn't even breathe, it was as if she'd

forgotten how. It took a moment of gasping and choking before she could both control her lungs and stay receptive to the imagery of the Dzall.

It was as if the Dzall had been waiting for her, eagerly, to show her what the future held. The symbols they sent to her were an onslaught of images, flickering so fast she could barely take them in. It engulfed her and threatened to drown her mind. She wanted the images to stop. She saw a bear with three heads and Naomi riding on its back, and then fire in the temple, a burning light, a tower made of lightning, and a door in the rain. That door glowed and sang and she wanted to open it, and see what wonders waited behind. And then Mazi and Talia. So strange, seeing them, and they felt like a lantern in the darkness, burning brightly.

And then she saw El, who was naked and androgynous again, just like in her dream. The child was carrying something in her hands, a fine dust, a pile of ashes, and she was taking it to the bone labyrinth. That was when someone ripped the blindfold off, and pushed her out of her reverie. She turned around, saw El standing behind her, holding the limp blindfold in her hands.

The connection was closed abruptly, and Sash realized she was on the ground. Her limbs were weak, and standing up was far more difficult than it should have been. Even breathing now was labored and hard. For a moment she wondered if she'd had a seizure. She'd seen some of the other seers fall into seizures during ritual, and she knew it was a danger, that a mind could crumble so easily when they left themselves open and vulnerable to the primitive forces.

El pointed, and spoke inside of Sash's head. She spoke not with words or a voice, but instead the language of thoughts.

Pure, undiluted by existance. *Something is about to happen, and you need to be there. Follow me.*

Sash nodded, and followed where El led her. The two of them ran through the ruins, struggled through the damp half drenched portions, and then up to the temple proper. They ran as quick as they could, holding hands so as not to lose the other in the dark corners. They'd become close in the past few days. As close as Mazi and Talia, Sash supposed. And it was a good feeling, a feeling of family. A feeling that she hadn't had in so long, when she had taken those other seers with her into the darkness, deep below, into the terror that waited for them out of sight. It was so good to have that feeling again. And yet here it was, tainted with that fear. She was about to lead them into darkness again. That was the only way out now. To move through the darkness and come out on the other side alive.

It wouldn't matter if she lost her other eye, just as long as no one else disappeared into the shadows with the ghosts.

24

MAZI CROUCHED ON THE GROUND, the lantern dim and flickering as she held the heart aloft, beating in the direction they needed to move. She was trying to light another candle quick, before the lantern extinguished itself and they were plunged into the dark once again. The fog moved inward, obscuring everything else into a thick soup of haze. Mazi plunged the candle between the glass doors of the lantern, cramming the flame against wick, and watched the fire kiss between the two objects, and then extinguish on the candle. Too much of a wrong angle. The wax dripped down and exhausted the flame.

"Let me hold the heart."

"No, Talia. No... you keep your bow ready, something waits for us beyond the fog."

She dropped the candle and grabbed her wrist as pain spidered out from the wound to her fingers. She felt something changing, and held her breath. No, no, she must hold her breath and hold her hand. It would go away soon, it had to. This curse was not meant for her. She had a thought then, a quick idea. She unwrapped a portion of the ghost heart, not the whole thing, just a small portion of it. And she held it up, bowed her head down, and placed the ghost heart against her temples. She closed her eyes, and allowed herself to breathe again. The air felt pure against the heart, racing inside of her, and the pain eased just a little.

"That's better," she said, "I can think now. The fingers of the curse are out of my head."

"Good," Talia said, and held out her hand, "Give me the candle, I can light it. If something in that fog wanted us dead, it would have done so by now. I doubt me dropping my bow for a single second will destroy us."

Mazi nodded, reached down with a free hand, and scrambled against the earth for the candle. She grabbed it, held it up to Talia. Her other hand did not move, it kept that heart still against her skull, both of her eyes still closed. She needed this clarity. Everything had been so occluded in her mind. But now? Every thought was clear, and she realized how foolish it had been to throw off her mask. Of course the curse could still enter her lungs and her pores through the mist, of course. Just because her arm had been tainted, it did not mean the curse was done with her, not by a long shot.

There was a familiar crackle of a dry wick, catching flame. She could see that light even now, that candle light coming through her closed lids. She breathed with the heart against her, and in that clarity she saw something. The curse, right now, was only in her arm. When she breathed, she felt it invading her senses, but it was not infecting her. It was not changing her, yet. Maybe, she could survive this. She had to do it, even though it sounded mad, and it was risky...

And yet, keeping her arm attached to her body was even riskier, still.

It was a honeycomb of pain, the wound splintering out towards her hand and shoulder. She knew what she had to do. She had to isolate and remove the infection from her body, and she had to figure out a way to not breathe in the fog, to keep the curse from entering her body anew. For now, she could hold the ghost heart against her head, but it was not a permanent solution. Even using the ghost heart would only put the curse to sleep. There was only one way to cut it out before it infected the rest of her, and she fell to the changes.

She remembered Lens' brother. He didn't even recognize Lens. Would she do the same to Talia, once this curse took hold? They did not have much time. If she was going to do this, she had to do it now.

"Talia, I'm going to need your help in a moment, I don't think it's possible for me to do this by myself."

"Shouldn't we keep moving? I have no idea how much further this is, how much deeper into the labyrinth you need us to go."

Mazi coughed. "I need you to help me cut off part of my arm."

"What."

"The infection is starting to spread, it's already gotten to my fingers again, making it hard to do anything at all. I need you to help me cut off part of my arm, at the base of the infection, to keep it from changing me, permanently."

There was a hand on her shoulder. She could not turn and

see her sister. "Mazi, my love, just take the ghost heart and use it for yourself. Just a sliver, right? That's all you need, and then we can keep going."

"No. That's just a temporary solution, not something I can keep doing. I'm lucky, in a way, the curse is isolated. We can cut it off, stop it off before it does any more damage."

"I... I can't do that. I just can't. We won't even know if it will work. Wouldn't they have done that at the temple if it works?"

She opened her eyes, moved the heart for a second, and held out her arm to her friend. "It has to work."

"What about your bow."

"I cannot fire it now. Let's just do this. You know this is our best bet for me to survive."

"No," Talia growled, "Using the ghost heart and then leaving is the best bet. Saving the ghost heart for Naomi would only be destroying yourself."

"I have not changed my mind, and I will not change my mind. Now, do as I ask. Cut it off."

Mazi turned her head and closed her eyes. She did not want to see this, she had a feeling if she saw it happen it would be too much, and she would give in and use the ghost heart. She felt Talia's knee on her elbow, pushing it down, holding it still, her eyes closed as the bowstring tourniquet was wrapped around her arm, just above her elbow. So tight, she felt the blood pulsating and it hurt. The curse wriggled inside of her, as if it knew what was about to happen.

A hand grabbed her hand, and held it rough against the dirt. They gripped each other, fingers enmeshed into fingers. And then came the biting feeling, the sharp pain that dug under skin, broke it open, a cool pool of blood on her arm and she bit down on her lip, bit down as the blade scraped against her bone and she couldn't help it, she screamed, and screamed and kept on screaming. The pain was bright and terrible, and darkness clouded her vision. She wanted to stay conscious and experience everything, to know for certain that it all went well and she would survive this ordeal.

But the pain was too much. Everything trembled, all of her muscles spasmed. She thought the pain of the curse was so terrible before, but she realized now that she'd had no idea what pain truly was. This was pain. And this was everything.

Her mind sucked into blackness. At the edges of her blurry vision, she saw shapes sinister in the dark.

She woke again not much later to a pain and the feeling of a ghost where her arm should be. The pain was a numb creature, stumbling along her nerve endings. She felt a bit woozy, and yet somehow energized. What was this? She looked down, and saw a bandage around a stump where the curse had been removed. Rough guaze barely hiding the herbs and tinctures Talia had spread along the cauterized areas.

Everything felt distant, broken and in a grey haze.

"How are you feeling?"

She nodded. "I don't know. The curse was pain, and now that pain is gone. But it's been replaced by something else."

"We should rest for a bit more."

"We've rested enough."

She stood and was dizzy, but that was nothing new. "Did you cut all of the curse out of me? I feel dizzy still. Off kilter and broken, still."

Talia walked over to her, put a hand on her shoulder. "Yes,

I did. You just had major surgery. I did all I could to speed up recovery and minimize your pain, but herbs and poultices can only do so much. You need to rest."

Mazi pushed away her friend's hand. "We've rested enough. It's dangerous here, we'll die..."

And she stood and immediately fell back down. Everything spun quick and her legs were like noodles. She hated feeling like this. Talia sat down next to her and drew her bow.

"We'll go in a bit, but you have to let the herbs do their work. I added a bit of the ghost heart as well, just enough to make sure the curse was gone and to speed up the healing process. The concoction may make you feel better than you are, so rest. Recuperate for now, and I will protect you."

And Mazi turned her head, and looked towards the shadows beyond. "Thank you," she said. And then fell into the pain tinged shadows once more.

She woke to a start, the pain mostly gone from her arm right now. She'd forgotten just how amazing Talia was at this sort of thing. "I think I'm ready now," she said.

Talia nodded, and helped pull her upright so that she was standing. For a moment dizziness and she almost fell again. She grabbed Talia, and steadied herself. Her arm was there on the ground, and she watched it get eaten by the darkness, just outside the light of the flickering candle.

"See," Mazi said in half laughter, "I told you there was something out there, something dangerous."

Talia's expression was pained, and she turned, and could not look at her friend, could not even gaze at her. "You ready now? Can we move? We should probably get going, whatever is out there is hungry for more."

Mazi felt weightless, light and airy. She reached down and grabbed the ghost heart, which was laying right next to the lantern, just where she had left it. The mist drifted away from the heart, as if a single touch would burn it away. She held it up, put it next to her mouth, inhaled deeply.

This was so much better.

She moved the heart away a little, and said to Talia, "I think I might need your help againI just... I need to filter out this terrible air, can you at least wrap some gauze over me in a makeshift mask of sorts?"

"I have a better idea."

"You do?"

Talia turned around, and still looked past her, unable to look at her directly. She reached to her face, pulled her own mask off. Now she was able to look at Mazi, and she smiled a lopsided grin, and held the mask forward. It fluttered against her fingers, wanting to take off, but still a captive to her palm.

"We'll take turns," she said, "Passing this back and forth. It's not ideal, but it might just have to do."

"I hate that we have to do this. I have no idea why I threw off my mask. I wasn't thinking. The curse was thinking for me." She paused and looked at the ghost heart in her hand. "You'll have to place the mask on my face though."

"I know. We'll go a little further, than trade. Back and forth. Okay?"

Talia leaned over, and slid the mask over Mazi's bent face. She smiled when she was done, and walked further on, further, the heart leading them towards the center of the city turned labyrinth.

The maze folded around them, herding them towards the center of the labyrinth, where the tower and the bear awaited. The walls closer now, claustrophobically so, made of a red and yellow stone. Sections of it were obscured by mist, and in other portions were vibrant in their candlelight.

Mazi had given the mask back to Talia. It was now her turn to wear it. The ghost heart hung on a leather throng around her neck. It beat rapidly, always going in the right direction, a bare portion of the heart still pressing against her chest. The heart was warm and it felt like Naomi, pressed right up against her. She missed Naomi so much, and having her heart only made her yearn for her even more.

She gripped the lantern in her good hand, holding it as steady as she could. It was her left, and she was unused to using it. She felt a phantom twinge where her right hand used to be. She guessed it was a ghost now, and she was haunted by the missing limb. They had only two more candles left to last them the night. She wasn't sure they would make it in time. Talia was right next to her, the bow at the ready, looking out for anything that might attack or hurt them.

The maze kept moving, and changing, and herding them forward. It gave this whole evening a sense of terrible inevitability. Mazi fiddled with her stump from moment to moment, her fingers grazing the bandages, searching for that ghost of a hand.

Was that phantom arm carrying a phantom curse? A silly thought, yet a troubling one, none the less. She'd spent the majority of her life with ghosts, and she knew that they were more complex than anyone could ever imagine. She tried to picture the disease again. Could she tell if she was cursed again? The ache of her stump throbbed. It distilled all sensations into pain, and she couldn't figure out if the curse was there still. It could be like an egg inside her skin, waiting to hatch. The pain of her missing limb was so great it drowned out any sign of the curse.

She took solace in the fact that she felt different now. No longer foggy headed or feverish, she felt clear and sharp in her pain. For the moment, she let it be, and kept her thoughts focused on the task at hand. Now with the ghost heart around her neck, she was calmer, the gentle touch of something so close to Naomi giving her solace. So, when they reached a large series of arches that spread out into an infinite of fog and darkness, and Talia moved to take the mask off, Mazi just held a hand out and said, "No, I think I will be all right for now. The heart is keeping me safe, I think. It's Naomi, filtering the air out for me. This isn't like the last time. I'm not delusional. I really do think I'll be fine for a little bit longer, and I'll let you know if that changes."

Talia nodded, stared at her for a few moments, and then spoke calmly. "Yes, I see it."

Mazi did not respond right away. She thought about what Talia said, and remembered how she had felt when she was breathing that putrid air. It felt like her head was filled with a million voices, that she could sense everything and anything in the labyrinth around them. It was as if her nerves where the labyrinth itself and she was connected to everything. The only connection she still felt was her feet on that corrupted soil, and her spiral scar which still seemed to be connected to the maze around them. She didn't want to tell Talia about the connection between maze and scar. She wasn't sure Talia would understand, and didn't want her to think she had gone crazy from the curse yet again.

Finally, after much thought, she said, "Thank you."

Talia stopped for a moment. Paused, hesitant in her words. "For... what? Cutting your arm off?"

Mazi laughed and realized it felt good to laugh. It had been a rough few days, with little sleep, a bodily mutilation, a friend disappearing, a curse spreading, all of that, and she hadn't realized how badly she needed to laugh. And when it finally appeared, it took over her whole body, shaking with laughter. She couldn't stop if she wanted to, it was feeding into itself, each laugh making her laugh even more. Until the laughter broke something fragile inside of her, and she started crying. Just a little bit, a few tears and then they were like a torrential downpour, and she couldn't hold them back anymore. Sobbing, she collapsed.

Talia did not say a word.

"It's nothing," Mazi said, "I feel so rubbed raw and burned to the bone," she dried her eyes with the gauze on her wound, the light flickering with each movement. "Thank you, though. For coming with me, for helping me do all of this. Thank you."

Talia reached a hand down, "Get up," and with that she helped Mazi stand again. It was not an easy task. Her body was still woozy and shaky, and she was not used to using only one arm yet. "Now," Talia said, readying her bow. "I'm doing this for you in the same way you're doing it for Naomi. Because I would go to the ends of the earth for you. I would do anything by your side. Do you understand? If you wanted me to jump into another fire, I would do it. And I have a feeling you feel the same for Naomi. I can see it in your eyes. We are alike, in that way. We will go to the ends of time and murder the sun, if that sun in some way means to harm the ones we love. Understand?"

"Yes," Mazi started walking forward, the beating heart guiding them further in the labyrinth.

25

THE HEART STRUGGLED AGAINST THE leather strap, violent and brutal in its syncopated rhythm. That was both a good and bad sign. They were close to Naomi now, close to the center of the labyrinth. Her own scar was covered in tingling sensations now, radiating out from the beating center of her heart and spiraling out. Her one hand held the lantern high, the light illuminating her face so clearly, so perfectly. Her hair tied up, thick and tight, her stub of an arm resting next to her body, as if it was searching for some kind of meaning. All the while, the heartbeat so rapid and fast. If this had been her own heart, she would be worried that she was having a heart attack, and it gave her anxiety just to hear it.

Please let this be a sign that you're still alive, Naomi. Let the connection be true and right.

Talia followed, the two of them distinct figures in the circle of candleglow. They pushed onward, crawled over debris where the maze went to reconfigure itself and failed. Bits and pieces of broken granite scurried away at their approach, as if it still contained some knowledge of its failure. Mazi remembered the way the curse had called to her earlier, when she breathed the air all stark and vivid. It commanded her. It forced her into thinking with all thoughts. She saw the designs, the geometry of movement, the perfection of possibilities. In that moment, she was no longer in control over her own thoughts. The curse thought for her, and it thought with a multifocal mind, a million connected thoughts racing all at once. It was glorious to lose oneself in the wave of the infinite.

She was glad that was behind her now, the curse in her dead arm and no longer connected to her body. They moved on further, crawled under makeshift holes that tried to trap them inside. They pushed aside webbing and vines, making their own way towards that center tower. Would Naomi be there? The heart said yes. No matter what else, the heart said yes.

They climbed a series of broken, half formed steps. They then jumped from edges, clung to stone precipices, pulled their bodies up, and kept going, following the beating of the heart and the burning of her scar. Closer now, closer. Through long stone tunnels, like towers laid on the ground, going under the earth and climbing back upwards. The fog crept down below, even inside of those ancient, subterranean passages.

When they reached the ground again, they stood for a moment and caught their breath. It had been a long journey. Mazi had to switch candles, this one had burned almost all the way down, and she had to move quick, before the flame extinguished. Using the flint to build another flame would just take too long, and they did not want to be standing in one place here very long. She pulled the old candle out of the lantern, and stuck it into the ground.

She bent over into satchel while the candle flame sputtered, and illuminated them in a hollow light. The heart beat even faster. She pulled out another candle, lighting it quick and sticking it back in the lantern. "This other one is almost dead, best to just leave it here."

Talia cleared her throat. And then she said, "This is bothering me, it's bothering me a lot."

"What's that?"

"This place is empty. Can't you feel it? Nothing is alive, and that is so strange for this labyrinth, don't you think? Everything had been alive, even moments ago when the granite scattered away. But now? It's quiet and motionless and I don't like it."

Mazi nodded, and then bent over and blew out the candle stuck in the ground. "I see what you mean, but what can we do? We just move on and that's it. Finding Naomi, that's the key to all of this."

And then Talia grabbed her arm. "Wait, shhh, wait. Listen," she whispered, "Do you hear it? Listen, and try not to make a sound."

Mazi concentrated, closed her eyes so her sight would not distract her from any of this. She heard only the crackle of the candle at first, but then, after a moment, she began to hear something else. A multitude of voices, talking, chattering. And then if she listened even closer, concentrated even more, she heard singing, like a hymnal.

And she stopped. She opened her eyes wide. She could not

move. She wanted to move. But. She could not. Move. "I... I know that..." she said it in a broken voice. "I haven't heard that in so long."

> *The key, the crown, the mirror, the sword.*
> *The key, the crown, the mirror, the sword.*
> *The key, the crown, the mirror, the sword.*

"We can still turn around, turn back," Talia whispered, trying not to draw attention.

"No. It means we're almost there."

Now the chanting was all she could hear. Before it had been a vague, almost whispering sound, distant and muffled by fog. With each cycle of the chant, she remembered the last time she had heard those same words. The brother, Lens' brother, so long ago. That night that had started it all, that night of the first curse Mazi had ever seen.

There was a worried anxiety and a touch of melancholy at that memory. She wanted to hate and despise Lens for what he had done to Naomi, for how he had cut her open and stolen this ghost heart from her own cursed ribs. She wanted to be full of rage and anger when she remembered waiting for him to return after all those years. Instead, she just felt a hole that opened up in reality the moment he had died.

She remembered the way he looked, after his brother had devoured his face. She remembered him falling. And then she remembered that last night, so long ago, when they were staying up all night staring at stars and just existing in perfect, contented silence. She missed that. In a way, she missed him.

So quickly he had died. In an instant, it was all over. For a moment, she thought of her own death, to no longer be piloting this body of meat and bone. To be nothing... to be nothing more than... nothing.

She made her bones into steel, hardened her mind, tried to put those memories in a box and bury them deep within her mind. She had to stop dwelling on this. They moved forward, pushed onward, with Talia at the edge of the light, her bow drawn taught and ready for a fight. Mazi only hoped that a fight would not come, and that they would survive the night without any more death.

Daylight broke the world. Mazi thought momentarily of sleep, but knew that it would not be a good idea right this moment. The fog still moved and surrounded them at all times, masking that light from the sky and making it a dim, diffused golden bulb. Mazi blew her candle out, and stuck the still warm lantern back into the satchel. The chanting was close. She had to figure this out now. Could she use her bow, if that was needed? She tried a few different ways. She tried using her stub to pull it back, but that was of no use.

She tried putting a stick crosswise into her bandages, and used that to draw it back. But that only snapped the stick in two, leaving small pieces scattering on the ground. Talia watched her for a moment more, and then said, "Try this."

Talia bent her neck down, and pulled the bow back with her teeth, let it fire without arrow, just to prove a point. "That seemed to work," she said, and then rubbed her hand against her mouth. "Hurts your teeth, though. And a bit harder to aim."

Mazi tried it, biting down, the string caught inside of her teeth, and pulled it back. Nice and taught, she opened her mouth wide and watched it fire. The sound of the melancholy wailing of her bone bow was right near her ear, and it gave her the chills to hear it so up close.

"You're right, it does sting a little. Good to know it's an option, right?"

"Right."

Mazi kept her bow out, holding both it and an arrow with her one still good hand. They moved forward now, side by side, no longer Mazi leading with the candle. The sun gave them enough light, just enough to keep going forward and not needing a lantern at all.

The miasma gave way to a large archway of yellow stone, coated in different species of moss and a patina of filth and scorchmarks. There were chips and cracks in the edifice, as well as strange bits of graffiti that looked more like sigils and symbols than the usual defacement. They were dwarfed by the sheer size of it, gigantic, larger than anything that either of them had ever seen up close. In the center, just beyond the arches, rose that tower from the fog. Mazi felt it in her chest, in her scar, and in the ghost heart bouncing against her skin. This was it. They were at the center of it all. She stopped directly beneath the arches.

The enormity of the whole situation exhausted her. She felt so small in the center of everything and dwarfed by the arches and the tower beyond. She felt like she had experienced this moment before, in a dream maybe, or another reality. Along the path to the tower, they saw a line of lanterns, with strange figures shuffling in the fog between them. They clicked when they moved, and they sang that hymn they'd heard earlier.

The key, the crown, the mirror, the sword.

The lanterns were not just lanterns propped up on sticks, or hung on stone outcroppings. They were organic and alive, undulating with tense expectations. At one time, the lantern keepers might have been human, Mazi was sure of it, just by the shape of their bodies. There was a human angularity to them all, a strange construction of spine and limbs that suggested human, without exactly speaking it aloud. And their heads looked like Lens when he had died, that strange slurry of meat and blood and bone, with a singular mouth directly in the center of that mess, wide open and gurgling. They were unable to make sounds directly, but instead spoke with the echo of words.

There arms, if you could call them that, were raised up like a crescent moon. And where the hands should be was a giant, bulbous, translucent hunk of flesh. And in the center of that was a blue, flickering glow. These were the lanterns of the changed, illuminating through murky orbs of skin.

Mazi's urge to shout had passed, and now she resisted the urge to move closer, to see if they were really human or not. Instead, she shook the thought from her head, and moved against the wall. She tried her best to stay invisible from those hunched shadows that walked through the fog. She moved a bit more through the courtyard, going towards the front door. She tried to see Talia, but she couldn't even see her shadow. She searched some more, but nothing. The fog obscured all but the lantern keepers, their movements slow and methodical, searching in the fog for *something*.

She did not want to be alone. She did not want Talia to be hurt. She didn't want any of this.

The ghost heart's beat was louder than anything, and she wished she could quiet it. Please, she wished, pleased don't draw their attention to me. One of the tall figures turned towards the sound. It gurgled hoarsely, and pointed towards her. Other heads moved, followed his lantern light in the fog. The one who had spotted her moved towards her, and the other sentinels in the dark turned as well and followed suit. She couldn't get the bow right, not just yet, she kept trying to string it, but dropped her bow instead. She wished that heart would stop beating.

A sound like a harp string plucked rang out, and then another, and another, as the shadows fell right to the ground. Straight shots, right to where Mazi had hoped were their heads. They gasped as they fell, a sound that was almost human, but not quiet. There was still something off about them, even in death.

She stood still, against the wall. Another shadow moved towards her, and Mazi knew that outline anywhere. Talia bent down and retrieved the arrows from the dead flesh, pulling back hard, the shadows wrestling with the unseen. Eventually she made her way to Mazi and said, "That was close. It's really hard to aim through this fog."

Mazi nodded, and then the two of them moved a little closer to the entrance. "I think," Mazi said, "I'll stay here and you look in, get the lay of the land? I have a feeling this," she held up the ghost heart, "Will probably bring them right to us. If you look first, we can at least come up with a plan."

Talia breathed in deep, preparing herself for the dangers ahead. "Right," she spoke plainly, calmly, "You're always right, you know that? Always."

Talia moved towards the entrance. "Be safe," Mazi said, and Talia nodded. "You too."

26

AZI COULD NOT TELL HOW much time had passed, for the sun was still obscured almost completely in the sky. It could have been minutes, it could have been hours. She couldn't take it anymore. She had to move and check on Talia, it was a matter of survival. Maybe that was what the curse wanted? Would Talia even find her if she moved in this thick fog? Mazi just had to be patient. With each second that went by, she fidgeted more and contemplated going back and looking for her yet again. Hurry up Talia, please. She wasn't sure how much more of this she could take.

Staying here was madness. Moving forward was madness. She stood back up, spine straight, pulled out a knife in her good hand, just in case. It was a dull, broken thing, but it would work in a pinch, if she needed it. She couldn't do the bow. At least, not yet, that bit with her teeth was just too complicated. She wasn't even sure if she could aim it like that, it was like aiming under water. So different, almost weightless.

She had to check on Talia, even it was risky. It had been too long, something had to have happened to her sister and best friend. She slid along the edge of that wall, keeping eyes towards the fog, counting the shadows and shapes. She had to stay safe. This would be it. She was alone now, with only her wild erratic thoughts and the ghost heart to guide her. This would have to work. If it didn't, she risked everything for nothing.

She breathed heavily, focused on each of her breaths. She held her dagger up, parallel to the ghost heart. She timed her breathing with the heart itself, making she it would purify each inhale of the fog. This was risky enough as it was, if she got out of sync with the quickly beating heart, that would be it. She would be cursed.

And then she slid towards the opening in the arches, keeping a keen observation of her surroundings. The chanting was nothing more than a hum and a drone from behind the tower walls. She slid further, moving slower than she wanted to, but still being cautious. Any second now, and it could all be over. They could be destroyed, the plan failed, everything doomed. She tried not to think about it, too much was riding on this.

Naomi, Naomi, Naomi. What if the ghost heart didn't work? Did she have it in herself to murder Naomi? She would have to turn her head and let Talia do it. Mazi turned now towards those large tower doors.

They stood over her and made her feel tiny and insignificant when compared to their brooding height. They were decorated with complex designs: swirls, spirals, knots and trees.

A fourteen foot tall stone statue of a woman stood still with her hair on fire. A sword was gripped in her left hand, pointed towards the ground, and in her right hand was a twig pointed towards the sun. Her paint had peeled, her sculpture lined with various cracks. She stood still, watching Mazi with stone eyes, asking her to come inside.

The door was opened a crack, and revealed a cavernous room with chairs, and pews, and a large procession of people. For a moment, Mazi thought of the temple, and the rituals they held there. Only this procession was different, everyone had a haunted look in their eyes. Instead of leading up to hollow stones, it led to massive bear torso. It's neck disappeared into the rubble of broken tower above.

Naomi!

Naomi dangled from the bear's chest, her body crucified in fear and meat and sinew. Mazi held a scream in her throat. It burned her, and she felt the heart beating against her chest. She wanted to run up and free Naomi. She wanted to howl and set fire to the building. The sight of her mother like that, in so much anguish and pain...

She had to think of the bigger picture. She couldn't just rush forward with the heart, not in this crowd, not with her missing her one arm. She had to find Talia, and then devise a plan.

To the right of the bear was a man in ragged, piebald robes. He waved his hands, swooned and spoke in gibberish that edged towards insanity. Everyone followed him. Everyone mimicked his movements. They seemed hypnotic and dangerous, and he was unchanged by the curse, and yet still it's servant.

He would break the chants to shout out words of religious

rapture, as the procession moved forward. And for a brief moment she understood. She felt the pull of his movements, his hypnogogic gaze a cord around her soul. *Follow, chant, the bear wants us. She is the mother of the world.*

No, wait. She was not the mother of the world. She was Mazi's mother. Naomi was hers and only hers and no one else could have her. She pinched her arm stub and felt the pain riot through her nerves. It snapped her out of it, brought her back to reality. She looked through the crowd, watching them, trying to find Talia.

Each person that came to the bear got swallowed by fog, devoured by it, and when it parted they rose changed. Mazi had to hold her hand to her mouth to stifle her gasp in shock. Never before had she seen anyone change that fast. Each time this happened everyone screamed and clapped and the priest danced and howled. The bear did not move. The bear did not seem to care. Naomi struggle and tried to free herself from her fleshy manacles. She saw Naomi's head point directly at her, the blind eyes searching her out and finding her. A connection. Electric.

Mazi felt rapture. She turned her head away, could not look into those blind eyes any longer. She had to save Naomi, not worship her. The heart still beat erratically against her skin, and she looked to see if anyone noticed it, if anyone could hear it. Nothing. She was invisible. She was a ghost.

Her own heart beat with the ghost heart, connecting her to Naomi. She went up on tiptoes, her mouth dry and aching with thirst. Where was she. Wait. Was that Talia? Was that her, right there in the crowd? That couldn't be her. She wasn't wearing a mask! Talia? Why weren't you wearing a mask? And as she moved, and she chanted, and Mazi held the knife against her lips, closed her eyes. This could not be happening. Not to Talia. Had Talia been cursed as well? What would she even do if she'd lost Talia as well as Naomi?

She knew what she would do. Naomi might be past the point of no return. She would use the ghost heart on Talia and heal her friend. She just had to get to her and wheel her away from all of this. Maybe she wouldn't even have to use the ghost heart. Maybe she could rescue Talia before the curse took hold.

Mazi opened her eyes again. There she was. Moving forward, one step at a time, chanting those words over and over again. Mazi saw the mask, it was fluttering over to the door, trying to escape the madness beyond it. Even the mask knew that this curse was a wild, dangerous thing. If she moved quick she could put the mask on Talia and they wouldn't have to use the ghost heart. They could go, rest up, and make a plan to come back and save Naomi. It might not save the world. It might be counterproductive, or even destructive? But it was the best that they could do.

First she prepared the arrow. She glanced around quick, made sure she was safe and not about ready to be attacked. She pulled away from the door, so she was out of their line of sight. This was not going to be easy, but it would be necessary. She pulled an arrow out, laid it on the ground. With her good hand she pulled the ghost heart off from around her neck, and then held it for a moment, the second lasting an eternity. She could not believe this moment was here, could not believe this was happening now. She felt an infinite expanse of seconds leading right here, right to this moment, and felt like she was outside of it all, as if she was experiencing it happening to someone else. A dream, that was it. This was a dream.

This one action could save them all. Talia, Naomi, everyone.

She moved quick, ignoring the dislocation she felt from her body, tying the heart to the end of the arrow. It hung down, dangled and swooped, and she knew that if she struck right, and this hit Naomi in her heartless chest, then the ghost heart would merge with her body and everything would be all right. She only had one chance at this. Only one.

She pulled out her bow, moved over to the gap in the door again. She aimed it carefully, placing the edge of the arrow directly in her mouth. It tasted like oak and mildew and feathers. The string bit into her teeth, between them, sliced into gums, and she could taste her own blood now, a tangy metal against her lips. She aimed between that door, aimed as well as she could with her face. With her teeth grasping tight, she drew the bow back, her neck muscles tense with fear and power. The spine of the bow sang, as if it was waiting for this exact moment in time to sing that song. As if all moments led up to this moment, this song, this spinal bow, this arrow heart.

She aimed, trying to get it right into Naomi's chest. Talia was right there, right at the end of the procession. She was about to be changed, and Mazi had to act now, she could not wait any longer. The fog consumed Talia's legs, crawled up them, moving now to her waist, her eyes closed, her head bent in rapture.

Mazi let go, let fly, her mouth opened wide and her hand steady and still. The bow made a loud funeral wail as the arrow sped over the crowd. It was a blinding ghost light tracing the heart as it flew onwards. Mazi closed her mouth. A bit of blood stained her lips, her teeth aching, her gums on fire. The arrow arced, and thundered as it reached the zenith, and it landed against Naomi's shoulder blade with wet thumping noise. For a moment everything seemed right and perfect, and Mazi exhaled and thought this was it, this would fix everything and we would finally be all right. The ghost heart did not touch Naomi's skin though, not yet. It was close, dangling still, almost touching, almost reversing the change. But she had missed.

Mazi exhaled, stunned for a moment. How could she have missed? It might still work. All it needs to do is drop a little and hit the bear's heart...

Alas, no.

The demon bear yanked the arrow out, and flung it violently to the ground. Its scarred paws nimbly avoided even the scarcest glance against the ghost heart. It fell right to Talia's feet, which dispersed the fog that had been changing her. There she stood, half changed, raven wings on her back, her legs covered in vines and tree roots. She seemed stunned, and she reached down to grab the ghost heart. It touched her hand, sparks flew about, and the change began to reverse itself in an orchestra of light and fire.

Alas, no.

The bear picked Talia up like she was nothing, and swung her against a pillar. Her skull smashed to pieces. There was nothing left of Talia. Her sister was gone. Her sister was dead. Talia, the best archer, the best dancer, the best in everything. Talia, who had followed her all the way out here because Mazi had asked her for her help.

No, Mazi screamed, No, No, No, and she could not stop watching as the bear picked up her friend once again, her little sister, and then smashed her against the dirt and stone like a ragdoll, all void of life. She repeatedly crushed her against the ground. And Mazi saw it, the ghost heart died when Talia died. It burned up Talia's body, leaving scorch marks against the skin, where the ghost heart had attempted to merge with her.

They all turned to where the arrow had been shot. Mazi was still in shock and screaming *no* over and over again. She couldn't hide. She couldn't move. She couldn't do anything. She wanted to die now, to have them tear her apart. There was no use in living any longer. She had the best intentions at heart, but she had ruined everything.

The chanting was over. Now they howled and wailed and began to run towards the door, and right behind them, barreling, hungry, there it stomped, coming right towards her. That demon bear, with Naomi still struggling to free herself from the curse. Their movements fighting against each other. Naomi attempted to pull herself free, and the bear tried to move forward against her limbs.

Mazi did not hesitate. She stopped watching the grim display. She ran with the bow left behind, her arrows scattered on the ground. She ran with the knife in her teeth and an overwhelming sense of panic and dread and failure rushing through her body. She ran so that she could live. She knew that she did not deserve to live, she ran anyway.

27

THE FOG ROARED AROUND HER, changing shape and dispersing around Mazi. She leapt over a crooked wall, crawled under a crumbling tunnel. The chants of the changed surrounded her, the words frenetic whispers. They weren't far behind her now. She wished they were farther, farther still. How could they be tracking her? They seemed broken and without conscious thought in their skulls. And so they moved liked insects moved, scattering in the fog. Beyond the susurrus of the changed, there came the thundersome steps of the bear. The ruins of the labyrinth city crumbled.

She could not shake this uneasy feeling. The stones, themselves, watched her every movement, and reported back to the demon bear what they saw. Each visible stone were covered insects, millions of tiny, small, dust sized creatures crawling over everything. And they all watched her, bright in the sunlight now visible that the fog dispersed. They gazed at her with their million eyes.

These things were more just uncanny. Mazi's mind tripped back and came to a horrible realization. She was doomed. The fog had been made of these creatures, so small, so minuscule, yet all connected to the demon bear. They were wardens of the curse, the central nervous system of it all. When she had joined with the curse earlier, she had felt a connection to all things. That's what she had been connected to. These insects. That fog.

Now the fog was so thin it was barely a haze. Why had it weakened so much? Mazi ran some more, further up ahead, breathing heavily. Yet with each inhale, with each exhale, she felt nothing. There was no putrid stench, nor any horrific thickness to the air. Nor did she feel connected to any curses, or the calling of any destinies, or the need to be purified. The fog no longer had any power over her.

That was why the labyrinth lay still and only watched her. She wondered with each run, trip, jump, skim and dive why the walls were not moving. Was it because the curse chased her? Did it have limitations to its powers? Range, maybe, strength maybe. Maybe sending all of these creatures after her, chasing her, it used up all of her strength, all of her mental capacity. Maybe, maybe, she could wear the curse out and ruin it that way. It was her only hope. There was no more ghost hearts.

She thought again of Talia and her own heart broke again. She stopped for a moment and screamed and sobbed. She'd failed and lost her best friend. And then the great bear roared behind her, followed by the sound of concrete smashing. Bits of gravel flew past her head, got caught in her hair. A rock hit her in the shoulder blades and knocked her out of her depression. She opened her eyes and looked at the curvature of the stone around her, twin circles overlapping, covered in stray leaves and riddled with those tiny insects. They flickered, drew the others towards them, a cacophony of ladybug chatter. She could not stop. She could not just let the curse take her and die. Not after all this, not after everything that happened.

The cries and horrors behind her were louder now, closer now. She gripped that knife in her hand, sucked in a deep breath, and concentrated. The sun was so visible, so bright, directly overhead. It cast long shadows across the world. She missed the sun, it felt like forever since she had seen it last. It was like she had lived in this labyrinth for a lifetime. More than that, two lifetimes, a million lifetimes. She felt like all she knew was that maze, and the fog.

And now it had all changed. The sun shone down overhead, and cast sharp light against the glitter of limestone glow. She stood for a moment, thought, how beautiful it all was, how breathtaking it was now in that bright light. A chaos of organic and artificial architecture, yet fully alive, extremely beautiful. As if it had not been cursed, but instead carved out of some mystical, primal, geometry.

She touched her fingers to her scar, and knew right away where to go, and how she could survive all of this intact. She breathed heavily, one last time, centering herself. She was anchored in this moment, breath caught, heart beating a steady, normal rhythm. She was calm in that second, serene almost, as she was surrounded by stray rays of sunlight coming through the living labyrinth around her. She bent to one knee, crouched in a runner's stance, and then breathed in deep, exhaled, and took off.

She danced with the labyrinth, as the millions of insects tracked her, leading the others towards her, hunting her now.

Her body burned as she moved, and she knew that this would only be the start. It happened each dance, each time the ritual would start. After maybe the first half hour or so and the body would rebel, would ache and cry out and ask her to stop. But she could not stop during the frenzy of the ghosts, only move faster, burning up, screaming loudly the words. Words even whispered in sleep, generations of seers haunted by the rituals.

And now, when her body did the same thing, when that psychic wall rose up and commanded her to stop, the muscles screaming and blistering on fire, she just kept going. The dances before would have gone on all night, lasting until the first light of dawn. Running through this maz was nothing. This was a small dance, a child's dance, one that she could've done when she was a young acolyte. A smile gripped her lips, and she was lost completely in this chase. The movements took her outside time. She ceased to exist in the present for a moment, and fractured into a million instances of herself, scattered across the hours. It was pure joy, sheer bliss, an epiphany of movement.

Even that moment where she tripped and skittered and almost fell, she felt the ecstasy of it all, and didn't even think to stop, to spin around, to fall, to do anything really. She moved like silk, like water, and changed the balance of her body. She danced into the trip and rolled and bounced right back up and kept on running. There was an art to it, all of it, and she existed in perfect harmony with her surroundings. Even though her surroundings were violent, and aggressive, and only wanted to destroy her very being. Such was the nature of transcendence. It wouldn't mean anything if death wasn't waiting as a promise.

The curse ripped through the maz. The stone pulsated in its claws as it made its own path through the light and shadows. Each head cried out, clacking and clicking and whirring. Sometimes it made violent, guttural incantations, and other times the voice was a death rattle, and other times a small voice, like a child, slipping out phrases of nursery rhymes. The words and the language were not in any tongue that Mazi could understand. She only heard that mixture of strange sounds, heard the ripping of the stone and the roaring of the labyrinth as it was ripped apart. The bear was closing in on her.

And it was larger now, even larger than before. It was not just the bear. It was more than the bear, more than Naomi. It was a conglomeration of all the changed bodies, all congealed into this gargantuan creature. The hills behind it that led to the sea were engulfed, and shadowed by the bulk of the beast. It moved slower now, with a rumbling gait, and paused to rip, to tear, to destroy. But it was so large now, it eclipsed the sun with its trifaced head. Mazi would turn each moment to see it, looking over her shoulder, watching as it burbled towards her. She had to keep one eye one it, and she had to keep running.

She owed that to Talia and to Naomi. She realized this now, and swore that she would live and carry on the life they had given her. So, she moved faster and faster and faster. But would it be enough? The beast lumbered slowly, but its strides were the strides of giants that toppled mountains and cracked open the earth. Mazi kept the dance going, but time was starting to wear on her. That lack of sleep, that ripping apart of her arm, the death of dear Talia, the defeat at the black tower, all of it wore on her, tore her down. It took all of this strength and fire in her heart to keep going, a survival instinct that ripped her apart from the inside, keeping her moving, living, even just a little longer.

What was the plan? She had no plan. She wished she had a plan. Getting outside of this labyrinth, and then what? Getting outside, yes, but the bear would still follow. Then what? She thought of the temple, but knew that would be worse, it had to be worse. The bear would not just kill her then, it would kill everything and everyone. The seers would be no more, the temple would be destroyed.

She dodged quickly, rolled out of the way as a stone pillar smashed at the space where her head used to be. The debris and gravel bit into her shoulders and the pain livened her, made her more real, more astute, more certain of her surroundings. Not much further, the scar on her chest ached, not much further. And then what?

A flash in her mind of the bone labyrinth. She looked behind, saw the rough beast getting sluggish and slow. The multiple arms and skulls twisted about, as it stumbled forward. It grew weaker, yes, weaker by the moment. She could hide in there from it until the curse burned all away.

The bear lurched forward. Mazi could see it perfectly now. The assemblage of limbs and faces, the patchwork of stone and vine that rose up out of the back, the arrows stuck into the giant bear arms and paws. The three faces, the bear skulls, now repeating nonsense, a chant maybe or an incantation. The words made no sense, yet it still lumbered towards her. Moving slow and wretched with outstretched paws. The legs dragged behind its body, and made large rivets in the ground. She saw Naomi in the center, still struggling, still trying to move forward, to pull herself free. But vines of fur entangled her and different hands pushed her in, kept her solid still in the center of it. Naomi searched around and shouted, "Mazi! Live! Run! Mazi! Go! Now! Mazi! You are here, it sees you, and it's trying to hide you from me. It's trying to get me to be quiet, but it's weak, it was burned by the ghost heart, when it murdered..." a gulp, a gasp, " Not enough to stop it, no. Just go. Survive! "

Mazi looked at her, watched the bear stumble, collapse, crawl across the ground some more. Even in its massive form it still looked weak and vulnerable. Naomi was scraped on the earth with each movement, and Mazi flinched as she watched. She wanted to turn around and do as Naomi asked and run. But she could not leave Naomi here, she had come so far, for so much. She couldn't let it end like this. This would not end on an act of violence. She knew that now. The bear was to weak to kill her. She saw that in its movements, and the pained look on her face.

"No," Mazi said, her voice clear, distinct. "No."

She lived in the defiant now, forever in the present, a seer in her own right. She walked forward, discarding the shadows behind her, the sun in her hair, the sun against her face. She moved up towards the large cursed thing, watched it crawl face first across the ground. The walls crumbled, and spat up large clouds of dust and grit. And Mazi walked through it all, a solid shape outlined with the cloud of debris. The cursed body finally lay still, unable to move forward. A paw would rise again, as if to pull it just a little farther. Instead, it fell to the ground, and everything shook. A tree or two fell, a few walls cracked and threatened to tumble, but did not.

Mazi walked through that cloud of rubble, as it painted her skin the color of ash. She climbed over that destroyed wall, the remnants like chunks of stone skin scarring the earth. She walked towards the giant body, her movements outlined by the light of the sun, making her every motion outlined by fire.

The beast was flat against the ground, the faces on its back slack and unmoving, with dead eyes staring up and dead lips perched in half words. The arms of the other absorbed were limp, flailing, flaccid things. For a moment Mazi thought it was dead, and moved a little closer, just a bit, just to see that it was still breathing. The back rose and fell, shallow ragged exhaling, a rattling sound coming from deep inside of the lungs.

The triface skull of the bear tried to open its eyes. They twitched, and one or two could view things through a crescent of eyelids, and then closed again. It opened one jaw and another growled between snarling lips. It made a sound that might have resembled a sigh, and might have resembled the sloshing of the waves on a beach, and might have resembled an exhale of death.

Mazi was dwarfed by the giant heads, as she climbed up and sat against the giant bear's body. Her knees pulled up to her chest, her head pointed towards the sky. She felt the slow rhythm of the body breathing, just barely. She knew if it had been at full strength it would have killed her by now, that was for certain. Could she kill it? Probably not, her weapons were too weak for something so massive.

So, she decided to just stay here, her back against the furred rib bones, taking in the whole world around her. Behind was the labyrinth that rose chaotic and solid overnight, once a city full of people and life and now a wasteland of corpses. She left it all sink in, those moments, the body against hers gigantic, yet comfortable.

There was a peace in this moment, and a solemn beauty. A

wake at the end of a war, for all of the fallen and discarded in the sorrow of battle. She let this moment stay for a little more, washing over her. She allowed herself to miss Talia, to realize she would be gone now, not even a ghost anymore. The cursed never become ghosts. It devours the essence of the humanity, leaving nothing behind.

Eventually she stood up, cleared the dust from her clothes. She walked up the back of the bear, scaling the body like a large hill. When she got to the spine itself, she had the most random thought in the world. And yet, in another way, it seemed like the most rational thought in the world as well. Why not? She plunged her knife into the skin of the back. The bear did not budge, it barely even seemed to register that anything was happening at all. She cut inside, pulled out greasy red wires, and cut even deeper, pushing herself into the body. Was she really going to do this?

Yes. She had to do this.

She would search through the bones of the bear for Naomi, hoping she was still alive.

28

SHE SWAM THROUGH THE BODY, ensconced in a sea of humming wires. Metronome beats ticked far off in the distance, echoing like the whispers of a heart. She pushed in, using the wires as balance, letting gravity do most of the work. There was no blood inside the curse itself. No fluid, except that strange slippery coating to those wires.

The curse reached out to her as she swam, a weak signal, yet still there. Shadowy fingers that tried to change her, attempting to enter her body through her lungs and her pores. She held her breath, not letting it inside, and closed her mind, keeping it at a safe distance. The curse was too weak and vapid, and so it bounced from her defenses. If it hadn't destroyed Talia... maybe, then, maybe she would feel sorry for it now. But how could she empathize with such a thing as this curse? It was impossible to feel anything other than hatred and fear. And yet, she did not feel either of those right now.

She felt weary, worn down. She had not won, she had merely

survived. As she swam down, deeper and deeper inside, the wires moved closer together, cocooning her in electric heat. She thought more of the meaninglessness of it all. If she found Naomi, maybe this wasn't all for nothing.

Deeper and deeper. All was red. All was humming. She swam by a large round flower bulb, covered in wires and light. From the center of the bulb came a flickering glow that called out to her. She wanted to reach out, to destroy it. Would that kill the curse? Could it somehow destroy its life? No, wait, no. She couldn't do that, this whole thing was still connected to Naomi. Killing it might kill her, and that very idea horrified her.

She wished she knew the rules of the situation. That had been her whole life, guided by rules in the temple. Every moment of their life until now had been choreographed, perfectly. Even eating food and sleep had become a ritual.

But here, inside the giant demon bear, there were no rules anymore. The curse corroded rules, created new structures, the purification it had promised was chaos. Further and further she pushed through the mess of wires and light. And then she saw Naomi's body, floating in a sea of internal night. Lit only by that strange glowing flower and the wires connected to it. She reached down, swam further, her one good arm outstretched, her fingers splayed and coming closer and closer to Naomi's body.

She touched Naomi's skin. It was still warm still and soft against her palm. She was still alive. Her breathe was slow, and her eyes did not open at the touch. Though, they fluttered a little, eyelashes playfully darting against her cheek.

She had to keep Naomi alive and take her back to the temple, a place where she was known and loved. If she were to die soon, this would be what she wanted. To be surrounded by friends, by a makeshift family of lost, abandoned people.

Mazi pulled herself up to Naomi , and curled up around her in a spiral. Bare skin touched bare skin, and it was like some primitive moment that extended beyond time. *Mother*, she whispered. *Please wake up. Please.* She remembered the times she had snuck upstairs into Naomi's room, candle in hand, and Naomi letting her sleep in her bed. Those mean little girls tormented her constantly, and her only reprise was coming up here, and being with Naomi. Here she felt safe and protected. Sash was the worst when they were younger, before she lost her eye. One night she had even set fire to Mazi's bed, while she was sleeping in it. But here, now, she existed in two moments. The moment of childhood comfort, the moment of adulthood sorrow. It echoed throughout time and comforted her when she needed it most.

I was so lost, so broken, so alone when you took me in. You kept the curse at bay, you lit the fires and prayed to the ghosts. You taught us song and dance, and the rituals of each hour. You showed us the glory of a clockwork life, of living out each moment in a specific contrived way. And yet in those moments there was joy. Like a spontaneous eruption of happiness, burbling out uncaught from the inner depths. And you did not chastise us; you did not tell us to bottle it all back up, to hide our joy in the rituals. You, our new mother, our Naomi, you taught us to live in that joy, to explode with excitement. That each ritual

was not just a recitation of all those memorized moments, but was instead an improvisation, a calling out and inside to experience all things. The rituals we learned were at war with sorrow, and were defiant to the sadness in our lives. They celebrated such misery, and in doing so taught us the joy in our pain, the laughter in our darkest moments, and the secret grins hiding inside our melancholy.

You fed us, washed us, and read to us each night. The other elders were there, yes, but the connection was different; the context was missing. Naomi was above it all, and when she rose through the ranks she became a constellation, a north star for our hearts. And that secret, the curse, it was always inside of you, a hidden part that only a handful knew about, and even fewer understood. It was the key to who you would become, a map of all your future actions. It made you act the way you acted, and it was hard not to see you as perfect, even now, even all these years later. It was how your daughters will always see you, untainted by the fog, unapproachable in love, always reaching into the shadows, always shining with a sparkle of light.

You gave this broken orphaned girl hope, and a life, and above all a reason to keep going.

So, breathe Naomi, breathe. Suffer through this little pain, it will only be a momentary thing. I have to cut you out in order to break you free. So, stay on, hold on, don't let death take you, and don't let your suffering pull you down. You need to come with me now, so keep on breathing.

Don't ever stop.

The bear's body was like a mound, collapsed on the ground, surrounded by the shattered labyrinth. Its back no longer rose and fell with thick breath. It was silent, still, the faces were slack and lifeless, and the eyes no longer tried to open. Everything was frozen in one single second. Death. That was what death looked like, a stillness, a silence. And then, the body jerked violently, a marionette of skin and meat. The bubble grew a bit more, a pimple on the mammoth back. It spread upwards, and then split, as a knife pushed through with a raw, tearing violence. A stump of an arm crammed forward and pushed the flaps of skin apart, as a head slid through, gasping and slick with electronic viscera. The head tilted upwards, the hair a slick mess of blood and wires. Her chin bent up towards the sunlight, eyes opening like newborn eyes, and seeing the sun for the first time in so long within the darkness.

Mazi's head turned left, then right. She placed her knife in her teeth, then ducked back down inside the bear once again. Not too much later, she rose upwards and pushed herself back out of the gaping wound in the corpse's back. Naomi was in her arms, with her neck cradled against her cheek. She carried her as best as she could with one arm. Wires and slippery grease tripped her up, and several times she almost fell, tumbling down the back of the curse.

But, she never let Naomi go. Not even once.

She stood for a moment, regaining her footing. Traction was difficult, and she had to pause on the spine of the beast. The matted fur and bones beneath her feet gave her traction, for the moment. Naomi's breath was against her neck, and even though it was the shallow breath of a deep sleep, in meant that she was alive, and here, in her arms.

Anyone else might have felt a flittering of hope in their hearts. She had found Naomi, this mission should have been a success. She had none of that. Instead, there was only a weary, exhausted, sense of duty. Skulls lined the corpse, stretching all the way down like stairs to the yellowed ground below. She picked Naomi back up and carried her down these grim steps. The skulls were of various animals and creatures, some human and some not. All of them had been changed. As she reached the edge of the bear's paw, she turned and stared at the massive thing. The sun was at the zenith of the bear's three skulls, sending out rays of pristine light. It shrouded the ruins of the labyrinth around the corpse, and outlined the body in pastel fire.

The three faces rotted away in highspeed. The fur and flesh gooped off, and revealed the naked skull beneath. The pool of skin lay flaccid, and twitching. It moved for a moment or two, silently, and then burst into a million tiny insects, scattering through the labyrinth. She turned, walked towards the entrance of the bone labyrinth, following the map on her chest, leading her out towards the human world once again. Naomi coughed against her, still weak and exhausted. She opened her eyes, revealing a bright sparkle of color, and a smile. "Are we safe again?" she asked.

"I don't know, mother." Mazi could not return the smile. She had seen too much, been a party to too many horrors. She was only glad that the final moment, the last reprieve of the curse was one that ended not with violence, but instead a rescue. That thought gave her some relief, but not much. She wished for more, for a feeling of pure infinite bliss to replace that melancholy ache that clung to her bones. They moved further now, through the stone walls. No longer living, no longer pulsating, no longer a physical extension of the very curse itself. Everything was drained of life.

"I can see again," and now Naomi was crying a little, "I was so blind, and lost, and drowning. It wanted me to think and see only what she needed me to think and see. But I fought back. Do you know how?"

Mazi kept walking. Naomi was weak and brittle in her hands, with scorch marks across her skin from where Mazi had yanked the wires and pulled her free. "No, how?"

"Wait," Naomi said, and placed a hand against Mazi's shoulder. "I think I can walk."

Mazi helped slide her down, and she stood with weak legs, the muscles barely able to hold her upright. She clung onto her friend for a moment, her knees wobbling, and then she said, "If you can help me like this, I think I can do it," and wrapped an arm around her shoulder. Mazi grabbed her back, helped her stand, and moved forward, together.

"Tell me, please. How did you survive?" Mazi tried to hide the eagerness in her voice. She hoped that Naomi had pictured her, her adopted daughter, and that was what kept her sane. Maybe that would make it all worthwhile.

Naomi coughed, smiled, the sun bright against her face. "By remembering. Most importantly, by remembering my wife, Sophia. She was the key to it all, her and you, and Talia."

She paused for a moment and stopped walking forward. Mazi stopped as well, but did not turn, did not meet her eyes. Neither of them could glance at each other, so instead they stared out, stared past, towards the world behind the ruined walls of the labyrinth. When Naomi spoke again, she sounded so small and distant. "Talia. Oh. She's... I killed her."

"No," Mazi said, "You didn't."

"I..." and Naomi was quiet again. "I killed her. I was fighting for my life, and the bear caught my memories, held them close, and saw what the ghost heart could do. And so it killed her. I killed her, simply by remembering. My memories saved me, and those same memories killed her."

She stumbled a bit, started falling towards the ground. Mazi grabbed her, held her upright, the two of them hugging for a brief moment. Then Mazi spoke, with calm, detached words. "No, you did not kill her. She... it was all... it was all part of it. All part of it. I... I don't know what to say. You did not kill her, and I'm so sorry, so painfully sorry about all of this."

Naomi then sucked in her breath, a violent motion, and then pulled away from the embrace. Her eyes were wild, horrified, manic. "That... that bastard who did this to me! The one who stole that ghost heart, and started all of that! Did you see him? Is that where you got the heart from? Is that it? Did you see him?"

"Yes," Mazi said, "He's dead now."

"Oh. And then, that heart, that was the one he stole from me?"

"Yes."

"Then, we don't have another, do we? I'm still cursed, this could all happen again, tomorrow, the next day, the day after that. It's only a matter of time, before I change again."

"Yes," Mazi said, and pushed a stray hair from her eyes with her stub. Naomi gasped, and said, "Your arm! What happened?"

But Mazi realized she didn't want to talk about this, that she didn't want to talk about any of this anymore. So, she just said, "Nothing," and kept walking, her back to Naomi. Naomi whimpered, and held out her arms, needing help, and trying to walk, and stumbling and falling again. Mazi turned around, hearing the commotion, and went over, and helped her back up yet again. They moved forward, onward, the sun blazing behind them, outlining the giant body of the now dead bear.

29

SASH HAD NEVER BEEN THROUGH those spiral trails in the daylight, the ghost rituals only happened in the cloak of hours, when even the stars were smoldering glimmers of light over their heads. It seemed strange to see it like this, well-lit and full of color and life. She walked with a walking stick she had carved a few months ago, when the steep hilly climb upwards gave her a little more trouble with each night, each ritual, each song. She didn't tell anyone about it, not really, it was just something she did, and that was that. Her pain was her own, her sorrow was her own, and she would not share it with anyone else.

El climbed up the steep stone steps in front of her, moving towards their final destination. She moved quick, darting between rocks and trees. Sash felt El's voice in her mind again, and the strange images that accompanied it, telling her to hurry up. *They needed our help*, El's psychic voice said, *something terrible has happened in the city, and we have so much to do to fix it and make things right.* Sash nodded, and moved as fast as she could, the pain in each joint a little brighter with each movement. She wasn't that old enough for that kind of pain, and yet, here was the pain, here was the sorrow. Even the socket that once held her eyes ached.

"What is it we're doing?"

A response in her head. The voice was sort of angelic, sort of trumpeting, kind of an echo of images and light. She winced visibly at that sound, almost blaring away at her thoughts. *We are doing what needs to be done*, the voice said. *We are going to burn the ghosts. It was what I was born to do, what my sisters have been born to do. We wander this land, waging our war against the curse.*

"Your sisters? You have sisters?"

Speak to me in images, speak to me with your mind. Open a gateway, and reveal yourself to me, as you have done before with the Dzall. Do not say these things out loud, in a speaking voice, like some barking animal. Show me respect. There are cursed things still in these pines, ones that would take the knowledge and go after my sisters.

Sash opened her mind, like she had been taught before, the water singing in her blood, the doorway sharp and poignant. A series of images flashed in a repetitive loop, creating a passage from her thoughts to El's mind in a long tunnel of fire. She asked again, *You have sisters?*

Sash had to stop for a moment to create this communication, her body freezing, her one good eye slammed shut. A response came back to her in a whooshing of nightmare waves. *Keep walking, it's hard, I know, but you have to keep walking, we don't have much time.* Sash opened her eyes, kept walking, kept concentrating, keeping the passage opened. It was much harder than it looked, doing these two things at once, her mind occupied on a near symbolic level, her body moving still, following forward.

Good, good, the trumpet voice called back. The words echoed in the hallway of her mind, reverberating around, bouncing off the mental tunnels that she had erected. *Yes, I have many sisters, all of them exactly like me, right down to the cold of our skin, the plasticity of our faces. We were grown together, in the ruins beneath the sea, waiting to wake when the three bells ring. The Dzall built us so long ago, and we slept.*

I see. And then Sash found it too hard to keep that connection open, so she closed that gateway in her mind, and almost fell to the ground. She gripped on her homemade walking stick, down on one knee, head pointing towards the earth, trying to keep her balance. She stayed like that for a moment more, breathing and catching her strength. When she raised her head she saw El up there, near the top of the spiral, almost at the hollow stones, waiting for her. Not impatient, only calmly watching and waiting, as Sash pushed herself back up slowly.

Once she stood up tall and straight, she pushed stray hairs behind her ears, made sure her eyepatch wasn't crooked, and then started to climb upwards again. El saw this and nodded, and then climbed the rest of the way towards the hollow stones. Sash felt the weight of this moment, of all the moments leading to now. There was a great silence to that weight, and it bound her to the moment. Everything was happening again, repeating in an infinite, recursive loop. She would not let the immensity of it all drag her down.

Sash made it the last few steps, right up to the land of the hollow stones. The outcroppings seemed to whisper and howl in the wind. And at other times they created a placid, haunting sound, like a wind harp placed by the waves. She leaned against the crook of a dead tree. The branches snapped against her weight, yet the trunk still sturdy. The air felt stale and hungry, and the sky was an evening bruise, the sun not yet setting, only getting ready to disappear into the ends of the world. El was in the center of the hollow stones, with a yew stick grasped tight in her fingers. The staff left marks in the dirt, a perfect circle. Sash had never seen anyone draw a perfectly round circle with just her hands. They usually used a protractor for their rituals, that and other tools to make certain everything was as it should be. Yet, here she was, El, moving in such a clockwork fashion, that pristine geometry rising out of her movements naturally and unforced.

Sash got up to move forward, to maybe see if she could help with whatever was going on. The minute she began to walk forward a blast of sound corrupted her thoughts, a single word blowing her back, almost physically knocking her down. *No No No.* She grabbed the tree, steadied herself, cursed at her own foolishness. She wanted to ask her why she needed to be here? Why this had to involve her? But she said nothing, she only watched. She felt that it was more important to only observe and nothing else.

Ghosts rose up out of the stones, translucent like blue sheets twisting in the breeze. A vague impression of something that used to be human, an outline of what used to be alive. Four, five, six, seven. She lost count, all of them, they were all here, all the ghosts they had prayed to through the years. They all clustered forward at once, and then surrounded El in a massive clump of illumination and susurration. They appeared to be stuck in the center of that circle, and they moved angrily then, trying to move outside of it, to break the circle, the break free. A massive wind tore at Sash, trying to push her away from the tree, but she clung onto it, needing to watch. Maybe this was her purpose, to bear witness to all of this.

El rose up through the ghost bodies, spreading her arms out to her side, and the ghosts turned into a solid beam of blue light, and she rose up a little higher, in the center of that beam. They turned to a blasting blue fire, and then El burned up, she burned up body and all, collapsing to the ground as the light turned to ash, and scattered itself in the circle.

El looked like a burnt toy. She had scorch marks across her face and hands, her clothes burned up and torn away. She herself was unharmed, but instead burnt to soot like a wooden doll. Poking out from shattered pieces were red and white wires, and her head tilted about, and her eyes dangled like glass eyes. Sash did not know if El could even move right now. She stared at the scene for a moment more, before moving closer, and then sitting down, outside of the circle.

She tried to open her mind again, to connect with El, but nothing happened. Nothing at all. El's mouth finally began to clack, and to move, and the voice that came out hollow and tinny. "Take these ashes to the tree in the labyrinth. Find my sisters. Let them know. Let them understand." And then a glass eye fell out of the socket and rolled on the ground, and the mouth stopped moving with a final whir and a click-click-click.

Sash leaned in, hesitatingly touched El's skull with the tip of her finger. It didn't move, it didn't respond at all. She poked at it a little harder, watched as it moved a little. It wasn't alive, not anymore. She touched again, and watched the head slump over, tumble off, roll on the ground completely disconnected. She knew what she had to do, even though she didn't want to do any of this anymore. She wanted to just maybe run off and hide and never speak to anyone again. This, she knew, would be the right thing to do. For once, she would do it.

She bent down and began to scoop up the ashes, as many ashes as she could, and placed them in the only thing she had on her that could carry it. She placed them in El's hollow skull, after moving aside some wires and disconnecting a few things.

A few hours later and she was done, and it was almost night. She pulled out a lantern and lit it, hanging it from the walking stick she had used earlier. And in her other arm, she carried that skull, filled to the brim with ghost ashes. She didn't realize as she walked down to the pines, back towards the temple and the bone labyrinth, that the skull was leaking a little of the ash as she went, leaving a trail behind her. And if she had known, she probably wouldn't have cared. Just as long as she had enough for this last ritual. A ritual she had read about, had talked about, but had never practiced.

She made her way back through the pines in the dark, coming at last to the bone labyrinth. Everything was silent all around her, not even a snapping of twigs, not even a single animal making a sound. Even the temple had been quiet, with the lights long extinguished hours ago. She wondered briefly of the rituals, and if they would still be performing them anymore, since all of the ghosts have moved on thanks to El. She felt a sense of loss at this, a sense of history slamming shut.

And then she anointed her head with a dot of ash, and said

the four syllable prayer she had learned years ago. She transcended being Sash for the moment, and instead took on the archetype of the wanderer, the sun chaser, the moon eater, the messenger of death. This template was a temple of a human being, a person who existed beyond sexes, beyond material existence, whose whole interior form became a shrine itself. Her intestines a labyrinth, her heart a burning lantern, her blood the water under the earth, her eyes the stars and the darkness beyond their light. She moved inside, the trail of ash still trickling behind, yet unimportant now. There was only the action, the subjugation of self towards the prism of identity, and the last ritual.

This was the only ritual that mattered.

The maze moved around her, changing location, leading a straight line right towards the center and that silver tree. This time, the maze withdrew its teeth and claws and let her walk with petals against her feet, as it led her towards that center of everything. The silver tree glistened, and she knelt, and said the first oath. When she finished she stood, and said final oath, and spoke the words that were forged at the end of time. Two words, whose meaning had not yet been written. Lakaf. Arayn.

Then, she spread the ashes into the roots, bowed her head, and curled up around the tree like a serpent. After sitting for an ageless age, she uncoiled herself and moved back. She picked up her staff and lantern yet again. She looked at the skull, now empty of ashes, and thought that it should not stay here. She had no idea why, but she knew that it needed to come back with her. Maybe, she might still be able to communicate with it, some way. She bent down, grabbed it, stood back, and felt something awaken in the forest around her.

She saw what looked at first like tiny moons glittering on the tree branches. These moons blossomed out to night flowers, petals unfurling, shaking their stamens as they opened. She could not turn away, she stood and watched it some more, holding the skull close to her chest, leaning solemnly on the staff and lantern. These glowing flowers then unwrapped themselves even further, petals bending back and shaping themselves into what looked like ripe apples, but then on closer inspection contained ventricles and arteries, chalky white in the shadows. They were beating and burning, and it took her a moment to realize that these were ghost hearts. All of them, each of them, ghost hearts.

She wept as she pulled them down, one at a time, placing them in the skull. Damn it, she couldn't take them all. She wished she could, if only she had brought a basket or something. She knew that the hearts would barely last until dawn, and then dry up and float away. So, what she grabbed now was of utmost importance. Who knows when it would ever happen again? There were no more ghosts in the hollow stones, no more spirits to bring burn up into ash and feed to the roots of the tree. This was it. Her last chance. She had to make it worthwhile.

30

THE SHINING CITY ON THE hill now lay transformed and changed, a murky reflection of its former self. What was once high towers like trees against the skyline was now a wandering maze of stone and rubble. In the center lay a huge hill of a rotting carcass. The curse had fled from the rot and body, wounded and ruined yet still alive, just barely so, looking for any life to cling to.

Two figures walked down in the night, their movements slow and aching, with a candle split between them for light. In the amber of their shadows, a weary solemnity flickered between their faces. The curse was out there and inside of Naomi still, and it would only be a matter of time before it rose up again. Mazi walked in the front of their two person line, with the candle burning against her still working hand. This was not a victory; this was only an exhalation of breath.

Naomi was walking better now, yet still moved a bit aloof. She weaved to and fro, not quite used to using her legs again.

Her body was wrapped in some rags they had found while scavenging in the ruins of the city, her body cold in the night air. In a way, she mirrored Lens, their bodies bandaged up in much the same way. And here they stood, at the exit to the bone labyrinth. An exact echoing of that single moment, that primal second that had changed everything. When Lens had approached her, had attacked her and removed her heart.

Here they stood, breathing silently for a moment, unable to move on. This second was weighted with all the other moments that had come before it, and all the other moments that will come afterwards. It felt like there was a choice to be made here, to move on, or to go back. To return to the hills and go to the sea beyond, maybe moving away from all of this, all of the life that had defined everything in their existence. Or, they could walk forward, keep going into that labyrinth, return back to the temple, and perform those rituals once again. Neither of them knew of the sacrifice of the ghosts, nor of the sacrifice of El. They only knew of one gateway, one doorway, one step into the liminal moment. This was a period of transformation that awaited them, forged in the fires of their experiences.

Like all moments in their life that carried meaning, they felt as if this had required a ritual of some sort, a prescribed symbolic way of marking the passage, from one state of being to another. Yet there was no ritual for this moment, it was uncharted territory. Naomi cleared her throat, and they stood for a moment more, neither of them speaking, neither of them needing to speak. Mazi realized how much of her life was made up of the silence that existed between conversations, and how much meaning existed inside the void of words. It was a devouring entropy of absence.

The ritual, she realized, was this. This whole moment, this silence, this was a ritual they were creating in this moment. It burned into their memories, striking the moment in stone. "Let's move on," Naomi said after a while. The sky above their heads raced with stars. "Let's just do it now."

Mazi nodded, still unable to break the silence, that holy quietude that enveloped them completely and totally. They moved forward, walking to that large arched doorway that led into the bone labyrinth. There were skulls lining the arches, and the pillars were a loose collection of femurs and humerus. Beyond the glint of their candle light they saw something else moving, and the shadows changing, and then another lantern flickering, moving closer, moving towards them. The shadows beyond the archway elongated, and made way for sister Sash, who walked towards them, with a solemn sense of urgency.

They saw the patch over her eye first, that key glittering in the dark. Then her features, stern and vibrant at once, and then the staff with the lantern, and then after the skull filled with ghost hearts, lying in her hands. She didn't seem surprised or happy to see them, her eye only lowered a little, as if in shame. "Talia," Sash said finally. "Where is Talia? What happened to her?"

Mazi spoke, clearing her throat. "She died in the city on the hill. How did you get…"

Sash held the skull up for them to see it clearly. The skull was upside down, with the lower jawbone removed, so as to fit as many hearts as possible inside of it. Petals of flowers lay crushed near the hearts, and strange red and yellow wires curled up around them. Mazi recognized those wires, they were the same that had been in the curse's body, when she had climbed in, to retrieve Naomi from the prison of its form.

"There was a girl, who came to us not long after you had left. She was a lot like Talia, in a way. And very different, I guess, in other ways. She caught all of the ghosts, and burned them all with her hands. This is her skull, she was destroyed when the ghosts became ash, burning her alive as well. She's... I barely knew her, yet I loved her."

And then that ritual of silence broke through again. Three figures standing alone, in the night, a candle and a lantern creating a circle of illumination around their bodies. Three figures, cutting shapes into the night with their shadows. They moved clockwise, trading places, another moment of silence, and then a hug passed forth, from one body to the next. And then Sash held up the skull for them, the ghost hearts vibrant and new in that amber light.

It was a moment for healing, for reconciliation. Naomi reached into the skull, grabbed a heart, and placed it over the scars and fresh wounds on her chest, where her own heart had been torn out. She placed it there, and knelt in the shadows, and watched as it merged with her body, a tendril of fire in her skin, and then she was whole again. She stood and laughed and said, "That will buy us some time," and then walked further into the bone labyrinth. She didn't have a candle or a lantern, but the tattoo of the ghost heart on her chest still glowed, faintly shedding enough light for her to walk by.

The bells rang out in the temple, calling out in an echo across the world. It started the minute one of the elders spied three figures walking out of the bone labyrinth, and realized that one of them was Naomi. She ran out, calling to the others to *come see, come see! They're coming home again, they're all coming home again.* The blazers were lit, the halls alive with torchlight, and the light of lanterns hanging by the lines of stained-glass windows. Various seers and acolytes and elders stretched out, groggy and muttering to themselves, but still very excited and awake. They conglomerated together, in the great hall by the front door, and opened it wide, swinging the doors far apart and letting the multitudes of light inside shine out and shatter the darkness.

A bunch of the acolytes could not wait, and they ran forward and hugged them and shouted with joy. Everyone came out then, slowly, spilling out into the night in a loose clump of bodies. Later, they would ask about Sash, and about El, that new girl that had come to live with them for such a short time. And even later still, the elders would hustle them into the shadows, into the quiet rooms where no one could go except them. And they would ask the three all sorts of questions, prying information at every turn, at every second, trying to gleam everything they could from the situation. What did it feel to be cursed like that, to turn into that creature? What had happened to the city? How did you get the ghost hearts? What will happen to them, now that all the ghosts are gone and the city is a vacant hole in the heart of their island?

But all of that would come later, much later. Right now it was a moment of joy, of love, of return from the edges of death and a revival of one they had thought lost and broken. Certainly quite a few felt sad about Talia's death, and even a few others asked about Mazi's arm, and tried to find light and laughter even in these grim moments. For this was a time of celebration, of feast, of love unbridled by the pain the three had witnessed.

They performed the rites of return, the rituals of merging, and spoke the oaths of blood and companionship. There was dancing and singing, and lighting of fires, and cooking of food that smelled like beauty itself. There was playing cards and games, and some people drinking maybe a little more than they should, and others running through the halls, howling and laughing. It made Mazi remember that time, so long ago, running feral through the halls. Was that the start of this whole thing? That moment when Lens and his brother arrived all those years ago? Yet she wouldn't trade any of it, not even one horrible second. This life was her life, a messy knot of memories and moments, of actions and inactions, of sound and silence. It was everything to her.

She stood at the whirlwind's heart. The entire temple exploded with excitement at their return. She watched in silence, and saw Sash and Naomi both just like her, two melancholy figures, surrounded by such light and laughter. How could any of them tell these laughing, loving, makeshift family of theirs that the real fight was just beginning? That this was only a momentary reprieve and nothing more?

They found they couldn't celebrate. Too much death, too much estrangement, too much sorrow and misery. It would take awhile to piece everything back together again, to make themselves whole once more. And really, it might not ever happen. They would carve pieces of themselves to replace what was lost, an arm, an eye, a heart. But really, it would only help for a little while. An exhale, and then waiting, waiting for that inhale. When everything would change again.

Mazi walked forward, pushed her way through the crowd, and ambled upstairs. She moved towards the one location that always called out to her. that carried meaning even in the moments when she had forgotten what that meaning even was in the first place. She made her way across the temple, to the far side, and crawled out of the vine covered hallway, and outside, onto that giant granite skull. She moved forward, remembering everything, slipped her shoes off, feeling the moss and tiny specters of grass tickle the edges of her toes. And then she walked out onto the grim forehead, and sat down, still, legs dangling over the precipice, remembering.

Soon the sun would rise again, over those hills in the distance, and light would return to everything once more. She heard laughter and voices mingling, the sounds of the party reaching her ears even up here. She liked the way this moment felt, even now. Being outside of the party, all of that commotion happening elsewhere. It felt peaceful to her. The way the lights of the temple now danced against the windows, it made her think of viewing the stars at night from inside a telescope.

She had come here so often, so many times, just to see the sunrise over those hills. Even when she forgot about that first night, decades upon decades ago, when her and Lens where there, and behind them was his brother and Naomi. Back when this all started. Each year, coming up here, seeing the same things, feeling everything all over again. She let that emotion wash over her completely, all the moments and memories of her life leading up to now, filling her body with a poignant, emotional ache.

And she just sat there, feeling that emotion, reliving those moments, waiting for the sun to rise once again.

CPSIA information can be obtained
at www.ICGtesting.com
Printed in the USA
JSHW021749191220
10391JS00005B/87